Ivy vs. Dogg With a Cast of Thousands!

Brian Leung

C&R Press
Conscious & Responsible

First Edition
1 2 3 4 5 6 7 8 9

Cover art: Laura Catherine Brown
Interior design by Ali Chica

Library of Congress Cataloging-in-Publication Data

ISBN: 978-1-936196-63-0
Library of Congress Control Number: 2018932455

C&R Press
Conscious & Responsible
crpress.org

For special discounted bulk purchases, please contact:
C&R Press sales@crpress.org
Contact info@crpress.org to book events, readings and author signings.

For my mother, Catherine DiTomaso, who listens and shares and loves; for Brian Yost who abandons his better judgment and leaps with me always; and for every home town whose children hear the whispering fists.

Ivy vs. Dogg

1

We're smallish. It's always been that way; but the committee has lots of ideas for improving things. And as you might imagine, it's a difficult thing to have to be right all the time. It sets up a lot of expectations, which, fortunately, we're always game for. Even in this case where two teenagers, Ivy and Dogg, nearly brought down our entire town. If it weren't for the committee stepping up to set the record straight there'd be people who'd be silly enough to want to read what follows as some kind of love story. But, of course, it's not, because, in this account, all the wrong people end up with each other and anyone who wants to see it different is just being willful. It's the committee, after all, who refused to stand idly by as an innocent little girl was being literally devoured before our eyes. So, yes, we're setting the record straight because we've had plenty of time to get the facts. And you're going to want to take a look at this not just to see how Ivy and Dogg pulled the wool over our eyes, but to get a sense of how two reckless teenagers nearly brought shame on us all and how the committee became the agents of redemption.

And this is part of what the committee does. We're the people of record. We set the standard in this town and, particularly in the space of these pages, we'll slip-in the benefit of our knowledge. All of us carry around Post-it note pads in case we need to let someone know about what we think is a good thing or infraction, like Kendy Smart's fence of vodka bottles which practically sprung up over night. All it took was a little yellow paper on her mailbox and we'd done our job. We're the ones responsible for limiting the number of signs on the front windows of Witherspoon's Liquor. We got a crosswalk put in over by the Presbyterian Church. And **(When crossing street you *must* look left, right, and left again. Repeat.)** - The Committee it was us who fought to get the Pepper trees cut down on Pepper Tree Street so the road could be widened—which is great for our annual parade. Besides, they're just nasty, throwing down pink peppercorns and tiny leaves that get into just about everything. The committee does lots of good, like cutting those trees, and whether people want to admit it or not, Mudlick isn't the sleepy little town it used to be. We're the suburbs now, just forty minutes to the city. It's not about milk cows and watermelon patches anymore. There's still a few of those *A Horse in Every Garage* bumper stickers around from years ago, and we'd tear them all off if we could. Maybe we could trade on that country charm way back when, but that's not good enough. The way the committee figures it, we've got the same three hundred and fifty days of sunshine as any place in the county and we've got to show that we know what to do with it. We've even got tract homes and apartment complexes with pools, and some people in this town just don't understand that we're on the move.

And it's not like we're trying to erase our past. Not too many years back, the committee put together a nice little book on the history of Mudlick and it all came from stories people told us. We took it so seriously that we even painted in small details here and there, colors and mannerisms and such, to really get across the flavor of our town. And in all modesty, people seemed to like our work. But being proud of the past doesn't mean you have to live in it.

Ever since the committee was formed, we've tried to get people to realize that Mudlick has to evolve. There are plenty of us on the committee, so we get this message out fairly well. And sooner or later we know who said what to who, and when. People like to talk. Over the years, we've gotten pretty good at cobbling together information to get at the truth. Though now and again there's a hiccup ... here and there ... a selfish person that just won't tell us what they know. Like Ivy and Dogg who refused to be accountable. What we do have of them is something we didn't ask for, a small black photo album thrown in our faces by Ivy's mother, the spiral kind that holds about as many photos you'd care to see of two people who've disappointed you so. We keep them just to remind ourselves how we were almost fooled, those photos and a letter from Vida Clark that lulled us into temporary complacency.

On the first page of the album is a photo of Ivy and Jimmy (Dogg) in First grade, Ivy in a too-small pink jumpsuit wearing a First Place ribbon, and Jimmy, already showing his trademark thinness, t-shirt blue as his eyes, holding a red ribbon. Second Place. Each of them smiling with missing front teeth, both holding hands. Just a photo full of hope and bright futures unless you know what you're looking at. Because that, in our opinion, is perhaps where all this mess might have been averted. If only their parents had been smart enough to have separated them back then we'd all have been spared this most recent summer of heartache.

But because people don't *see*, the committee exists to ask questions, sew together different versions of stories to make a whole. Like when Clay Cooper sat down in the middle of the intersection of Creekview Road and Vine Street threatening to impale himself with the business end of a pink flamingo lawn ornament. He kept that bird's steel legs, the tips, pressed right to his neck and, every once in a while, pushed them just hard enough to make two wide dimples on either side of his Adam's apple. Thin as Clay was, it probably wouldn't have taken much to run those steel rods right through to the other side. If anyone could've taken bets on who'd be most likely to pull a plastic bird off a lawn and threaten to kill themselves with it, the committee would've put its money on Clay. He'd been through five jobs in three years.

(Remain vigilant about potentially lethal garden decorations.)
- The Committee

Not the good kind of jobs either. Clay was poor, which

is something the committee wasn't too fond of. We have a long, generous history of reminding our downtrodden to lift themselves up. Not only that, we remind *others* to encourage the poor not to be a drag on the community. And so, over the years, the committee likes to think we've done a pretty good job making sure no one lets these sad folks get too comfortable with their station in life. Even our children know that poverty is nothing to be proud of.

As for Clay, the best he ever did was senior busboy at the Chinese Star 1 buffet, which is okay when you're eighteen maybe, but not when you're thirty-five. And it's doubly bad when a person doesn't display any other talents that might get him by, like singing or bee keeping, or . . . shoveling snow off driveways. Though, admittedly, it doesn't snow here. But a person could move. A person could choose not to be poor.

So, Clay was gripping that flamingo like he was really going to do it and what we could see of his jittery eyes from under those dark bushy bangs of his, was that he was crazy enough to see his threat through. All the while he's sitting there hoping that his girlfriend, ex-girlfriend, Melanie, would show up. And we on the committee know exactly what's going through his mind right then. He's thinking he's in way over his head and hearing all the honking horns and the sheriff crouched down in front of him slowly repeating, "Put the flamingo down, boy. Put the flamingo down." He's thinking about the crowd that's gathering and how the asphalt is getting hot and how next time he'll put a little more thought into it before using a lawn ornament to do something like this. He's taking all this in and wishing that Melanie would just hurry up and get there and give him a reason to stop. And, when she does get there, we all sigh because he smiles for the first time though he's got those metal legs right on his jugular. "Clay, baby," she says in her just-out-of-bed voice, brushing that blonde mane away from her face. "Clay, baby. Let me take you home."

"Don't want to go home," he says, standing up. He's wearing the same thing he wore practically every day of his adult life, white t-shirt with Marlboros in the breast pocket and faded blue jeans.

Melanie tries not to get exasperated but she's tired of Clay's dramatics and the fact she's always the one rescuing him even though they've been apart three months. She's thinking about her new boyfriend Max and how she won't go on a date with him anywhere in Mudlick. "Clay'd freak," she'd tell us later.

So there's Clay with that faded flamingo, holding a steel leg in each hand, pressing his neck. There's Melanie and the sheriff taking turns trying to convince him to give in. After two hours, there are about forty of us watching it all, and Burt Draeter suggests that maybe if we rush him as a group he might get scared and throw the flamingo down. Of course, Burt Draeter's not the one to ask about such things. He once mistook a rock thrown through his front window for a meteorite.

As you might guess, in the end we didn't have to do anything to get Clay to stop. He stood there sweating, the box of cigarettes the only definition on his skinny chest, when all of the sudden the flamingo torso slips off one rod, then the other, and falls to the ground, bouncing briefly with a drum-like thrum. And Jimmy Doggins runs out when none of the rest of us would and puts his arm around Clay, bringing him to the curb where forty people are doing a terrible job of not laughing, and Clay telling us later—after psychiatric evaluation and after landing a bus job at Denny's in another town—that even though he still had the metal legs at his neck, there didn't seem much point if people weren't going to take him seriously.

The committee knows all that because some of us were there and because we asked. There's not a soul alive that doesn't want to tell their side of things and if you hear from enough people, even just snatches here and there, you can stitch together a pretty accurate story. What folks don't tell, we fill in ourselves because we know how people are. Take that mess about Ivy, Dogg, Fern and the giant squid. We've heard from everyone about it all, everyone, that is, except Ivy and Dogg themselves, but we've got a pretty good handle on just what happened and what went wrong.

We don't exclude ourselves from this story about Ivy and Dogg, not at all. The committee has mostly rotated membership by now, so we're free to talk about certain members more so than if they were still one of us. Which isn't to say we aren't proud of our past, because the committee is the committee whether its 1902 or now. We have a proud history, a history of trying to help this town, which is why we have to know who's against us . . . those who just don't want progress. And there are plenty of small-minded people willing to stand in the way of what's good and right. We're not trying to change everything. We'll still have our rodeo and the big 4H fair, and, of course, the Junior Mr. Mayor elections, which gets us a lot of publicity each year, publicity that we sometimes don't want, like a few years ago when we had that ugly confluence of the elections and Ms. Colton's pornographic lawn topiary.

The committee was looking forward to that year because it signaled the end of Mumford Smith's tenure as Junior Mr. Mayor. Candidates run in the summer between their junior and senior year of high school. Usually we get some of our better students to run. But Mumford, a big, freckled, baseball catcher for the high school, ran unopposed. At first it seemed okay because, far from being a dumb jock, Mumford, named after his grandfather, was in the top ten percent of his class.

(Squash is an excellent brain food. Steam. Never boil.)
                                                    - The Committee

But what we couldn't account for was that he just didn't care. Junior Mr. Mayor isn't a big job, but it's an important position with a modest budget and ceremonial duties all year long, both of which Mumford horribly neglected. At the 4H fair, he was a no-show as guest auctioneer—"out playing baseball, I suppose," his father told us. And just six months after his election, without our approval, he'd spent his entire Junior Mr. Mayor budget on Calamine lotion (more on Mumford and that debacle later), and uniforms for our all-Mexican Little League team. So there wasn't anything left for the wreath that the children of Mudlick present each year to the V.F.W. hall on Memorial Day. Instead, they ended up taping to the wall dozens of red-white-and-blue construction paper ribbons which ruined the paint when they were taken down. Mudlick Elementary got a hundred-and-forty-dollar bill for the damage.

So, we were more than happy the following year when Jimmy Doggins announced he was going to run. Jimmy was a straight "A" student and the county's best tennis player. The committee had even voted him a nominal per diem when he went to the county tournament. The *Courier-Tribune* carried a full color photo of him in mid-serve, his long thin arms stretched high above him, blonde hair fanned out, grimace on his face. The headline for the story about him read "Dogg Days." And as we came to find out, that was his nickname, which we weren't too fond of at first because it had that back-slapping hick sound to it, an image the committee was trying to wring out of Mudlick. But it wasn't long before we, too, started referring to him as Dogg. We knew from the start he would be a fine representative of Mudlick. He looked good in a suit and even better next to his girlfriend, Charlene Hergis, one of the prettiest girls in Mudlick. Young love is a good angle, though, admittedly, Dogg surprised us with just how much love he had to give. But we were so confident of the total Dogg package the committee even approached him about endorsing our plan to change the name of Mudlick to Valhalla West. There were seldom "real" issues in the campaign, but we thought this might be one.

Jacob Alter, at 37, one of the younger committee members, went out to talk to Dogg at the swim club tennis courts. Jacob was a dependable kind of guy, regular and tidy with thin wavy red hair he kept pasted down close to his head. He went to church on Sundays, and, before his wife divorced him and moved, he coached the Electric Squaws, his daughter's Soft Ball team. Two years straight with losing seasons, but they had the nicest coach. Everyone liked Jacob and if they didn't, they probably weren't likeable themselves.

The way Jacob told it, the day he went to the tennis courts, Jimmy was all sweated up, shirtless, his torso hairless as a baby, and nearly thin as his racket. He was hitting balls shot at him from a machine. Charlene was sitting on a bench reading *Cliff's Notes* on *To Kill a Mockingbird*, the novel about a lawyer who surprises his children that he's the best shot in the county when he kills a rabid dog.

Charlene looked up and squinted her green eyes as Jacob approached. "I didn't know you belonged to the club, Mr. Alter."

"I don't. Just came to talk to your boyfriend."

The yellow and black booklet in her hands waved back and forth in front of Charlene's Kewpie face as if she were a Southern belle. "Good luck if you can get him to talk about anything but tennis. Meanwhile I sit here boiling, trying to catch up in English. Summer school. Like, right?" She offered a purposeful sigh and checked her ponytail. "I got a little behind in English because of Cheer and they won't let me back on the squad if I don't have at least a "C" in all my classes. But they've got Ivy Simmons and, like, a couple other nerdy kids as teacher's aids, so I'll get through."

Jacob, caught off guard, remained quiet. Charlene was exceptionally lovely with her small red lips and generously sized eyes. But she was also the kind of girl he feared in high school.

"Don't get me wrong." She tapped the *Cliff's Notes*. "The other kids, like, just watched the movie. But I understand the importance of reading." With that, Charlene, waving at Dogg, who was still swatting at machine-hurled forehand-balls, excused herself to get a soda.

The court was littered with yellow balls. Jacob called out to Dogg a few times but the boy kept swinging until the machine emptied itself, and then, as if Jacob had just arrived, he turned and said, "Hey, Mr. Alter. You joining?"

"I came to talk to you, Dogg." Jacob opened the gate and walked onto the court. He patted his hand over his head to reign in any fly-aways. He told us he was there just five minutes and his skin was frying. Out here in the county, down in this box of a valley, all we get is dry heat and all the pollution the city can send us. Melissa Robinson once baked a sheet of cookies in her mother's car as a science project for school.

(The ideal chocolate chip cookie should have no more than 7 chips in it.) - The Committee

Jacob said other than perspiration, and the mild pinkish tint of his white skin, Dogg didn't seem to notice the heat at all. "The committee wants to know if you'll stand with us on a certain issue."

Dogg toweled himself off and listened as Jacob explained to him that it was really unfair that our town had gotten stuck with the name Mudlick in a county where everyone else got named something that reflected the Spanish heritage of the region—Los Vistas, Coronadito, Mira Vista, La Tia, even San Pepe. But poor Mudlick got its name way back when because of our thin lake that simmered down to nearly nothing during the hot summers and left slick brown mud the mule deer learned to tromp and scrape at until enough water collected in one place for them to drink. That, of course, was back in the late 1890s when they built the 200 room Grand Mudlick Lodge for the rich people who wanted to take a day's ride out to the country and do some hunting. Back then, anyone could practically step out their front door and stare right into the inspiration for one of those old time Western paintings, dusky hills beneath a bleached blue sky. These people'd wake up and go right out to shoot rabbit, dove, quail, and the occasional duck. Hunting in the morning and still time for cigars by noon. Not a bad life. Just the name of our town made the rich feel like they were roughing it. Though the lodge burned down, the name Mudlick stuck.

Dogg was patient with Jacob's explanation. They sat on a bench, courtside. Jacob said the sun was so bright off Dogg's yellow hair that Jacob could barely avoid the distraction as he spoke. And he admitted, even, to being a little nervous when suddenly caught in the literally bright fame of Jimmy Doggins. This was Dogg as we saw him, the young man who'd carry out our vision for a better Mudlick, someone who in ten or fifteen years would make an excellent committee member himself. If only we'd known that Dogg had other plans. If only Jacob could have divined that Charlene, beautiful Charlene, wouldn't last, and that Jimmy Doggins, was taking up with the wrong sort just as we needed him to be the straightest arrow in the quiver.

"I know all about Mudlick's history, Mr. Alter." Dogg smiled and patted Jacob on the back. "But, you understand Valhalla isn't Spanish, right? I think it's Norse." He slapped Jacob on the knee to seal the point, then twirled his racket on the tip of his finger like a basketball. As if he didn't care about Jacob's answer and was just at that moment realizing his girlfriend's absence, he said, "Have you seen Charlene?"

Jacob was good at staying focused in spots like that, so he said the committee just wanted to choose something dramatically different. "We want to do a whole three-sixty if we can."

Dogg smiled again and stood. Jacob said that, up close, Dogg's about the handsomest guy you want to meet, the kind his daughter is always pointing at on her phone, the so-blue eyes, too-moist skin. "I'll think about it," Dogg finally answered. "Help me pick up some of these balls?"

Jacob said they didn't talk any more about the Valhalla West idea but that Dogg seemed receptive. He said they mostly talked about women and how Dogg didn't hear wedding bells with Charlene just yet, and that there were more important things to worry about. "The scary thing is," Jacob told us later, "I'm sure the kid can smile at just about anyone and get what he wants."

At that point, the committee felt really good. We had an excellent candidate for Junior Mr. Mayor, someone not likely to be opposed. Normally, for the show of it at least, we like two candidates, but, after a year of Mumford, the committee was more than ready for a sure thing. Plus, after we did a little checking, it was clear to us that Dogg was practically born for the position. Fifth Grade Student Council President, junior high school President, and just elected class President for his senior year. **(Cultivate the skills of attractive children.)** - The Committee And since the Doggins had money, he'd have plenty of cash for posters, maybe even a website. Because he would be running unopposed, even that didn't appear to be too much of a problem. The committee was imagining a banner year. We had no way of knowing another candidate would come along and louse the whole thing up.

2

There was a week left in the school year, nearly campaign season for Junior Mr. Mayor, and some people on the committee had even started referring to Dogg by that title. Plans were full steam ahead for announcing the idea of changing Mudlick's name. We'd planted the notion here and there, without mentioning, of course, the exact change. Dogg's year in office would really be a springboard for us to shoot for bigger and better things. So, we all got a surprise at our weekly meeting in the Mudlick Historical Society reading room when Ivy Simmons walked in. "I'm here to submit my letter of intention to run for Junior Mr. Mayor," she said.

There was collective quiet as we looked at this young, thick-limbed girl in a short red dress, holding out an envelope. Her brown hair fell at her shoulders in a stringy thinness that accentuated her odd, round face, the kind of girl you see around town but never notice until she's in the newspaper for keeping drugs in her locker or having a baby in a motel room. "I think this is all you require," she said, jiggling the envelope at us.

Gloria Valdez, our unofficial Secretary, stood, and took the envelope and read the letter. "Yes, dear," she said. "This will be just fine. We'll contact you soon with information." Some of the rest of the committee might have rolled their eyes at that moment, but Gloria, a collector of scarves, straightened the bright-orange one draped around her neck, and smiled.

(Keep holiday colors in mind when shopping for clothing accessories.) - The Committee

If you needed level headedness, Gloria was the one to turn to. In her youth, she worked on two presidential campaigns and it was there she learned never to let anything seem to surprise you. Which is perhaps why she was also able to run a successful non-profit ferret rescue program. People think they can keep those things but they'll stink up a place in no time and can practically squeeze out of a keyhole. Gloria didn't even much like them, but she kept the place funded and going. And that steadiness came into play as she looked the potential Junior Mr. Mayor candidate in the eyes.

Ivy wrinkled her nose. "I'm quite busy, so please don't take too long. I've got to organize."

Remaining calm, Gloria smiled. Though it had been a long time, she'd had experience with Ivy years earlier. Gloria volunteered with her niece's Brownie troupe, and, even then, Ivy caused problems, quit, in fact, because the troupe planned an outing to the water slides on the same Saturday as the community cleanup at the reservoir. Ivy lectured her fellow Brownies about their choice and when she didn't get her way, she stomped out of Ida Goss' living room. Ivy, selfish even at eight-years-old, spent that Saturday picking up trash.

So, at that moment when Ivy declared her candidacy for Junior Mr. Mayor, Gloria couldn't help but wonder what we might be in for. She looked at the envelope Ivy had just delivered and then up at the candidate, who turned to go but stopped, the pleats of her skirt flapping against her dense thighs with the unfortunate, but small, Port Wine birthmarks at each bend. She was not at all fat, but certainly sturdy, not so much graceful as sure-footed, more mountain goat than gazelle.

(Soak wild game in milk before cooking.) - The Committee

"I'm just doing this for the town, you know," she said, her slightly glossed lips rigidly parallel like an equal sign below her nose. "I really didn't think I'd have time, but I just couldn't stand the idea of that Jimmy Doggins winning one more thing. I kept hoping someone else would oppose him." We think of this statement now and have to laugh because Dogg tied one arm behind his back to make things fair.

"He's quite popular," Jacob said, to which a few on the committee nodded or affirmed with a humming "mmm hmmmnh." We were the kind of calm when a wasp first lands on your nose and you freeze because you're not quite sure how to react. But we did know a little about this older version of Ivy. She was sometimes seen with college boys and strange men no one in town knew. She was the kind of girl apt to end up in *that* kind of trouble. Clearly she was an apple that had fallen not too far from the tree, in this case, her mother Gwen, who never met a man she didn't flirt with. We know a bit about that family and we weren't too far off guessing the kind of trouble that seems to haunt their kind.

Ivy walked back to the table, placing her hands on the edge, leaning slightly over the bear claws and coffee, her unpleasant hair hanging stiff as grass. There's been a great many important matters discussed over that table, before and since Ivy, but never has it gotten so tense as when we sat waiting for what she was about to tell us. "I know you have to be impartial, so you can't thank me for running, but don't worry, I'm going to win."

3

To skip ahead briefly, there was a moment of calmness, a sliver of time where it actually seemed possible that our little town was headed toward the quiet perfection the committee was striving for. And we talk about it here because it helps make our point about just how wrong everything went despite our best efforts.

The Junior Mr. Mayor elections weren't going at all well and then, two evenings before the vote, nearly 500 Mudlick families got some very bad news. Just days earlier, Quixote Furniture opened at the former site of Cattail Saloon. On its first night, Klieg lights shone from the small parking lot, the hollowed-out building freshly painted and carpeted still somehow smelling slightly of beer. The room was filled with beautiful furniture at amazing Grand Opening prices... we all thought. Huge discounts for cash orders. All day long we signed bills of sale and made appointments to have our furniture delivered. Bright red sectionals and thick cushioned leather recliners, and hardwood coffee tables and Tiffany style lamps, and all manner of beautiful ceramic jungle cats, all of it so reasonable a person just couldn't say no, and we didn't.

The point is, those people just pulled out overnight, left everything behind except the cash we gave them. And you might have thought we'd be angry and depressed, which would be natural, but Camille Kwak had a conversation with Fern, who we'll detail presently, and Fern said, young as she was, pretty little thing that she was, that we ought not to worry.

The Kwak's lived in what we called Little Tokyo, the pair of houses occupied by Camille's family and her widowed mother. Admittedly, we found out after a long while that they were Korean, but we were used to using Little Tokyo by then, so it stuck. Both Camille and her mother had put out cash for new furniture. "They have your money," Fern said in her soft way, "but it's not your fault there are tricky people." The innocent rationale of a child set us all more at ease, which isn't to say we didn't feel just a little taken advantage of.

So maybe we were handed kind of an unconscious mantra, "nothing is your fault." And just maybe that's why two days later, when we didn't have Fern to comfort us, after we'd lost her to the evil whim of Abigail Colton, maybe that's why we didn't all just break down. Even the news Mumford delivered, reluctant and willful at the same time, even that wasn't enough to destroy our desire to press on. Mumford reported shortly after "the disappearance," as we've come to call it, a somewhat sketchy detail about his official arrival at the Junior Mr. Mayor election site with our two candidates.

"Ivy," Dogg had said, "are you sure you want to do this?"

"No," she said, "but let's do it anyway."

Now we understand that it was not only an election between Ivy and Dogg. It was also a contest, a battle, them against the committee. **(Seek the opinions of people who are smarter than you, and vote like them.)**
- The Committee

4

Now for those people who want a love story we kind of have to go back a ways to show how it might be misconstrued as that and why it's really not. We have to show why you really wouldn't want to see these two, Ivy and Dogg, together no matter what the circumstances.

The committee didn't have to ask around much to find out that Ivy and Dogg had a rivalry from their elementary school days. It was she that Dogg had beaten for President of Mudlick Elementary. From all accounts, it was a bruising campaign. And again, a few years later, it was Dogg who bested Ivy for the Student Council presidency of Eucalyptus Junior High. What interested us more was that, up to fourth grade, these two had on-again-off-again crushes on one another. Farla Simpson remembers their first kiss when she was playing with them in the bamboo near the dry creek bed. Ivy hadn't thickened yet, and Dogg, still with his baby fat, wasn't the thin young man he became. Dogg, being the boy, led Farla and Ivy through the bamboo, warning them about the stalks and leaves that might brush against their skin. Bamboo leaves will sometimes give you a painful cut if you aren't careful. Ivy was wearing pigtails that shook like loose springs as she plodded along. The three of them were headed for the clear spot worn from years of junior high students who smoked cigarettes before and after school.

(Make your child smoke a full cigarette as a toddler to discourage the habit later.)   - The Committee

This is also the same place where, in the early 70s, high schooler Daphne Roberts dropped a match on her Polyester mini-skirt which immediately caught fire and melted onto her skin. At the same time, as she ran, she set the bamboo on fire, which also set ablaze the Pennfield's chicken house. For years afterward she visited Mudlick schools giving emotional talks about the odor of burned poultry and her scarred thighs. "Smoking did this to me," she'd dramatically conclude as she revealed some of her scarred leg.

When Ivy, Dogg, and Farla arrived at the opening, Farla tried to arrange some leaves to sit on but Ivy plopped down on the ground, leaning back on the embankment. The sky was an off-white glaze above the barely touching bamboo tops that stretched out and over the rotunda-like clearing. "So, what are we gonna do now?" Ivy asked, kicking off her tattered sneakers.

"Dunno," Dogg said. "If you were guys, we'd play pirates." He pulled at the waist of his blue corduroys that hung a couple inches too long at his ankles. It gave him something to focus on. In those days, Dogg wasn't nearly as assertive, so he barely looked at the girls when he spoke.

"That's stupid," Ivy said, standing up. "I can be a pirate easy." She held her hands near her waist as if she were a buccaneer about to draw a whale tooth shiv.

"There aren't girl pirates," Dogg countered, this time looking right at Ivy and Farla, who had stood up as well.

Ivy shook her head forcefully, her pigtails violently bobbing. "Are too. I've seen them in movies and they look just like me."

"Farla, tell Ivy there aren't girl pirates."

Farla took in the stare of both her friends. She liked Dogg a lot, and was jealous that all his attention seemed directed at Ivy. She studied the little beads of sweat broken out across his freckled nose, then Ivy's white neck which had gone red in patches. "I guess," Farla said pragmatically, "that you could capture us and turn us into lady pirates."

Ivy looked suspicious, but surprisingly, Dogg shouted, "Great, everyone find their swords." The three dispersed to look for fallen bamboo.

That's when Farla remembers the kiss. She spent a few minutes looking for a stick or piece of bamboo that looked like a sword. It took her longer than it might have otherwise because she hoped to pick out a weapon that would impress her crush. When she returned to the clearing, there were Ivy and Dogg in the bright sunlight, lip to lip, not moving, nearly grimacing, but they were indeed kissing, if not in the passionate sense.

A year later, after that kiss in the bamboo, the pre-adolescent courtship of Ivy and Dogg was squashed by politics and an unfortunate, if accurate, nickname heaped on Ivy's shoulders. As a rule, the elections at Mudlick elementary are tame. But Ivy enjoyed a popularity in the early grades that she would never know again. Though she was often a bit curt, and boyish, she was honest and helpful and stuck up for even the least popular child on the playground. The willingness to fight even the largest boy combined with the magic shield of her gender—no boy at Mudlick had ever struck a girl in a fight—conveyed upon her a great deal of power and, particularly among the less stout, a preserving respect.

Craig Marston was one of Ivy's protectorate. A pale diabetic with skin so thin he looked like a medical book's illustration of the blood system, Craig couldn't ride a swing or get in line for Four Square without being in someone's way. Once, in third grade, from across the playground, Ivy caught sight of Adam Kaiser pushing Craig aside for a turn at Tether Ball. Even though Adam carried the weight of two boys his age, in seconds Ivy was on the spot, and in even less time a circle of children gathered as she pummeled Adam while sitting on his chest. Even in his teens his broadened, camel-like nose showed signs of the encounter.

Jimmy, on the other hand—he wouldn't be called Dogg until his final year of Junior High—Jimmy became popular early on because he had money, and because he was a celebrity of sorts.

His father owned two auto dealerships out of town, one foreign, one domestic, on the Mile of Cars and Jimmy appeared in all their commercials. For tax reasons, they paid Jimmy union scale. With each commercial since he was nine-months-old, Jimmy's college trust fund grew, plus he always had money on the side. At lunch, if a child needed a little change to afford a second milk or a juice bar, Jimmy was the boy to see. From his end, it wasn't so much as generosity as it was a real need to get rid of his money.

(Providing children with cash of their own builds self-esteem.) - The Committee His father was always tucking dollar bills into his pockets and sending him off to play. Jimmy never wanted for anything. What a family like this was doing in Mudlick, the committee could never quite agree on, though the large house they lived in had been in the Doggins family for three generations.

After a year of stealing innocent kisses in the bamboo, behind the Safeway, and in Ryan Neifert's tree fort—"No girls allowed, but Ivy's okay"—it's easy to imagine that Ivy and Jimmy spent little time talking about their political futures and that it came as a surprise to them that they both intended to run for school President of Mudlick Elementary.

"She can't run," Jimmy told Ryan as they waited for Ivy in the thick Fruitless Mulberry of Ryan's back yard. Quite a few years earlier his father had helped him and his brother build a clubhouse in the branches when Mrs. Ryan was away getting a treatment for the prescription drug dependency she developed after breaking her neck from being thrown from her horse, Burrito.

Ryan fiddled with the tan patch his parents made him wear because the stillness of his glass eye, true blue as it was, made them uncomfortable. "How come she can't run?" he asked, cocking the brow above his good eye.

And then came the two-word response that altered Ivy's young life, the albatross that Jimmy had no intention of hanging around her neck, but which flapped and fluttered her direction the minute he opened his mouth. "She's poor," he said, and even as he did so, he must not have understood the implications. The committee, having done our job over the years, established a great deal of power in that label—there's little dishonor in being poor, but *staying* poor long enough for the title to adhere isn't acceptable. **(Shame is the helium that lifts the poor.)** - The Committee Who would have guessed the impact of that simple, honest phrase, "she's poor," would cost *us* dearly years later.

"She don't seem poor," Ryan said.

"You ever been to her house?"

"No."

Jimmy looked out the window of the tree fort. Four years earlier, Ryan's brother, Martin, who died in a drunk driving accident when he was seventeen, abandoned it with the acquisition of his Learner's Permit. They were at the very top of the backyard hill and twenty feet up in the middle branches of that fifty-year-old mulberry. From there, through the plywood cut-outs, the boys saw the entire street, and, beyond that, the elementary school and the lake shining as if it were yellow mercury. When Jimmy was sure Ivy wasn't anywhere near, he continued. "She doesn't even have a house. She lives in an apartment."

Ryan shrugged. "Lots of people do."

"You're not getting it. I haven't even been to her place. You know why? Because she lives in the Pink Ghetto."

A late afternoon breeze came up and rocked the tree, the wood slats creaking against one another. Ryan nodded because he understood. The Pink Ghetto was not one of Mudlick's better apartment complexes. In fact, it was the first ever built. Some say it got its name from the peculiar shade of stucco slathered on its sides like spoiled strawberry icing. Others say it's because everyone in the complex is poor and pink-skinned. It doesn't help that that's where the Broadback Murders took place, or that people who live there tend to sit on the floor in the evening in fear of a stray bullet flying through the window. Whatever the case, it's always been a rough bit of housing and if you live there, it says a lot about your position in life, whether you want it to or not.

(Home ownership is a foundation of moral stability.)

- The Committee

"Poor Ivy," Ryan said.

"Exactly," Jimmy agreed as if the statement would be nothing more than a definition. "But I kind of like her anyway."

Ryan fixed his sighted eye on his friend and tossed the moment of intimacy into the tree branches with a long, slack-jawed rendering of "Duhhh."

The following week, during the campaign, there was a palpable difference in the way the other children treated Ivy, though at first she didn't sense it. Suddenly, an invisible scorecard floated over her head in the eyes of everyone under ten: same old tennis shoes all week long; waits in line with the other free-lunch kids; wearing that dress with the spot *again*; mother works at Witherspoon's Liquor. All of these things and more floated about her like a tangibly dark aura, and though Ivy's campaign posters, stenciled with thick-leaved vines, proclaimed her slogan as "Climb to the top with Ivy!" the phrase that swept the playground instead was the simple, but true, "Poor Ivy."

Before a single vote was cast Ivy had been brought down. It mattered not that Witherspoon's donated enough nickel candies for her to pass out to the entire Third and Fourth grades, nor that her assembly speech about school pride and raising funds for computers in the library went over very well with the teachers—"Do we want to be children of the future, or mindless drones?!"— nor did anyone seem to care that Ivy actually had a resume, of sorts, as a Crossing Guard and class monitor. No matter what she did, it still all added up to "Poor Ivy." Few things diminish a person in the eyes of others more than publicized poverty, which in itself should be incentive for the poor to lift themselves up.

As for Jimmy, with his confession to one-eyed Ryan that Ivy was poor, he'd unknowingly started something, like a tremor in an ocean that spawns a surge that grows into a tsunami by the time it reaches shore miles away. The same wave that swamped Ivy would carry Jimmy as high and far as he wanted to go. No one would criticize his plain, "Vote for Jimmy Doggins" signs with the "y" and "s" squinched at the end to fit the paper size, nor the fact he rarely spoke of the campaign all week. And though the line his father wrote in his speech about "root beer in the water fountains" received the planned-for laughter, the truth is he could've stood in front of the entire school and silently peeled a banana and still have won the election. Jimmy Doggins was a winner, and everyone knew he understood this unasked-for projection of a future that spun out before him like stepping stones in the clouds. It meant for the rest of his life he would win, and win and win and win.

The only price Jimmy paid for all this fortune was the single friendship he valued most, the one person who should've cared, but didn't, that he had money, that he was Little Jimmy in the TV commercials. What it cost him were those few excruciating moments when they announced that he'd won the election 117 to 20, when he was called up on the stage to say a brief thank you in front of half the school, while Ivy, with whom he didn't dare make eye contact, sat defeated in the second row. She was the one everyone really watched, tears silently spotting her white dress, brand new from the look of its intense creases. Everyone remembers looking at her, then at him, as if there were a slow Ping Pong rally between them. And it was clear, even with her proud, straight-up posture, and her rare, tightly wound pair of skimpy buns, with the tears that she was almost keeping under control, that she knew, though no one could tell for how long, she knew what everyone was saying, "Poor Ivy," and that she knew, too, where it had begun. And in one feeble moment, Jimmy looked at her at the end of the thank yous his father had written for him, certainly by now sensing what everyone else did, Jimmy looked at her and said, "Thanks, too, to my worthy opponent, Ivy Simmons." With that, he abruptly stepped away from the microphone, walked through the applause and to the back of the auditorium where he whispered in the ear of his teacher, Vida Clark, the two of them leaving, she patting his back as the door swung slowly shut, separating them from an ecstatic student body.

Three years later, the committee learned, Ivy launched an ill-fated election in junior high, the results the same, but not so lopsided. Some say Ivy didn't expect to win, that she ran for other reasons, mainly to build a constituency. That her real object was becoming President of the Associated Student Body in high school. And, with her clever selection of Wide Receiver Joey Mathison as a running mate—"You won't have to do a thing," she told him—Ivy managed to drain away enough of Dogg's athlete base to pull out a slim victory just weeks before she walked into our meeting with the announcement that she was running for Junior Mr. Mayor.

But there are different ways of winning, different finish lines. It came out later that Dogg's ASB loss had really been of his own making. He decided he wanted a different position, so he shifted his attention to the class elections, where he was handily voted Senior Class President for the following year. High profile, slim responsibilities, stepping stone, usually, to becoming Prom King. While Ivy was worrying about how much concession money ASB was earning at the football games, and whether to hold a referendum on a new mascot—40 years of "Mudlick Crayfish, Go! Go! Go!" had never really caught anyone's imagination—while Ivy was immersed, Jimmy would be able to enjoy his senior year. In everyone's mind, he'd beaten Ivy once again.

5

We have no way of verifying this, nor do we particularly admire the source, but out of fairness, Thatch Hutchinson swears the following words were exchanged about the Junior Mr. Mayor race, though he wouldn't be precise about the context, nor the time and place.

"Ivy, I *do* care about you," Dogg said.

"Not enough," Ivy said.

"Enough that I don't want you to go through with this."

"I know it's dumb, but this is my last crack at beating you on your own territory and this is pretty much my last chance. Just once I'd like to feel..."

"Popular?"

Ivy shook her head. "Acknowledged."

(When on vacation, unscrew light bulbs in most rooms to prevent the house sitter from snooping around.)
                                                                        - The Committee

6

"But what do we call her if she wins?" Jacob Alter asked. Ivy hadn't been gone from the sign-up table thirty seconds. Jacob stood, his hands squeaking across the polished conference table. Pinned to the wall on his left was a "Mudlick = Valhalla West" prototype bumper sticker. Above his right shoulder was a large black and white photo of the failed Mudlick Vineyard, rows and rows of withered grapevines on a background of hazy, dry foothills. For a few years, we're told, Mr. O'Haloran almost made a go of it, but the soil and too-shallow well both gave out on him. "I don't think we've ever had a girl run before," Jacob added, pacing the perimeter of the room.

It was uncharacteristically shortsighted of the committee. There had been Junior Mr. Mayor elections for as long as any of us could remember, and of course, we should have realized that eventually we'd have a female candidate. What would we call Ivy if she were elected? The sash, with its red, white and blue embroidery, and the plaque, minus the winner's name, were already prepared. "How about Little Miss Junior Mr. Mayor?" Dillard Phipps offered. The women on the committee glared at him. Charming and exasperating all at once, Dillard, of *the* Phipps', was one of the older members. He'd once suggested, during a financial crisis at Mudlick High, that the school temporarily suspend girls' sports and consolidate funds into the football program. But, at Christmas, with his bulbous paunch and fountain of white hair, he made a fine Santa Claus, or simply a kindly looking old man when the committee needed a good, trustworthy ear somewhere in Mudlick. It was Dillard who'd informed us that several families in the tract homes built two years earlier planned to install satellite dishes on their roofs, which we pointed out was in violation of ordinance 1074.3B.

The committee agreed, of course, that calling Ivy Little Miss Junior Mr. Mayor was inappropriate, if not absurd. Without any of the committee getting rude, we all instinctively understood that a year of introducing someone like Ivy as "Little Miss" would be about like entering Francis the Talking Mule in the Kentucky Derby. Conferences broke out in groups of twos and threes to come up with something acceptable, a title that could easily be added to the existing sash and plaque, if needed.

In the corner of the room, Joseph Colton, owner of the burned Grand Mudlick Lodge of a hundred years earlier, stared down at us from a sepia photograph, his thick gray-yellow moustache hiding the ambivalence he held toward our town. Some suggest he may even have set the lodge on fire himself when the committee, just two people back then, challenged his claim of sole ownership of the lake. **(Arson is bad.)** - The Committee And it's reported, though his daughter never confirmed it, that his distaste for the community showed at the very end when he said on his death bed "Mudlick could have been something."

When the committee came back to order, it appeared there were just two viable options. Dillard Phipps, and Gloria Valdez fingering an embroidered daisy on her tangerine scarf, offered the first solution, which was to simply add "ess" to the end of Mayor on the sash and plaque and all would be solved. "For the price of three letters," Dillard said, "I can etch us out of this mess." As part owner of Kaplan's Trophy Barn, the suggestion seemed firm. "Junior Mr. Mayoress."

The competing notion came from Ruby and Flack Jones, the only married couple to ever sit on the committee. They were, as always, holding hands above the table and wearing nearly matching outfits, Ruby with her blue "I Love Hawaii" t-shirt and dangling aqua hoop earrings and Flack wearing a blue oxford, the sleeves buttoned tight at the cuffs to make sure no one saw the tattoos we all knew were there, the splotchy one of the bare-breasted woman coiled by a snake and one that said "U.S. NAVY" with a skull in place of the "A." Their inseparability, down to the fact they both dyed their hair the same deep black—"Elvis meets Vampira," a later committee member once said— their inseparability was driven by the single calamitous *near* infidelity of Flack shortly before their marriage.

In an inexplicably poor understanding of Ruby's color blindness, Flack had composed, under the imagined security of red ink, a sort of love letter to his previous fiancé, Josephina. Her parents, finally, would not let her marry outside the Catholic faith, and Flack, committed to the non-denominational First Church of our Savior, refused to convert. In his letter, however, written in erratic, line-defying script, he proposed they have one night together before his marriage to Ruby. "I want more than anything to be your first, as we'd planned," he wrote. Though the letter was less than poetic, Flack took days to write it, confidently leaving it in the top drawer of his desk, thinking that Ruby couldn't see the red words which were his heart and blood. Instead, patiently, she read every addition as it unfolded, waiting for the right moment to discuss the actual limitations of her vision, about which her future husband clearly misunderstood. To this day, for all we do know, we've never heard from either of them exactly what was said. But afterward, over years, Flack became a changed man, a male version of Ruby, veering now and then because of drink or joblessness, only to be reined in by her public reminders of the letter she carried around in a plastic freezer bag, zipped into the side pocket of her black leather purse, ready to be quoted from at any given moment.

(Use grudges wisely, and sparingly.)   - The Committee

"Well," Ruby said after presenting their idea to add "Ms." to the beginning of Junior Mr. Mayor, "what do you think?"

After considerable debate, the committee reasoned, though both ideas had merit, that on a practical level, the "Mayoress" suggestion added three full letters to the title, whereas "Ms." was simply two and a bit of punctuation. And, the latter had the advantage of sounding more professional. So, it was decided on a nearly unanimous vote that in the very unlikely and unwelcome event that Ivy Simmons won the election, she'd hold the title Ms. Junior Mr. Mayor.

7

As fast as information flows into the committee, it some-times flows out just as quickly. Less than twenty-four hours after Ivy announced her candidacy, word got out that the committee was less than happy about her entry into the race. Most of the contacts we had merely wondered who Ivy Simmons was. But the reply from Vida Clark was much more invested. She was someone with whom we had a history and were inclined to hear her out given the fact that her ex-husband was a former committee member who served quite honorably. That, and the fact that Vida was a member of the school board. We keep her letter to the committee tucked in the back of the black photo album later foisted on us by Ivy's mother.

For a very brief moment, Vida's letter convinced the committee that Ivy's candidacy would not be a problem and that we need not worry. Events would prove otherwise.

To The Committee,

This sheet of paper has been sitting on my kitchen table since early this morning, and now a little square of light from the window shines on it like it's telling me to get going. I'm sitting here with about my thirtieth cup of coffee of the day, working up the courage to write you all about Ivy and Jimmy and this year's Junior Mr. Mayor election. I've heard already your displeasure with Ivy and I can only imagine what you're about to do and if I'm right, I don't like it. I don't like it one bit.

As I sit here, I see out to my backyard where that messy olive tree I'm always complaining about is bravely taking the summer heat. Below is perhaps the reason, despite my complaints when it drops its fruit, that I've never had it chopped down, why that gray old thing will stand as long as I live here. Because, when you sit beneath it at the picnic table my ex-husband built, you are sitting in the best kind of shade. The best kind of shade a mother and father and their son can share on summer afternoons. A shade that forgives burned hamburgers and soothes bee stings.

Impatient as I know you to be, you're already wondering what this has to do with Ivy and "Dogg," as Mudlick seems to want to call him. Indeed, Jimmy is a treasure. As you undoubtedly already know, I had occasion to be well acquainted with him because of school. I was his teacher when he and Ivy first ran against each other, and I know how sensitive Jimmy was to the way things devolved, the way, as I heard the kids say then, he "creamed Ivy." We talked after his acceptance speech the day he won, and let me tell you, that little boy had his face practically buried in his desk trying to fight off tears because of what had happened to Ivy. I remember he looked up at me, eyes watery and red, a half-painted paper-mache pterodactyl looming behind him. And he said something no child should have to ask. "Ms. Clark," he asked, sniffling, "do people like me just because I have money?" At that age, he understood the double-edged sword of how the election had turned, that the "revelation" (goodness, who didn't know?) that Ivy was poor said something about him as well. And let's be honest, the committee makes it clear how the poor should feel about themselves regardless of their individual circumstances.

Though I'm no longer teaching, I will always remember that afternoon with Jimmy. Through my ex-husband it lead me to encourage the committee in moderate directions. Mostly I failed in that effort, though, fortunately, Jimmy seems to have only grown into the young man I'd suspected he would. He is one of those people whose wonderful reputation bears out, and then some, when you meet him. Jimmy will do well in

life, whether the committee stands by his side in this Junior Mr. Mayor
election or not.

Had the letter stopped there, the committee would have probably been more than happy with Vida's comments. Just a simple
"Sincerely, Vida Clark" would have been perfect. But, maybe too
many years on the school board and all their yackety yack yack
(Scented stationary is a sign of moral laxness.) - The Committee
taught her some bad habits about not knowing when to quit while
you're ahead. In this first part of the letter, Vida managed to confirm every reason we knew Dogg could be the best Junior Mr. May-
or we'd ever had. But, unfortunately, there was more to the letter.
Much more.

So, about that shade in the backyard. There are times when
you're sitting at the picnic table and the wind comes up a bit and sud-
denly light is sparkling all over. That, and the percussion of the leaves
make it feel like you're sitting beneath a shower of invisible confetti.
The table, peeling green paint and all, seems lonelier these days. Some
afternoons I look out the window and expect to see Cole Junior there,
where he spent a lot of his time, especially at the end when we were told
there was nothing more to be done. But this is not a letter about how
much a mother misses her son. It's about how that teenage son found a
bit of happiness as he waited out the inevitable, how, I often think, he
was able for a couple hours at a time to take his mind off the worried
look that was certainly always on my face. I see myself now, hovering,
watching as if at any moment it would happen.

They traded services, Ivy and Cole Junior. She came to him for
tutoring in Physics, he, never a fan of subjectivity, needed help in His-
tory. "You mean to tell me," he said in his first high school history
course, "Abraham Lincoln never did or said one asshole thing?" Not
exactly the quote a mother hopes to hear attributed to her son, but now
I cherish the individualism.

When I close my eyes, I can see Cole Junior and Ivy talking,
sometimes with their books open, sometimes not. Cole, even with his
black hair thinned to a wisp, looking renewed and relaxed, as if he'd
forgotten what was happening to him. And Ivy usually laughing, or

snapping her hands to her waist when she was making a point. So many times I wanted to slide the window open to hear what they were saying, to maybe give myself a chance to forget.

Just like with Jimmy Doggins, I knew Ivy from my earlier days at Mudlick elementary school. I knew of her, that is. I knew she was the girl in the white dress who found out in front of the entire school that she lost the election. But it was teenage Ivy I really came to know during my son's last few months. Sure, maybe she wore the same clothes more often than most people would. And yes, maybe without the makeup and hairstyle young ladies wear she could seem a bit conspicuous. But I'm coming to understand that noticing such things says more about the observer than about her.

All this is to say, I'm concerned about what might happen this summer. I know the committee well, how certain you are about your role in this community, and to what lengths you'll go to press your opinion. If my ex-husband were still living here, was still on the committee, I might be saying all this to him. But I don't have your ear the way I once did, fraction that it was. Still, I write this to ask that you let that young lady be. Don't turn the Junior Mr. Mayor elections into Ivy vs. the committee.

I'm not sure what effect this letter will have on all of you, or even if you'll read this far. But maybe I'll end this way if I haven't convinced you yet.

There was a day about a month before my Cole Junior passed away when Ivy and he, as usual, sat beneath the olive tree. It was a warm afternoon on a day scrubbed clean by Santa Anna winds that blew all week but seemed to have calmed. Cole Junior and Ivy were immersed in building the foundation of her balsa wood suspension bridge. Even now I question whether she ever really needed tutoring in Physics, but never-the-less there she was, asking my son for help. I was struck as I watched Cole Junior instruct Ivy using the tip of his pencil like a pointer, that I was seeing the peak of his potential, that there was not time for more, and that maybe I'd not be able to think of that moment without also thinking of the generosity in Ivy's responsiveness to his direction, the way, as I think of it now, she feigned uncertainty, pushed her hair back behind one ear and smiled a question or two. That was Ivy. That was my son.

When she came in to get glasses of water, I hesitated to speak to her, worried I'd break the spell, though we'd had many brief conversa-

tions since she started her visits. But also, though I know better now, I was concerned that maybe Ivy didn't understand the gravity of the situation, or at least the immediacy of it. "You know," I said hesitantly as she retrieved ice from our freezer and filled their glasses from the tap, comfortable in our kitchen—and I, happy that she was—" as difficult as it is for a mother to admit, I want to be sure you understand that there's not much time left for Cole. We can't set our hopes on the future."

Ivy stood next to me, setting the glasses of water on the table where I'd made myself an audience, an excuse of bills in front of me. Both of us looked out the window at Cole Junior inspecting the work they'd done on Ivy's bridge. He was pale and thin, even a bit unsteady, but none-the-less focused. "He only needs a little Now," Ivy said quietly, picking up the glasses of water. "And it just so happens that Now is something I have plenty of."

In that, I felt the assurance that Cole Junior must have felt. I don't know what more I can say to you. Tread lightly this year in these Junior Mr. Mayor elections. Certainly, Jimmy could represent Mudlick well. But don't be blinded by pedigree. Ivy's heart would benefit us all.

Yours,
Vida Clark

Of all the nerve. What could the committee do with a letter like that? Though, admittedly, that's not exactly what we thought the first time we read it. Caught off guard, we were momentarily persuaded that Ivy's entry into the campaign, though undesirable, wasn't something to get worked up about. In any case, she'd surely lose to Dogg and no action would be required on our part.

8

It didn't take long for Ivy to give us cause for worry. In a town our size, it's not hard to run into folks and of course Ivy ran into Dogg and Charlene at Borgner's Stationers. The Borgners were long dead, but when Theo and Doris Tuttle took over, they had a choice of installing new carpet or putting up a new sign. Which is really just as well because after the divorce, Doris got the store and she would've had to change the sign again when she switched back to her maiden name. Doris (Yoder now) volunteers at the food co-op. For her efforts, each Friday and Saturday for four hours of work, she comes home with two pounds of cheese, celery, saltines, two cans of soup, apples or oranges, (depending on availability), and a dozen irregular eggs.

And it was on a Saturday, as Charlene was opening up the shop for Doris, and Dogg was kissing her goodbye, that Ivy walked up. In retrospect, the committee feels that Ivy had to know Charlene worked there—having tutored her nearly every day as a student-assistant in Charlene's summer school English class—and even that it was common for Dogg to drive Charlene to work on the way to his weekend tennis practice. It was an intimidation tactic, we've decided. But in that moment Ivy feigned innocence (surprise) in finding the two of them in mid cheek-peck, watched by the smiling, bright orange, cartoon sun decorating the glass storefront—*Sizzling Summer Savings on Picnic/Party favors!*

Ivy had come from around the corner, locking eyes with Charlene. "Precious," Ivy said. "Who would've thought I'd be able to get office supplies and young love all in one trip?"

Dogg spun around. He was wearing the red striped shirt he had on when he won his last tournament. "Ivy. Let's keep this fight between you and I."

"Between you and *me*," Ivy corrected, pushing her stringy hair behind her ears. "And don't worry. *Everything's* between us."

Charlene did not like confrontation, perhaps because her father, Sergeant William Hergis, did, sought it out, in fact, on the base, at home, even at the ice cream store sampling different flavors. Charlene turned toward the door, her French tipped fingers shaking as she turned the key in the lock.

(Absolutely no red nail polish unless you want people to think things.)   - The Committee

"I can't stand politics," she said, pushing into the store and pulling Dogg with her.

"You're the only guy I know who plays with dolls," Ivy said as the pair retreated inside. She stepped close to the window just under the word "sizzle" and looked directly at Charlene who was already looking back from behind the counter. "And I do mean dolls as in plural," she said before walking away.

To be fair, as we like to think we are, this is Charlene's version, and certainly the most believable. But, Harold Palmer reported being there for the exchange as he was finishing his fast food breakfast in his truck before opening up his locksmith shop next door. He didn't see it like Charlene at all. Of the two of them, Harold is hardly the more credible, given the fact that, even to this day, he refuses to remove the god-awful home-made birdhouses in his front yard even after the committee has posted several stern notes on them.

But he claims he remembered the conversation because of the coincidence of seeing Ivy and Dogg together. Years earlier, when they were in elementary school, the pair of them had come across Manna Johnson stuck at her wrought iron gate. She'd closed her bright red muumuu into the lock of her gate and couldn't extricate herself. The committee asked her why she didn't just slip off the dress and she said, "Because I wasn't about to walk across my yard in the all-together and stay in that neighborhood." So, it was Ivy and Dogg, fortuitously riding by on their bikes, that found her and went for help at Harold Palmer's locksmith shop.

In this most recent encounter, Harold recognized them even in their teenage forms. And he claims that Ivy did indeed show up as Dogg let Charlene off to open the store. In his flimsy version, Ivy doesn't say a word to Charlene at all, just waits until she goes in and has a few words with Dogg on her own. She says hello and he looks away at first.

"I'm just a little stuck, Ivy," he says to her. "But I'll make it right."

"No, Jimmy," she says pretty firmly. "Making it right just means you think there's something wrong. This situation doesn't need to be fixed, but one of *us* does. Nothing's ever hurt me so much. How many more times in our lives are you willing to discard our friendship?" She turns to leave but stops, holding up a single finger, tapping the air. "That's the wrong question," she says. "How many more times am I going to come back?"

And that's the whole of Harold's version. Ivy walks into the store and Dogg drives away in the time it takes Harold to drink the last of his coffee. But really, the committee has concluded Harold's version is just a bit too simple. Charlene's account clearly reflects Ivy's true antagonism. If anyone ever needed evidence that Ivy was spiteful and out of control, the committee could certainly high-light Charlene's version. Not that we're looking to vindicate any of our decisions or actions, but all we have to do is look back at the way Ivy hijacked the Junior Mr. Mayor elections, how she made a mockery out of the whole thing, and we know we were right to do the things we did.

9

At the same time the Junior Mr. Mayor election was shaping up, Abigail Colton displayed her summer topiary, as she did every year, new botanical art that amazed Mudlick, and would, after all was said and done, assume immense importance during the election. The topiary stood in the center of Ms. Colton's lawn, protected by a wrought iron fence and her one-eared German Shepherd, Collie, named for her half-brother, General Collin James Colton, who died in Vietnam, crushed to death by a half dozen barrels of Agent Orange after a ceremonial inspection of troops near the Mekong Delta. **(Encourage young men with no college prospects to enlist. War is useful.)** - The Committee The hour before his death, he'd told the semi-doomed soldiers, in his famous manner of connecting with the fighting men, that their "efforts in this Gook-ravaged country will go down in history as the bravest moment in American military history."

Ms. Colton was and remains the youngest daughter by a second marriage of Joseph Colton. She was the only family member by her father's side when he died and carries on his banner of bitterness toward Mudlick. In her gray years, Ms. Colton represents the last surviving link to the Grand Mudlick Lodge. Though she was born years after its demise, she inherited all the furniture and art saved before the fire brought the lodge to the ground. Some of the paintings, we're told, seventy in all, including ten by Olaf Weighorst, were purchased very late in Mr. Colton's life and would revise the landscape of the history of Western oil painting if they were ever allowed to be exhibited publicly. Now, we assume, it all sits in the Victorian home erected by Joseph Colton himself, the property whittled down to ten sloping acres on the upper side of Mudlick. And there, Ms. Colton resides within the walls of her great house, with its sparkling white wooden shingles and gray, duel turret roof complete with the obnoxious curly-q trim of the East coast Victorian homes Joseph Colton admired, that look-how-much-money-I-have kind of house.

Though the Colton family relationship with Mudlick is dubious—the committee has pondered for years why they never moved out altogether—each year Ms. Colton attends the Friends of Colton Library potluck fundraiser in support of the granite institution her father built with his own money and left to the town. And each little league season she trots out to the mound at Colton Field, built on property that was once the family's private airstrip, to throw out the first ball. But most significantly, every year up to the time Ivy and Dogg ran against each other, Ms. Colton provided a pleasing display of topiary art on the expanse of her lawn.

In years previous to the Ivy vs. Dogg election, Ms. Colton presented topiaries of the animal variety, geese, rabbits and the like, and there were always persistent rumors her exceptionally large greenhouse contained something very, very ambitious. And despite our general dislike of their creator, to some degree, these little creatures became real to us. It was easy to imagine their private barnyard and forest dwelling lives and those thoughts often lead to intricate histories and simple names like Goosegoose and Whiskers. But we all agreed the year Ivy and Dogg went at it head to head for Junior Mr. Mayor, that year's creation of a small girl was by far her most perfect—life-sized right down to her swaying green pigtails and uplifted hand with its distinct fingers that seemed to wave at us when we walked by. And it wasn't uncommon to see someone waving back. That poor little thing. Destined for so much tragedy. If only we'd known how much trouble she was in for.

By the first day the committee was able to visit as a body, word about the new topiary spread through town quickly and the sidewalk in front of Ms. Colton's vast lawn filled up. The air was shot through with warm breezes, and in the distance, thunderhead clouds rose and cauliflowered over the dessert. But above Mudlick, the sky was blue and empty except for the flight of a Red-tail hawk riding updrafts in lazy, sometimes wing-tottering circles.

"Isn't she a pretty little girl," Audra Webster said of the new topiary. "I wonder what grade she's in." None of us thought it was unusual that she would ask such a question. Audra had just retired from teaching first grade for thirty-nine years. Practically everyone in town had gone through her class at one time or another. But just the previous year, during Mudlick Elementary Art days, we discovered something rather sad. The children had been allowed to use their colors all wrong and so the wall of the V.F.W. Hall dedicated to her class was full of paintings with green Suns and orange grass. In some, the clouds were purple and raining brown. One little girl had merely drawn in pencil what looked like a backward "S" and titled it "only the skin of a seahorse." It was then we realized some of the children, having extended their teacher's laxness into their lives, were wearing mismatched clothes, too. As much as we loved her, Audra Webster needed to retire. So the committee met and decided the matter quite neatly which is how we do things here.

(Before having children, map their lives carefully to avoid unpleasant surprises.) - The Committee

"Bout Fourth grade," Emory Case guessed in response to Audra's query as to what grade the little topiary girl might be in. It was a surprise to us to see him so soon after having his colon surgery. Emory, a grayish blonde Abraham Lincoln, complete with sunken cheeks, had suffered from ulcerative colitis for years. When, finally, his stool just became too bloody to bear, he submitted to his wife's request to get the surgery. "I agreed to 'for better or worse,'" she'd told him, "but not for incontinence." Not one to relax, there he was, just as eager to view the new topiary as the rest of the town.

There was quite a group of us that day, maybe thirty. The topiary was installed about halfway between the house and the fence, Collie panting at her feet—his single ear doing double-time scanning—a pair of Japanese persimmon trees flanking the topiary to its left and right.

"More like Third," said Emory's wife, guessing what grade the little girl would be in. She held Dolly in her arms, a scarred, mostly bald, but always well-dressed doll. The Cases were a nice couple but they tended to argue a great deal and pretty much everyone agreed that the reason Marjorie Case carried Dolly around was because they couldn't have children of their own. But none of us really minded because Dolly's baby-cry squeaker went out quite some time previous and Marjorie had glued her wobbly black eyes shut to keep her in a constant state of sleep, a powder-cheeked corpse in ruffles.

In our little black album, there's a photo of Ivy and Dogg holding Dolly between them, she, characteristically unexcited by her surroundings, trim lashes in their permanent sleep pose, Dogg looking straight at the camera with that perfectly white smile, a peace sign beaming from his two strong fingers, Ivy, smiling, but not looking at the camera, looking beyond the frame at Marjorie as we would find out.

"She asked me if the books helped," Marjorie told us, though she would not say what that meant, only that months earlier Ivy had written down several titles for Marjorie to look up at the library. "I was surprised that she remembered me," Marjorie said. "And the books did help."

The day Abigail Colton introduced the new topiary was hot and some of the committee, impressed as they were with this new green citizen of Mudlick, began to wilt under the sun. Dillard Phipps, digging so deep into his pocket it appeared he was stretching one side of his brown striped suspenders to its limit, drew out a handkerchief. His forehead was shaded by the wave of his white hair where he patted softly in a familiar motion that followed his neckline down to the pink dimpled scar at his throat where he'd had a tracheotomy after inhaling the cap to his great-nephew's baby aspirin bottle.

Maybe our reaction to the heat is why we immediately fell for the little girl topiary, why her greenness didn't suggest to us a Martian or some sort of swamp-creature. Because, as we'd see more and more, in heat and controversy we were concerned for this girl, initially because every year some of the high school boys stole Ms. Colton's topiaries and abandoned them in odd places. One year, we discovered a leafy menagerie placed in a circle outside the firehouse. Another year, in the center of Mudlick Lake, the boys floated Ms. Colton's green ducks on a wood raft. It was that prank, in fact, that Cole Clark Junior had been involved with, almost a year before his diagnosis. The same Cole Clark Junior who Ivy was quoted in the newspaper as eulogizing as "a friend, and a bridge builder." Nothing was mentioned of his hoodlum activities.

The little girl topiary newly on display in the Colton yard was more precious than any of the cute but lifeless animals that came before, and which were snatched from their intended home. This beautiful topiary was stable, too large to move, this time set into a hole in the ground rather than atop it, so that the little girl looked as if she was standing on Abigail Colton's lawn rather than potted above it. She stood in an unruffled green dress of living leaves, her body language offering a friendly out-stretched hand and the smile that, if it wasn't actually there, all of us were willing to imagine.

Even home schooled Susan Baker, the little nine-year-old repeat-offender arsonist—also referred to privately as Film at Eleven—whose mother brought her on a "field trip" to see the new topiary, even she fell in love with her viney counterpart. "What's her name?" Susan asked her mother as she poked her head between the wrought iron fencing. She wore an orange jumper that suggested a highway worker or prison inmate.

"I don't know, honey," her mother said, tugging at the collar of her daughter's coveralls.

"Then let's call her Fern, since she's a plant."

At first, the gathered crowd giggled at the suggestion, but after a few moments, there was a growing realization that the idea had merit. One by one they looked toward the committee. Never ones to decline an opportunity for decision-making, without conference we agreed that Ms. Colton's topiary was Mudlick's new daughter and her name was Fern.

(Strive to be a silent hero. The less you say, the smarter you are. Eat more asparagus.)

- The Committee

10

Ivy and Dogg sat directly across from one another. Gloria and Lucille Otto—with all our responsibilities, we can't all possibly attend every little meeting—brought them together to get the rules of the election straight. This was a step that hadn't been necessary until ten years earlier when Gordon Harley ran against David Vicar, young men whose campaign strategies consisted mainly of sabotage and vandalism. Even today, where the Vicars used to live, there's a faint white shadow on the brown stucco garage wall where someone, presumably Gordon Harley, wrote in fuzzy chalk lettering "Vicar Doesn't have a Prayer!"

At the meeting, Dogg's parents sat on either side of him. Mr. Doggins who was much shorter and balder than he looked in his television commercials, had already distributed to each of us the ubiquitous rubber key chains in the shape of two interlocking "g's," the symbol of his car dealerships—"We spell GGuarantee with a double-G!" Dogg's mother, always quiet, sat with her pale hands folded on the table, the sleeves of a pink Cashmere sweater tied loosely around her neck. They were an odd couple to be sure, opposites, but they'd produced Dogg, and so something was working.

We were waiting for Ivy's mother, Gwen Simmons, who'd arrived and begged our pardon to smoke a cigarette outside before she sat down. "I need a smoke first," is what she actually said. The room remained mostly silent, each of us staring at notes, or the key chains that sat like shiny dead minnows in front of us. Ivy looked the most relaxed. She wore her hair back in a pitifully thin ponytail that narrowed down to rat tail proportions. But she was smiling and looking around the room at the mounted arrowheads and black and white photographs of Mudlick during its brief flirtation with importance. She took special interest, it seemed, in the photo of the washed out railroad bridge, a silver-eyed man standing in the foreground of the collapsed structure and the floodwaters beneath it. Mostly, Ivy seemed unaware, or unconcerned that we watched her as she took in the room, noticed that she wore the same red dress she'd had on when she first announced her intention to run. Only now, it seemed to fit her more tightly, the ruffles at the collar forced upward around her neck as if her head were a rosehip.

(A messy collar indicates a messy personality.) - The Committee

Finally, Gloria looked up from her pad of paper and broke the ice, turning to Lucille. She brought up the Bud Wagoner situation, wondering if in the few minutes available we could make any headway in that area. Bud owned fifteen acres near the freeway and had been approached by a do-it-yourself home improvement outfit to buy the property. It's just the kind of business the committee works to bring to Mudlick, though we had nothing to do with this one. Unfortunately, Bud wasn't interested in selling. In the Forties, his father purchased seventeen pecan trees and a pair of Chinchillas and set up a fur ranch on the property, housing the rodents in a huge, cooled, concrete bunker surrounded and covered by earth. Connor Wagoner imagined a kind of Chinchilla empire and took to wearing sharply creased fedoras and smoking cigars he couldn't afford. "Chinchilla is the fur of the future," he'd say to anyone who had even the slightest doubt. But, like most people, he forgot that the future we envision never arrives.

Five years after buying the first pair of Chinchillas, during a long rainy spell, the mounded dirt on the roof collected so much moisture that it caved in on top of the caged rodents. Those few that weren't killed scurried about town for a couple weeks and gradually died off, most of them thinned and dehydrated by our dry climate, reduced to bony mounds of gray fluff. But it was the pecan trees that Bud prized, the tall, scraggly reminders of his father's efforts. For the most part, they were barren, occasionally giving off a few nuts. "They'll cut 'em all down and my heart too," Bud told Jacob at the suggestion of selling his property. The committee was sensitive to his response, but also realistic about the uselessness to Mudlick of a bunch of dusty trees. We resolved that we would just have to convince Bud that it was time to retire, maybe take the money and buy a smaller plot and we'd give him a seedling pecan as a gesture of good will. Though most people can't see past the end of their own noses, so we didn't hold out much hope for changing Bud's mind.

But the truth is, the last time that property did anyone even a mild bit of good was when the elder Wagoner, attempting to recoup some of his chinchilla losses, allowed a traveling flea circus to set up on his property on a Memorial Day weekend. The one faded canvas sign was painted with clumsy red lettering. *See Death Defying Chariot Races! See the World's Smallest Maestro Conduct the World's smallest 200 piece Orchestra! Thrill to the crackling Whip of Banzar as he Tames Blood-Thirsty Wild Animals! All in the Amazing Armstrong Circus With a Cast of Thousands!!!*

Of course, that "cast" was thousands of glued-down, semi-costumed fleas, and "blood thirsty" was perhaps the only part of the advertisement that was literally true. But for 50 cents it wasn't too bad for an hour's entertainment. The committee at the time remarked in gest how useful it could be if they had the ability to glue down people in Mudlick now and then to get them to do this or that thing we needed done.

Just as Lucille was about to offer a further course of action on Bud's property, she was interrupted. "I'm ready, Baby," Ms. Simmons announced to her daughter as she walked inside. She was a small woman, but her voice registered deep and loud like the low range of a pipe organ. She wore a bright lavender tank top that failed

to hide her bra straps and most obviously allowed a clear view
of a shoulder tattoo done with crisp green lettering spelling
her daughter's name and underscored by a sparsely leafed vine.

(Snug undergarments are a sign of a confident person.)

She sat, a dark red pack of Pall Malls still clutched in her^- The Committee
hand, and the room suddenly heaped with the smell of cigarettes.
"So, what's the skinny?"

Lucille Otto, who agreed to chair this session of the committee,
cleared her throat, touching her crisp gray collar in the way that always let us know she was ready to speak. She put on the gold frame
reading glasses always hanging around her neck. "We just want the
children to be aware of the ground rules." She gestured to Ivy and
Dogg, who was picking at the cuticles of one thumb. Lucille's specialty, as a secretary for 41 years, was organization, and she had at
hand copies for every one of the relatively brief "Rules of Conduct"
we'd shaped over the years. After each person at the table had a
paper in front of them, Lucille read aloud, enunciating in her hum-
mingbird voice, even the numbers.

1. Above all, candidates must remember that more than representing themselves during the campaign, they are representing
Mudlick.

2. Candidates must coordinate and direct their own campaigns.
Strategic assistance from outside organizations or adults, including parents, is prohibited.

3. Candidates may accrue no debt as a result of campaign costs.
All products and services required for campaigning must be paid
in full by Election Day.

4. Vote tabulation will be performed by the sitting Junior Mr.
Mayor and the candidates themselves immediately following the
closing of the polls.

5. Untrained livestock may not participate in any campaign event.

Ivy and Dogg both laughed after Lucille read rule number 5. They clearly didn't have a memory of the poorly planned "Running of the Piglets" planned by Donald Barns. "I thought we'd shoo them out of a pen at one end of the street and into a pen at the other," he told us after we spent six hours rounding up the 34 piglets he'd let loose in front of his grandfather's barber shop, each of the squealing little hams marked in black with the initials D.B. from a stamp he carved from a large russet potato.

"I'm not so sure about number 2," Mr. Doggins said, patting down the matt of hair combed over center of his bald scalp. "I got a lot of resources that could help Jimmy."

Lucille looked above the top of her glasses at Mr. Doggins. "Strategic assistance is different from financial assistance. This is about how motivated the candidate is. Not how excited his parents are." Of course, we were in fact hoping that Mr. Doggins would help Dogg pay for anything he needed.

"It's cool, Dad," Dogg said, tapping his fingers on the table matter-of-factly. "I can do it." His mother smiled and patted his shoulder.

Then it was Ivy's mother's turn. "As for my little girl," she said, leaning back in her chair, "she can vouch for the fact I've hardly helped with anything her whole life. She was smarter'n me by the time she was four." The room laughed as Ms. Simmons poked her elbow in Ivy's side. "But I do got one thing to make real clear," she continued, more seriously, and seemingly with the full knowledge of the resonance of her voice. She leaned in and spoke to Dogg directly, her blue eyeshadowed lids lowering halfway as she focused on him. "I don't want none of that Poor Ivy shit going on this time."

Mr. Doggins slammed his hand on the table. "I object."

"That was a long time ago, Momma," Ivy chimed in.

Gwen turned to her daughter. "All the same, Baby, I just want to make sure they ain't looking down their noses at you." She paused and scanned the table. "I don't have any idea how it got started or why we put up with this committee crap, but I will say this: It ain't a bad thing for a town to look out for each other, especially our babies like these two here. I know first-hand how much help I've needed raising up Ivy. Hell, you might say it takes a town. But you all go too far, so I'm saying straight out to let these kids alone during this junior mayor thing. Let them confide in their mommas and you stay out of it."

"I object," Mr. Doggins said more strenuously, only stopping because Lucille held out her hands, a long, thin finger pointed to each side of the table. It's amazing how much power can be found from bone and blue vein.

Lucille waited a moment, her hands quivering slightly, but no less purposeful for it, the nails like pale red stoplights. "This is exactly why the committee wants these young people to run their own campaigns."

Dogg raised his hand and Lucille nodded, only then lowering hers to the table. Dogg looked at each of us, finally arriving eye to eye with Ivy. "I just want to say publicly I've always felt shitty about what happened . . . "

"James Andrew Doggins," his mother scolded lightly.

"I've always felt *badly*," Dogg corrected. "But this is a whole different ball game. Lots of people we don't even know will be listening to us and I'm kinda into that. So, no tricks, Ivy. I promise. But I also promise I really want to win. And no offense to my Dad, but I really want to win without his help. Okay?"

As Dogg exhaled a quiet but noticeable sigh of relief, Ivy stood up and walked around to her opponent's side of the table where she stood at his back, sternly quiet for seconds, arms folded. Behind her, a group of mostly white pigeons swooped across the frame of the window, catching the sun like a thick curve of lightening. "You going to tell us anything else, James Andrew Doggins?" Ivy said. Dogg scanned each of us, looking guilty, as if there were something further we should know. But when he said nothing, Ivy answered her own question. "I didn't think so," she said, waving to her mother that it was time to go. "That's it, right?" Ivy asked Lucille. "May the best man win and all that?" Lucille nodded her agreement, and Ivy and her mother were out the door.

"What was that all about," Dogg's father asked without looking at anyone. "You can't let that little maniac run for mayor."

"Drop it Dad," Dogg said, as if it were a phrase he'd uttered hundreds of times. "Ivy's done a ton of stuff for this town. The only difference between us is that I have a father who makes sure everything *I* do makes it in the newspaper. And for the record, it's Junior Mr. Mayor."

"Well if anyone here wants to vote for a little skunk like that, be my guest," Mr. Doggins said. With that, Dogg shoved himself from the table and mumbled something about waiting for his parents in the parking lot. At the slam of the car door, pigeons flashed across the window again.

"I wouldn't worry," Gloria said as if she'd been holding something in. "If she's anything like the Ivy I remember, she'll quit her campaign the way she quit our Brownie troupe." But beyond that, Gloria held back out of our remnant of respect for impassioned Vida Clark's letter about what Ivy had meant to her son's last days.

Still, as expected, it was a tense meeting. When the Dogginses got up to leave, Lucille stood and held her hand out to say goodbye. "So we can count on you to let your son run his campaign?" she asked. We clearly had a favorite, but we had future campaigns to worry about and didn't want to let things get beyond our control like so many let loose piglets. **(High school biology students must have access to fetal pigs.)** The trick is getting people to live by the unwritten   - The Committee rules, and to trust the committee about what those are.

"Of course," Mrs. Doggins said. "And I must say, though I plan to support my son, I remember Ivy from my volunteer days at the library. She's curious and smart and, between you and I, might even have a better resume than Jimmy." Lucille was a bit stunned as Mrs. Doggins extended her hand. Mr. Doggins didn't stick around for the niceties. He rushed out the door, Gloria and Lucille sensing he was definitely not on board with his wife's sentiments.

11

We should have seen the signs, though how is that possible when certain people aren't awake enough to report them? After the meeting with Ivy and Dogg, the committee remained behind to talk things over. But our candidates were out and about, though apparently not separate and not with their parents.

Cupper Franklin recalled later, much later, that he'd seen them sitting side by side behind a dumpster on Railway Street which is a little dead end where no one goes unless they're walking out the back door of Big Sally's pool bar. Big Sally's of the Feltzer brothers armed robbery fame, the bar where those young men felt compelled to stop and buy rounds of drinks for everyone; bought enough rounds to get slopped up to the point where they let it slip just how they came by all the money to pay for those drinks and how easy and profitable it was to point a gun on a person.

Though he was pre-cataract surgery and being pulled into that blunted street by his Corgi, Ben, Cupper noted Ivy's red dress and Dogg's blonde hair. And he also noted one more thing, *the* thing the committee would have liked to have known: they were holding hands. And maybe it was a bit gauzy, but Cupper wasn't so blind that he couldn't tell that the pair was engaged in some sort of serious conversation, and that Ivy's primary gesture was wiping at her eyes.

"That girl," Cupper would say later, "she looked about like someone died and the boy kept patting her on the back and saying 'I can't. I just can't.' I didn't stick around to stay in their business. I just turned Ben around and left them kids alone. But maybe I did hear a couple more things. Her saying something about needing someone by her side who would support her independence. And him saying she was a good person and he was sure that someday she'd find what she wanted. But that the election made it that much less likely it would happen in Mudlick."

It's understandable that Cupper didn't think about mentioning Ivy and Dogg earlier, though he did recognize Dogg from the high school section of the sports page. And Ivy he knew by sight, if not by name, because she was always going door-to-door collecting donations for some unfortunate Mudlick resident. Though, whether by design or accident, she'd never knocked on any committee member's door.

So Cupper didn't think to say anything to us. He never was one for communicating. His claim to fame in Mudlick was the battered and rusting iron rocking chair from which he presided over a perpetual yard sale mostly made up of unsellable folding chairs and glass dishes filled with mosquito larva, kept blissfully moist by the careless use of an oscillating sprinkler. And in the summer, the piles of junk in his front yard were nearly concealed by a spectacular row of Russian Sunflowers, each one tied to six foot stakes and yet even taller than that, their heavy black faces framed by yellow petals, kind of menacing as one passed by them.

(Limit the blight of yard sales, but seek them out for good deals on classic bakeware.) - The Committee

As solitary and disconnected as Cupper was, had the committee just that little bit of information about our candidates, we might have averted the whole mess that was to follow. We might have sat Dogg down and told him just exactly the kind of trouble he was headed for. We might have pointed out that Ivy had made her own bed and that he couldn't allow himself to be dragged down with her. We would've told him that whatever her feelings were for him, that in Charlene he had a much smarter, more compatible future.

Though, even after all that, we probably couldn't have said anything that might have made him understand that Ivy was manipulating him, and that guilt is compassion's dangerous sword.

In short, at that point Dogg was still salvageable.

12

Some people have more clarity in their memories than others and we don't get to choose which of these memories we repeat and which we don't. It's the record that's important, a record that will confirm the soundness of the committee's actions. Mumford's recollections, the previous Junior Mr. Mayor, for example, are troublesome, but important to the whole. And though they may seem contrary to the story we're trying to tell, we can't, in good conscience, eliminate his accounts just because they don't suit our immediate purposes. Like when Alan Bursford tried to make the ridiculous case for maintaining a riparian habitat in the very place where Constantine Drilling planned a gravel pit. Well, we gave Mr. Bursford all the public time he needed to waste in what was an inevitable business proposition. The little birds, or whatever he wanted to save, would clearly have to move upstream in favor of the reality that the committee was supporting the prospect of local jobs. And it goes without saying maybe he'd be better off watching fewer animal documentaries and more time hunting for work. Without cable, he probably wouldn't even know what riparian means.

(Commercial radio is a problem. Question free entertainment.) - The Committee

Which brings us to Mumford lying in bed in the gray hours of the morning quietly watching the silent throb of red light coming from the top of KMVP's radio tower. Some mornings, awakened by a siren or discomfort, the light in thin fog reminded him of a beating heart. Most often, Mumford used that red pulse to send him back to sleep, but that particular morning his future whirred in his head and he refused to drowse. Dogg remained asleep, a faint white fleshiness on the floor expecting to be awakened for a fishing trip. A Mourning dove fluttered by the window, its wings whistling as it landed somewhere on the roof. Mumford's window had always given him a vantage of Mudlick's dull roof tops, its smattering of trees, and the radio station that changed ownership and formats every few years. Sometimes, if he lay perfectly still and concentrated on the red light, he felt small again. In just two months he'd be in Kentucky on a baseball scholarship. Next to playing in the big leagues, it was his dream to play on a top-notch college team. But the reality of leaving home was just beginning to hit him. He looked at the Charlie Brown clock radio his grandmother gave him when he was ten. It was 6:23, an hour later than he intended for heading up to the reservoir.

"Dogg," he said in a scratchy morning-voice. "Bro. If we're gonna do this, we gotta get up." His friend mumbled and stirred.

Mumford's twelve-year-old Doberman, Crow, jingled into the room, favoring a lame hind leg. It licked Dogg's face until he sat up. "What time is it anyway?"

"Almost 6:30, Bro."

"Damn. It's late." Dogg rubbed his eyes and leaned forward, corralling his knees with his arms. The two of them planned this last minor getaway before the campaign started in earnest. Technically, Mumford was obligated to remain publicly neutral on his preference.

"I've been thinking," Mumford said profoundly.

"Yeah?"

"What if I suck? What if I get over there and I can't even catch the fucking ball?"

"Isn't going to happen, Mum. You're The Mummy, the force that keeps on coming. You'll catch whatever they toss you. You'll hit the ball farther than those hillbillies have ever seen, and you'll do it with a straight "A" average."

Mumford scratched the soft diamond of red hair in the center of his chest. "You think?"

"Sure. You hold almost every single record for Catcher in our school." Dogg megaphoned his voice with his hands, "Now batting for the New York Yankees ... "

"Dodgers," Mumford interrupted.

"For the Los Angeles Dodgers, number 17, Mumford, The Mummy, Smith."

Mumford laughed, staring at the dimness of the ceiling in the quartz-like light of morning. His crib had been in this room, his racecar futon, and this same twin bed. "It's Match point for Jimmy Doggins, the scrappy young American from Mudlick, California. He needs an amazing serve against the defending champion to take Wimbledon."

"Hell," Dogg interrupted, "I'd settle for the quarter-finals." The two of them laughed into silence. "We're missing the bass," Dogg said, standing and searching the floor for his jeans. Crow, easily startled, hobbled out of the room.

"Fuck the bass. We'll sit on the bank eating baloney sandwiches while we fish for Bluegill."

"Whatever," Dogg said. "I just need to get away for a day."

Mumford sat up and slung his thick legs off the edge of the bed looking around the dark floor for his pants and a plausibly clean shirt. "You still worried about this election, Bro? I don't even know why you're bothering."

Dogg was already fully dressed, tying his shoes and sitting against the wall beneath pages of a *Sports Illustrated* swimsuit issue Mumford had tacked at odd angles. Each bikini-clad woman sported a drawn-on moustache or devil horns. One, relaxing on a black sand beach in a white swimsuit, was covered in a gorilla suit of inked hair. "At first," Dogg said, "I only signed up because of my dad. He wanted the publicity. But then I *really* wanted to run because it turned out it was something I had to do myself."

"It's not all that. Trust me," Mumford said, fishing under his bed for his left shoe. "If I'd known what I was getting myself into when I ran . . ."

"You don't get it, Mum. I don't have to read any of my dad's speeches with all the stupid car metaphors. I don't have to pass out his key chains. I don't have to be Little Jimmy Doggins, TV's favorite child car salesman. In this election it's all me."

"So what's your problem? Don't tell me it's Ivy?"

"Kind of. I know I'm going to trounce her and I don't want to go through my last year of high school feeling like a dick every time I see her. And let's face it. I have the name, but she has the qualifications."

Mumford put on his baseball hat. "Well, I have to give her credit for one thing, Bro. I've never seen anyone lay themselves across the railroad tracks as much as her."

"That's kind of the point. She does all this great stuff and she's practically invisible until it's time to knock her down."

The room was growing brighter. Outside, the light above the hills was pink and tufted with small clouds. Mumford saw the serious expression on Dogg's face, his hair wildly cowlicked from a night of sleep. The two of them had probably slept over at each other's houses a hundred nights since they were kids and Mumford suddenly had the sense that this was the last time. He said nothing as he led Dogg out to the pickup where they'd stored their fishing gear and cooler the night before. As they got on the road, Mumford reached for the radio.

"KMVP is playing Country now," Dogg said.

Mumford put his hand back on the steering wheel. "Shit," he said. Then he offered what had really been on his mind for the last few minutes. "You *are* going to try to win, right Dogg?" He was referring to the fact that his friend had recently all but backed out of the Student Council race for President in its last few days. It had been Mudlick High's best-kept secret—almost—that Jimmy Doggins *wanted* people to vote for Ivy instead of him.

"She keeps trying. It gets old, you know, publicly humiliating her every few years. She and I . . . " Dogg paused and inhaled the end of his thought. "I don't dislike her."

"Ivy Simmons humiliates *herself*, for Christ's sake. Maybe she should wear some new clothes once in a while. And you know what they say about her and all those college dudes she knows."

"Watch it," Dogg threatened. "That's exactly the kind of shit I don't want to hear. I think she's got those college friends because maybe we're not smart enough for her. And besides, I have to try. She was even more pissed off when she found out I ditched the last election."

"She's toast then, Bro. Live with it. As long as you got Charlene on your arm, a sweet backhand, your pretty-boy smile, and all that shiny blonde hair the chicks are always gawgawing about, you're the next Junior Mr. Mayor. I guarantee it. And I spell guarantee with a double g!"

Dogg soft-punched Mumford in the shoulder and smiled. "Sometimes," he said, "that's exactly what it feels like. Charlene is *on* my arm. So far, the only thing I've felt about her is that we look good together in pictures, which she keeps reminding me, as if that's a plus."

"At least," Mumford said, "at least you have that choice until something better comes along. Got anyone in mind?" Of course, he did, though he was entirely mum.

"Charlene makes me feel like I'm a pretty head of hair. Her and my Dad both. If I wasn't who I am, or who people think I am; if I was braver, I'd make other choices. Know what I mean?"

Mumford nodded. The gray light of morning thickened the cab, as if the air itself were holding he and Dogg down. "I know *exactly* what you mean." And presently you'll get an idea of just precisely who Mumford had in mind as he said this.

"Sure you do," Dogg said, sounding doubtful. "All I know is

that this election is a chance for me to finally achieve something without Dad's money or interference, which is going to piss him off. And if I win, I'll hurt Ivy all over again."

Dogg stared out the window for a few minutes, running his hand through his hair, and, almost as if it came out accidentally, he laughed nervously. "Man, Ivy is going to kill me. My dad is going to kill me. The committee is going to kill me. Why does it feel like I have to push everyone away in order to do something healthy for myself?"

Mumford patted Dogg on the knee. "Bro, if you can figure that one out, you win no matter what."

13

Had we known, had Mumford and the others come to the committee before instead of after, we might have averted a great deal of trouble. But, as it was, we didn't hear a thing until events were well beyond our control. It wasn't until the days following the election, when the committee was desperately trying to figure out what had gone wrong, that Mumford and others helped us to piece everything together. Of course, by then everyone was willing to give us his or her two cents. Everyone wanted us to know their corner of the truth, their brushes with the intimate details. With these kinds of things there is always a war between reputations and the facts. But by the time people spoke up, it was too late.

Perhaps we should have known, taken it as a sign, when the Japanese Beetles, or June Bugs as we call them, descended on us like a plague out of the Bible. Most years, as the peaches and nectarines in our back yards ripen, we pluck off these large green beetles that, in numbers, devastate the fruit. But usually, there's just a few, and we take them off, smash them under our shoes, or give them to our kids to play with. For a couple weeks each year it isn't uncommon to see the children of Mudlick in their front yards watching the flight of a June Bugs they control with lengths of thread tied to one of the insect's legs. There are spontaneous, if forced, June Bug dog fights as the frustrated bugs buzz and circle in the air, tangling themselves together.

(Write a name and phone number in children's underwear. Update when you relocate.) - The Committee

A favorite move is to get two of the beetles flying in opposite directions, their tethers winding together, forcing them into tighter and tighter flight patterns until, when there is no more thread, they crash into one another. Some children, who lack the patience, simply tie the opposite ends of the same thread to two beetles and let them go in a frantic battle for flight direction, betting on which one will get its way. The possibilities of experimentation are endless. Cole Clark Junior, in fact, once attached eight beetles to a tiny plastic Santa sleigh, the insects successfully pulling the weight hundreds of yards and into Tomlin Joseph's swimming pool.

Ivy and Dogg squared off just as the peaches ripened and the June Bugs came from out of nowhere. The beetles covered our fruit and thudded into windows, many bugs hitting the glass over and over until they knocked themselves unconscious or fell to the ground, exhausted. Our yards and driveways were littered with their shiny green carcasses, under tire or foot they gave off the full-bodied sound of eggs cracked on a skillet. In circumstances like that, it's more than a temptation to look around for Moses.

Sherman Fields stepped into his backyard one late morning and saw, absent his glasses, dozens of fat, iridescent green ornaments dangling in the peach tree at the rear of his property near his barbecue grotto. He assumed it was one of his wife's attempts to keep the birds away. When he walked nearer the tree to inspect her work, he was startled by the reality of hundreds of beetles sopping at the tree's fruit. Without thinking, he ran to the barbecue and retrieved a bottle of lighter fluid, the spray of which he thrust at the insects sword-like until the bottle wheezed its emptiness. When only a few of the beetles flew away, Sherman impulsively lit a match to one dangling pod of beetle-covered peaches. Within minutes, the entire tree was ablaze as well as the neighbor's fence. The neighbor being Vida Clark, who ran out with her garden hose to protect the olive tree she loved so much.

After the firefighters and effusive apologies to Vida along with promises of repair, Sherman and his wife sat staring at their charred peach tree. Only the uppermost branch had been spared, a damaged but still green section of branch with one heavy piece of fruit. As they stared at what remained of their expected summer harvest, what sounded like an uncertain joy buzzer—zzz, zzzzzzzz, zzzzzzzzzzz—erupted beneath the tree. As the Fields turned their attention to the wet and blackened ground, they saw a single June Bug extricate himself from the muck, test its wings and, in a final insult, fly up to that last remaining peach.

Mudlick had never known such an infestation. For a few days, all of us were set back on our heels. It's hard to think straight when you're being bombarded with insects from all quarters, when more than once you see a little girl screaming because of the June Bugs caught in her freshly shampooed hair.

Drunk on our fruit, these June Bugs were bloated and stupid. And stupid comes with its own brand of unconquerable persistence. Things got so bad that the committee voted to briefly delay announcing the idea of changing the town name to Valhalla West. We also held back on our plans to get one of those chain coffee merchants to locate in town. It was the committee who successfully got a McDonald's franchise to come in. And after they agreed, it wasn't hard to get Taco Bell and Burger King, though there was some fuss about the fact that the last remaining open tract of land in town from the Goble Dairy was being built on. But the committee successfully lobbied for the pragmatic notion that our citizens couldn't always be expected to stop by Wishbone Café, or The Country Cupboard. We needed something faster and nice new buildings with good landscaping like every other successful town.

The committee might not be able to stop hordes of beetles, we understood, but there wasn't much else about Mudlick we couldn't improve, given the chance. And even if it was God himself who rained those awful bugs down on us, we were determined to press on with our ideas and we were eager for Jimmy Doggins to carry our message forward.

14

Ivy Simmons, like most apartment dwellers, hardly noticed the June Bug invasion. She was focused on a campaign strategy that would, as the campaign progressed, not make the committee happy. On the day that Dogg and Mumford went fishing, Ivy convened a group of young people who would form her campaign committee, including Thatch Hutchison, who came from one of Mudlick's generationally poor families and whose father died several years earlier of a form of rare male breast cancer. Thatch was notable for his impeccable cleanliness and the excruciatingly precise part in his thick brown hair. Thatch was also known for actually being a homosexual. That is to say, he was effeminate or girly. We use "he," "him," and etc. because it's less confusing and because the committee decided they didn't want to get into all the trouble the school got into when they tried to block Thatch from attending school.

In addition to being Ivy's good friend, Thatch was the smartest student at Mudlick High. Gathered at Ivy's apartment that day as well was the same misfit menagerie which Ivy assembled for her charity collection efforts—among other things, building a wheelchair ramp for Cole Clark Junior, uniforms for the new Ladybug League soccer club for girls, and for little Cassandra Jenks' countless surgeries. We know all this because this was just before kids started planting their faces two inches from their phones, when they were still paying attention.

Helping Ivy this time was always-in-braids Elizabeth Lipton, ever-silent Raul Montes, Alice Dennis with her gold tooth, and one-eyed Ryan Neiffert, whose fortunes had dwindled since elementary school. Though he remained friends with Dogg, in high school he found that a missing eye was just too big a target for teasing by the kids he hadn't grown up with. By then, he'd given up the patch against his parent's protests, choosing instead to brave the taunts from teenagers who couldn't resist commenting on the unmoving orb in its dead socket.

"Thanks for coming, everyone," Ivy said. She wore jeans and a baggy white t-shirt with an iron-on teddy bear holding a stick of lit dynamite. "As you know, nobody gives me the slightest chance of beating Jimmy Doggins."

Thatch picked up two semi-burned chocolate chip cookies from the coffee table Ivy's mother recently bought from Glass 'n' Brass. "Geez, it's going to be tough," he said, biting into one cookie and tossing the other to Ryan.

"But not impossible." Ivy stood and squeezed herself past the knees of her guests. The room was too small for so many people, especially with the buzz coming from the eight large fish tanks lining one wall. For the past four years her mother dated a man who delivered tropical fish and small birds to pet stores. He always gave Ivy's mother any fish a shop wouldn't accept, striped Angelfish with tattered fins, anything mucusy, dull tetras, thin guppies, dispassionate kisser fish, and a temporarily blind Oscar that devoured five black mollies before Ivy's mother realized her mistake and put it in its own tank. The living room gurgled and buzzed with noise from the air pumps and fluorescent bulbs as Ivy spoke. "What's the worst thing about this town?" she asked.

"It sucks in general," Alice said, slouching down into the blue couch with its random mustard yellow design that looked as if someone had, in fact, squirted that exact condiment across the fabric. Alice, perhaps, had reason to resent Mudlick. She came from a peculiar family that never quite fit in. Her grandmother was a respected seamstress and champion hog caller; her grandfather had made a kind of name for himself by painting wedding vows on grains of rice. Her father, though not exactly following in the footsteps of his father, was an artist as well, painting temporary window signs for car lots and, in season, Christmas scenes for any business that would hire him. Unfortunately for their family he wasn't able to get work in Mudlick because, whether intentionally or not, he'd painted a Santa with a bundled up little girl on one leg and an unfortunate brushstroke that looked like an erection paralleling the other leg.

"No, Alice," Ivy said. "See, every year this election is never about anything. I figure if we can make it about something, get some real issues out there, I'll have a chance."

"I don't know, Ivy," Alice said, still slouched and doubtful. "Don't the adults mostly want to see their cute kids parading around, passing out balloons and making speeches about how great our town is?"

"Well, isn't that kind of the point? We've done a lot of good stuff together, but just once wouldn't it be nice to be heard?" Ivy touched her fingers to the tips of a three-foot-tall mother-in-law's tongue that grew near the window. She looked at the plant, and back at the group, all of them eating cookies. "But okay, let's be really honest here," she said. "I'm not pretty or rich and Jimmy Doggins is both."

A giggling, braid-twirling Elizabeth interrupted: "He *is* really cute." What Elizabeth was thinking right then, even though she was helping Ivy, was that she'd probably end up voting for Dogg. They were juniors now, but she never forgot that in the Seventh grade she was paired up with him to do a report and presentation on Mexican-American culture. She learned to play the castanets while he sang "La Bamba."

"Exactly," continued Ivy, looking at the rest of the group. "And she's on *my* side. So, let's be honest about the obstacles. Jimmy is good-looking and charming. He comes from money and he's almost a celebrity. And lately he's been waving that Charlene Hergis around like she's some sort of Nordic flag. He's a perfect candidate." She shrugged her shoulders in admission of a very important truth.

Raul sighed and shifted his position but said nothing. He'd only been in town one year and wasn't quite sure how this circle of teenagers had become his friends. "So why bother if you can't compete?" he finally asked.

"That's why I'm saying if we make campaign about something, bring up some real issues, we'll hit Jimmy so hard between the eyes, he'll be blind."

"Hey," Ryan piped, pointing at his glass eye

Ivy bit her bottom lip in apology. "It's just that I know something about Jimmy. He's boxed in by that supposedly perfect life. The sad thing is it's just cardboard and even though he knows that, he won't just bust out." But no one was looking at Ivy, they were looking behind her, at the plump old woman who was standing in a bra and slip and nothing else. In her gray-blue mottled hand she held a wad of red floral print cloth. "Gwen, why didn't you tell me you were bringing your friends over?"

"Grandma," Ivy yelped, taking the cloth from the woman's hand and snapping it out to its muumuu proportions. Her grandmother had been staying with them for nearly a year. Not long before she moved in, they'd noticed how forgetful she'd become, sending two cards for the same birthday, walking home from the store instead of driving the car she'd gone with. But finally, Ivy's mother received an early morning call from her mother's neighbor. "Gweny," the woman said, as if she were still speaking to the little girl who once lived next to her, "your mother is picking roses out of my garden and she doesn't have any gloves or clippers. Her hands are all torn up but I can't get her to stop." That day Ivy went with her mother to pick up her grandmother.

"Gwen, is everyone staying for dinner?" As her grandmother spoke, Ivy helped her on with the muumuu, directing the old woman's arms above her head effortlessly, as if this were an act she'd performed a thousand times. "I'll have to go to the store if they're going to eat with us."

"Grandma, they're not staying for dinner."

The woman didn't seem to notice Ivy's response as she walked closer to the group. Her white hair was short, almost a crew cut, and there was hazy denseness about her brown eyes. Just four years earlier she retired from Phipps Hardware where she worked for thirty-seven years. "Do your parents know you're staying for dinner?"

Everyone looked at Ivy, who was caught between a frown and smile. They were thinking how she never seemed to catch a break that it was a wonder she'd done as well for herself as she had, given the circumstances. Her grandmother was just one of the reasons she never had friends over, even Thatch. No one ever knew what to say to her grandmother. "Grandma," Ivy finally said, grabbing a cookie, "I made chocolate chip." She led her grandmother to the small breakfast table just outside the kitchen where the woman sat and regarded the cookie as if confused, then cracked it in several pieces before beginning to eat.

Ivy returned to the group. "So where were we?"

"Why is she calling you Gwen?" Alice asked

"Sometimes she thinks I'm my mother. But can we get back to the campaign?"

"Ivy, I want to say something," Ryan said. "Just for the record, Dogg isn't a bad guy." He too, was ambivalent about taking a counter position to Dogg. It said a lot about a person if they hung out with the likes of Ivy as opposed to her opponent.

Ivy sighed and sat back down in a square brown chair with its threadbare arms. "No, he's not. At worst, he's confused and kind of spoiled. I already know we can't have a campaign trying to drag Jimmy down. I want to show you something." Ivy hopped up and ran into the back where the bedrooms were. When she returned she was carrying a medium-sized cardboard box labeled on the outside in black, permanent marker. "Ivy Simmons: Campaign materials." She sat the box on the coffee table and opened it. "Ta da," she said, pulling out a two-foot-long poster. Everyone in the group looked at each other. It was a real poster, not handmade, all the lettering white on a clover-green background.

Vote Ivy Simmons
Pride
Progress
Preservation

"That's sharp," Thatch said. He was her sidekick and he knew it. Even his nickname came about purely out of his association with her. This, of course, was understandable since his given first and middle names came from his grandfather and his grandmother's maiden name. So, without Ivy, he was Harvey Harvey Hutchinson.

"And it's the wallpaper on our website," Ivy said.

Raul looked at his phone and brought up Ivy's campaign website, drawing his finger across it as if he'd never touched glass before. "I think we're going to win." The committee has always believed the minute he said that is when Ivy's campaign took on momentum. There, in front of her, were suddenly people who believed in her. And, except for money, few things will spur someone to run for office like the unwavering confidence of a constituent.

Each person pulled out their own sign and examined it. When they agreed to help Ivy, they'd imagined the usual, poster paints and flyers designed by Thatch on his computer. But this time, Ivy had taken them to a whole new level. The scrappy but futile campaign they'd imagined suddenly blossomed with possibility in their minds. They read and reread the poster's four lines, looking up at Ivy in between as if to pinch themselves.

"Got them donated from Ray's Print Shop," Ivy said. "Well, the labor. I have to pay for the paper." Ivy kneeled next to Thatch and he patted her on the back as she spoke. "When Mudlick wakes up on Monday morning, I want these all over town."

"Surprise attack," Alice said.

"Exactly." Ivy looked at the fish tanks and then back at her grandmother who had finished her cookie and was now quietly spindling a paper napkin as if toward some purpose. While the group all but congratulated themselves on a victorious campaign, Ivy stood and disappeared into the kitchen. She returned with a glass of water, which she set in front of her grandmother, and an orange box of fish flakes.

(Do not donate frozen items such as fish sticks to food drives.)
- The Committee

She gave each tank two pinches of food, the fish instantly spearing to the top as if magnetized. "There's one other thing," she said, without facing her friends, her birthmarks staring at them from the rear of her legs like two purple eyes. "It might be a problem. I'm not sure. So you can't tell anybody." She turned, fish food clutched in front of her like an inefficient shield. "But it may come up in the campaign because two other people already know." She paused and took in a heavy breath. "I'm pregnant."

15

The Mile of Cars is a half hour away from Mudlick and, in the way everything was a contest for him, Carl Doggins liked to beat traffic. When he left for work early that first Monday morning of the campaign, the air was unusually damp and foggy. Like every morning, he was immediately on his cell phone with his stockbroker in New York. Though there was not much he could do about it other than move, he resented the fact that the East Coast got a three-hour jump on him, a frustration he took out on Vida Clark who he honked off the side of the road as she took her morning power walk. So immersed was Mr. Doggins inside his morning routine, he didn't see Ivy's campaign poster tacked to the telephone pole across from his driveway, nor did he notice the three signs Thatch conspicuously placed along the route he imagined the Doggins family took to get anywhere in or beyond Mudlick. But the sign Mr. Doggins did notice was beneath the "Go" light to the onramp where he got on the freeway. "That's cute," he said out loud, pausing briefly to examine Ivy's green and white slogan.

"What's cute?" his broker asked from three thousand miles away.

"Nothing. That campaign thing my son is doing. His opponent made herself a little sign and set it next to the onramp. Looks almost professional."

"What's your son planning?"

Mr. Doggins laughed. "Oh, he's got plans. I'm not allowed to help, though. But, you know, the kid's got as much money as he needs. His opponent doesn't have a chance." In truth, Mr. Doggins didn't really know what his son might do. They'd had it out the night before over just how much help he could be to his son, Dogg telling his father to stay away. Mr. Doggins was used to getting his way and he probably knew that the committee preferred that Dogg use whatever resources his father could offer. But like us, Mr. Doggins had gotten a good look at Ivy, knew her, in fact, from the times his son had won over her before. So, as he looked at her professional sign, he acknowledged to himself that she'd done a good job. But he wasn't worried. His son was Dogg the tennis champ, Jimmy Doggins, and Little Jimmy Doggins from the television commercials. His opponent, well she was just Ivy Simmons, Poor Ivy Simmons if his memory served.

Dogg had a 10 a.m. call that morning for what would turn out to be his last appearance as Little Jimmy in one of his father's television commercials. By now, for both of them, it was pretty much routine. Dogg would say something to the effect that Carl Doggins Motors had the best deals on the Mile of Cars. No matter what, he'd always end with "Right Dad?" which gave his father a precise cue to begin reading his own lines from the cards just off camera—Dogg was originally brought into the commercials to help mask his father's on-camera cardboard persona. Of course, seasonally, they'd don costumes—Dogg's elf to his father's Santa, his George Washington to his father's Abe Lincoln. Throughout the county they were a recognizable pair and the effect Dogg's participation had on his father's business was measurable. Even the papers, when writing about Dogg's tennis accomplishments, often included the fact that he was the son of "notable car dealer, Carl Doggins." His election, too, was sure to bring more of the same kind of publicity, and Mr. Doggins knew it.

For that final shoot, Dogg told his father he needed to meet him at the dealership because he was spending the night at Billy Larson's—the Billy Larson of two-DUI's-by-his-eighteenth-birthday fame—to put together a campaign strategy, which they did. But in their planning, they also figured in enough time to catch some waves before Jimmy had to meet his father and for another stop he wanted to make before they caught him on camera one more time. So, he and Billy Left Mudlick and stayed the night at Billy's grandparents' condo near the beach.

It was nearly 10:30 and still overcast when Dogg finally strolled onto his father's car lot. The cameras and light reflectors were set up in their usual places. The lot PA squawked to life. "Mr. Doggins. The set is ready," a female voice offered uncertainly. It was the signal Dogg's father had asked for when his son arrived. He stormed out of the showroom doors, patting down his thinning hair as he unconsciously did every time he walked outside. His blue tie flicked back and forth across his torso like a snake's tail. **(Always wear a tie clip. Never tape.)** - The Committee
He stopped and looked at the set across the lot.
Dogg was nowhere to be seen. Just the crew people. He stomped forward looking around, not noticing the sales staff standing at the windows, nor did he pay attention to the guys from the service bays, all watching as he marched across the lot. Within twenty feet of the set Mr. Doggins stopped again, looking for his son. A pair of crew guys were talking near the camera. He recognized the smiling one facing him, Skip, with his fat black moustache. The other guy, with the waxy shaved head, he didn't know until he turned around. "Pop," Dogg said, running a hand over his clear-cut head. "Like it?"

There are two versions of Mr. Doggins' response. In his own account, which he sticks with to this day, he admits the phrase "What the fuck did you do to your hair?" It's what follows where there's dispute. In the Carl Doggins version, Jimmy laughs and says, "It's on the floor at the Chopping Block. Now let's get this fucking commercial over with," mimicking his father.

Mr. Doggins' face was tinting red, his lips quivering like a dam about to burst. "You can't represent Doggins Motors as a fucking Skinhead."

"I think it's perfect," Dogg sneered. "Because you're a fucking Nazi."

After that harsh exchange, Mr. Doggins claims that he and his son, both startled at their outbursts, embraced and set about figuring a way to make the commercial. Clearly, since the entire county knew Little Jimmy Doggins with a shock of blonde hair, they'd have to do something. Not to mention the fact that his shaved scalp, where the sun had never touched since he was an infant, looked like a pinkish-white helmet above his tan face. The effect of his new baldness was like lopping off the crown of a fresh pineapple.

In the other version, which the committee generally finds more credible because it comes from neither Dogg nor his father, the exchange is slightly different. After Mr. Doggins says, "What the fuck did you do to your hair?" he takes off his suit coat and throws it on the hood of the car that was supposed to be featured in the commercial.

"I can do whatever I want. It's my head." Dogg says.

His father's face is flushed. "Are you fucking crazy? You can't represent Doggins Motors with a bald head."

"Why not," Dogg calmly says in response to the biggest straight line he'll ever get in his life. "*You* do."

After that, it's said that the commercial's director, a tall, red haired woman, leaps between the two as Mr. Doggins rushes his son. It's all she can do to hold him back. "Wait, I've got an idea," she says, straight-arming her client. She leaves Skip and his intimidating black moustache between them while she walks to the show room. The group watches as she drags a chair across the floor and stands on it next to the window, making her just tall enough to bring down the thick curtain rod. **(Keep living room drapes open at least once a week to avoid suspicion.)** - The Committee When she returns, she holds, carefully folded in her arms, the white lining of the showroom drapery. She tosses it to Dogg. "Put this on," she says. "And get some makeup on that head before we all go blind."

Whatever version of the story contains the most accuracy, the commercial itself exists. In it, superimposed clouds part, revealing Doggins Motors and Mr. Doggins in his suit and on his knees, as Dogg, garbed in the curtain liner Gandhi-style, sits in near-lotus position on the hood of a car. Behind them, like rows of shark's teeth, sit the gleaming windshields of a lot full of new cars. "Oh Master," Mr. Doggins pleads, acting all the part of a truly tortured soul. "What is the secret of enlightenment?"

Dogg looks at his father with a perfectly serene face. You can almost tell from his expression that what he is really doing is presiding over the funeral of Little Jimmy Doggins. "The answer, my son," Dogg says in a kind of falsetto, "the answer can only be achieved by taking advantage of one of the great deals at Doggins Motors."

"The place where they spell guarantee with a double g?"

"Yes, my son," Dogg says looking straight at the camera, satisfied and serene. "And right now I can promise you zero percent interest."

16

Dogg's first public test of his shaved head came the same day he shot the last commercial he'd ever make for Doggins Motors. The committee scheduled an appearance for him and Ivy at the Republican Women's Club mid-afternoon luncheon buffet in the community center attached to Mudlick's main firehouse. It was a room large enough to hold two-hundred, though it rarely needed to anymore. The membership of service organizations, Kiwanis, Optimists, Soroptimists, and others, had dwindled to the point where holding meetings and events in a mostly empty hall with its ticking fluorescent lights and outdated announcements—JULY 18!!! DIME-A-DIP FUNDRAISER TO RE-ELECT RONALD REAGAN FOR GOVENOR!!!!! ALL WELCOME!!! BRING A DISH AND A POCKETFULL OF DIMES!!!!—things like this, made the remaining members feel insignificant and they started having their meetings at restaurants and private homes.

As always, the table for the Republican Women's Club was packed with homemade dishes; three kinds of deviled eggs including one made without any yolks, cold fried chicken, a small, spiral-sliced ham, Maxine Colby's strange gelatin dessert pocked with green pimentoed olives—politely taken but never eaten—a large bowl of iceberg lettuce sprinkled with carrots and red cabbage, white dinner rolls, cucumber sandwiches without crusts, and two perfect Angel Food cakes which, for the willing, were ready to be spread with peppered sour cream.

(Use national brand recipes when serving food to others.)

Before the food portion of the afternoon, Ivy and   - The Committee
Dogg were introduced separately to each table, giving the ladies a
chance to ask questions if they wished. The room swelled with female voices. It was arranged with seven round tables, covered in
white butcher paper, each table centered by a small bouquet of red-
white-and-blue carnations in ribboned jelly jars. The brightly dressed
club members sat, chatting with one another, their hair, puffed up
silver, various shades of brown, red, and powder blue, giving the
impression of a room full of talking dahlias. Of Ivy and Dogg, the
ladies mostly asked questions about her "cheery" green and white
signs that had appeared all over town that morning and about mod-
ern high school life—"I'd be so afraid everyday I was going to be
shot," Katie Farmingham blurted out. And each table remarked,
fondly, that Fern, the topiary, with her perfect little dress of leaves,
her apparent wholesomeness, seemed to represent old-fashioned
values and didn't they think that we needed to get back to that?

After meeting everyone, lunch itself began. Ivy and Dogg sat
next to one another at the same table with the club President, seventy-year-old Bernice Klein and other office-holding members. That
was the summer Bernice outfitted herself with a new wardrobe, a
splurge after her husband's death. He'd hated her in any form of
purple, so nearly everything she bought was a variant of that color.
At the luncheon, she wore a lavender silk blouse, violet slacks and
purple faux-alligator pumps with matching handbag. The two young
candidates sitting next to her said nothing to each other, and at first,
none of the ladies said much to them either. They knew Dogg, of
course, who couldn't? And Ivy they had a vague recollection of as
the girl with the donation can. But Bernice and the others were more
interested in Ms. Colton's new topiary, Fern. A number of the ladies had visited the topiary that morning and though they'd been
delighted by the bunnies and baby deer of previous years, there was
something special about Fern.

"She's just lovely," Bernice said to her table, then turning to her young guests. Fern had become a genuine celebrity in Mudlick and not just with the older set. "Have you two seen her?" At first, not realizing they were being addressed, neither Ivy nor Dogg responded. "Well, have you?" Bernice persisted.

Ivy put her fork down. She'd only taken salad and a deviled egg. She tugged her white blouse uncomfortably. "I went by yesterday," Ivy said.

"She's holding a silk rose today. It's so sweet. Such a nice little girl."

"My mother told me about it," Dogg chipped in after swallowing a mouthful of cold ham. "I plan to go this afternoon."

Bernice delicately bit the corner off her cucumber sandwich, then lightly patted at the loose curl she always imagined dangling from the back of her thoroughly set silver hair. "It's not so hot in the mornings. It might be too hot this afternoon. Better wear a hat." She pointed to Dogg's shaved head.

Dogg smiled and rubbed his scalp. "I better."

"Are you sick," one of the women asked, now that the subject had been broached. It was an understandable question. Why would this beautiful boy shave his head if he wasn't undergoing some kind of treatment like chemotherapy?

Dog smiled. "No."

"Head lice?" Ivy offered, a deviled egg in her hand hovering near her mouth.

"No. Just wanted to do it."

"But you had such pretty hair," another woman said. "I remember when you were a little boy in your father's commercials. Such pretty hair."

"Well," Dogg said, "I hope you won't vote against me because of my hair. I have some good ideas for when I'm Junior Mr. Mayor."

"Really" Ivy said suspiciously. She set down her half-eaten deviled egg and turned her chair toward Dogg. "Like what?"

Dogg looked around the table. Five women and Ivy were staring at him, forks filled and in mid-air, waiting for his answer. Without his hair, and with the tie and shirt collar that rested loosely around his neck, he seemed thin and not nearly as confident as they'd imagined. "Like," he began, "like this idea to change the town name. I'm really in favor of that."

Bernice nodded. "We've heard something of it. But what would we change the name to?"

"I've heard," Dogg said uncertainly, "that some people want to change the name to Valhalla West."

Ivy snorted a laugh but quickly capped her face with her hands. "You're kidding," she said a little deviously. "Valhalla as in the myth where the guy eats people's souls?"

"I'm not sure that's right," Dogg said, fidgeting.

"That sounds a little gruesome," Bernice said.

"Cannibalism?" one of the woman asked.

"I'll find out. I mean, no." Dogg's cheeks were going pink. "That's just one suggestion. We could call ourselves something Spanish, like Bonita Vista."

"There's already a Bonita Vista, dear," Bernice said, looking around the room at the other tables.

And then Ivy laid down the hammer, showed her hand and how she was against the committee and its push for progress. "I was just testing to see if you even knew what Valhalla means," she said, standing up adjusting her long navy blue skirt before she leaned into the table. "This sounds like one of those kooky ideas that committee is always hatching up." She turned to Dogg, who sat looking at her with his mouth slightly open. "Was Valhalla West their idea?"

"Yeah," Dogg said, looking slightly relieved he was off the hook.

Ivy sat back down. "You see. Those people have their hooks in everything. Who asked them, anyway?

"Let's not forget all the good the committee does," Bernice said.

Ivy softened slightly. "Did any of you get a call asking your opinion about whether we should change Mudlick's name? It may not sound glamorous, or pretty, but our town name is part of our history. You'd think these people are embarrassed to live here. I, for one, am not ashamed to say I live in Mudlick, California. If it's good enough for Fern, it's good enough for me." And then, almost magician like, Ivy produced and passed out business card sized versions of her campaign sign. "Ivy Simmons," she said. "Pride, Progress, Preservation."

17

The only true ghosts are the mistakes of the past we hold on to. And for the committee, we're proud to say we aren't haunted. We're as forward looking as we can get, which means not getting caught up in what happened a long time ago, except for maybe setting the record straight on a few things. For instance, Charlene Hergis might have come to us at any time about Ivy and Dogg, not only about the encounter outside the stationers, but maybe with her little memento shoe box, a kind of Jimmy Doggins shrine covered with photos of him playing tennis, newspaper clippings, and cut-out red and pink hearts, the lid centered with a white pair of kissing plastic doves forming the handle. All of it cast grayish in the dusty patina of the jilted. The contents, as we came to find, might have given the committee pause had we been informed in a timely manner.

But there was finally a day things became clearer when the committee was doing its best to recover from the Junior Mr. Mayor fiasco, complete with its new, highly unwelcome office holder. We'd done some coaxing of Mrs. Hergis to see if there was anything her daughter could tell us about what had been going on in Dogg's mind during the election. It wasn't long before Charlene walked into our meeting room clutching the box, her mother behind her with a hand on her daughter's shoulder, both of them in pink. Charlene looked tired and sad, like she hadn't gotten over, even so many months later, Dogg's terrible treatment of her. But if we were reading sadness into her face, we could also see determination. Her blonde hair was pulled back tightly in a ponytail and when she arrived next to the table she plopped the box down firmly. "This might give you some answers," she said. Some of the contents were indeed enlightening.

From Dogg, on printer paper and crosshatched with fold lines (with a notation in Charlene's bubbled cursive, hearts dotting each "i" "*His first text!*"):

> *Yeah. Dad told me he talked to urs. Pizza sounds good. lets meet at 6:30 instead. have kind of an important thing before that and not sure how long it's going to take.*
>
> *J.*

From Charlene on mother-of-pearl colored stationary embossed with her initials and bordered in snapdragons and hummingbirds:

> *Jimmy,*
>
> *Who would have guessed that you'd be the quiet type. But I kind of liked that. I'm glad our parents introduced us. I've always thought you were a cutie but since I moved here I never really got around to checking out your crowd. I guess I should have studied up on tennis though. I'm afraid I don't know much about it (except that you're so cute in your tennis outfits!!!!)*
>
> *And I want you to know that I'm sorry about the Peace Corp crack. It wouldn't be a waste of time at all. I just meant that what if you actually got going in tennis professionally? I know that when I'm a fashion merchandiser or designer that it's going to be so competitive that I just want to focus on that. Sometimes people don't think I'm that smart, but the thing is, I am, but mostly just in one area. I should show you my drawings for my prom dress next year.*
>
> *And! And! And! I totally agree. I don't think I can handle kids for a long time either. Luckily we don't have to. Especially us. My father was soooo embarrassing. Of course we would have kept the door to my bedroom open. Kuddle Kat says hi.* [Here she inserts a small and crude drawing of a stuffed toy cat.]
>
> *Who knew you were so serious!? But I like it. It's so cool.*
>
> *XXOO Charlene*
>
> *P.S.*

Did you see how well our mothers got along at dinner?

On the same stationary, on the back, Dogg scrawls his reply.

Charlene:

How many notes a day do you plan to stuff in my locker? I appreciate the attention. Don't get me wrong, but I feel like I can't give as much back. My life is so complicated. You probably don't want to get mixed up with me, though I think I've said that a million times and yet you just press on. In some ways that's an admirable quality. The double dates, getting our parents together for dinner. Remember, though, we've only been hanging out for a little while and you can talk about the future all you want, but in so many ways I can't express, I'm just trying to get through right now.

J.

(Never write notes you wouldn't expose to public scrutiny. Boil eggs for 4.5 minutes only.)
- The Committee

None of us will forget the day Charlene brought us a sequined love note box and placed in front of us that little archive along with a slim journal and a stack of writings too personal to share. A second stack contained the few notes she thought we should read. "I knew they were in there, but I haven't opened this box again until now," she said.

One pile contained things too personal to share, including a slim journal. The other pile contained the few notes she thought we should look at. "I knew they were in there, but I haven't opened this box again until now," she said.

Mrs. Hergis stood looking out the window, her pink blouse glazed in light. It appeared she was only half listening as we read each note aloud. But then she turned toward us, regarding her daughter from behind, crawling her eyes along the table until directing her attention to the committee. "Broken Heart Reveals All," she said, gesturing broadly above her daughter's head as if creating a marquee.

Charlene handed us what would be the second to last note. Some of the hair from her ponytail had begun to pull loose, rising into two distinct bumps like the emerging horns on a kid goat. Again, on her stationary.

Jimmy:

Sometimes I just don't know about you and I'm more than a little surprised at your reaction. It should should!! be a campaign issue. You're just like that father in Too Kill a Mockingbird *who can't see what's right in front of his face. The black guy didn't hurt his daughter. It was someone else. Well it's the same thing with this Ivy thing. She's gotten herself into some trouble and now she's bringing her mess in front of the town. Well if that's what she wants to do she has to expect that people are going to have to say something about it. And I don't know why you aren't one of those people. Where is your thinking at??*

Whenever anyone makes fun of my Abstinence Pledge I just think of people like Ivy and I know I'm doing the right thing. There was this girl I knew once in Junior High, Katrina Forbes. We were in P.E., after, and she had her baby right on the shower floor. Well, I wasn't actually there, but I heard about it and I had P.E. two periods later and they wouldn't let us go into the locker room. So instead of running the mile that day, the school guidance counselor, Mrs. Lopez, this woman with polio legs, the braces and arm things, she came and talked to us about miscarriages.

The point is that you don't owe Ivy anything. She got herself into this mess. But you do owe the community in speaking out against Ivy's behavior. At least you might say something about where is the lousy father? Don't get me wrong, she should have said no and it's all, all on her, but from what I can tell she's on her own. And maybe if you spoke up you could be some sort of role model. You could be an example for the rest. People look up to you, guys do. And think of that guy that got Ivy pregnant. He's probably some strung out kid from a broken home and with no male figure to inspire him.

You can't let Ivy off the hook and in the end she's brought this all on herself. HERSELF! But if the guy who got her pregnant were a real man he'd be at her side and hopefully talk some sense into her about running for Junior Mr. Mayor, though obviously neither of them have much sense. Think of that story about the lady and the tiger where I think he gets her pregnant so she sends him to the wrong door. That solved things!!!

At church on Sunday they were talking about Ivy and this whole mess. The pastor had a message for all of us about her that makes sense. He said that if your neighbor doesn't keep the weeds out of her yard, sooner or later they end up in yours. Amen, right?! So if you're serious about this Junior Mr. Mayor thing, taking a stand against Ivy is your first test to show if you're up to the task. Jimmy, a man doesn't run away from his responsibilities.

Your Charlene

When Charlene got to the bottom of her shoebox, her "personal" pile had become by far the tallest of the two. "This was the last one he wrote before he ... broke up," she said, holding out a still stiff 3x5 card. "It's at the bottom because I don't like to look at it." We asked her why, then, did she keep the note? She looked at the ceiling, bringing her shoulders up in a frustrated gesture, as if holding back tears "I told you," she said, "It was the last one he wrote."

From Jimmy, in green ink in hurried print.

Charlene—Got your texts. Yes, I've been avoiding you because this is too sad for a text. Plus, my handwriting sux. I'm sorry it didn't work out and that you're getting the news this way. But there's no time and the more I talk to people the more they confuse me. I think maybe the best thing I can do for this town is just disappear—Jimmy

18

It's almost hard to talk about Mudlick now, and by that we mean the people in it, when we compare it to some of those who came before us. Some of their stories we've told so many times they're almost committed to memory word for word. And these are why we carry on.

This Junior Mr. Mayor contest wasn't our first test, after all. The committee had been challenged before. In 1916, after years of drought, Claude W. Huxley appeared in Mudlick wearing a double-breasted gray suit, a bowler hat, and a pencil moustache that curved along the shape of his wide upper lip. He was a thin man, pale, with a curiously purposeful gait. He spoke to no one at first, sitting alone for half a day in Mudlick Saloon drinking brandy. The population of the town in those days was less than five hundred, so word of the odd-looking stranger got around quick. Some suspected he'd come to stay at Joseph Colton's burned down lodge and was too embarrassed to say so. Others figured him for a land speculator who'd arrived to cheat people out of their drought-ridden property. But at 2:55, Huxley pulled a gold watch from his pocket, checked it against the chime of the clock hanging above the bar, and walked outside. Apparently unaffected by the brandy, he aimed himself right down the center of the dirt swath that was Main Street, a black leather attaché swinging at his side with each confident stride.

It was January. Like nearly every day for the past four years, the sky was cloudless, the air so hot it was almost yellow. It hadn't rained since early December and even that was barely enough to keep the dust down. Some days there wasn't a person in town who didn't have a handkerchief pressed to their face. Back then, the committee, just three people, held its meetings on the loading dock in front of Lakeview Hay and Feed. Records show that Jarvis Smith, Parnell Gotley, and Thomas Morton conducted their meetings every Tuesday at 3:00. They saw Huxely coming down the street, though they had no idea he was planning to speak with them. They sat, as usual, hats on their knees, Smith and Morton on short wood stools, and Gotley, with his great weight, on a rickety bench that seemed each week on the verge of collapse.

Huxley arrived at the meeting precisely at 3:00. He stepped up onto the dock, his leather heels making hollow clomps on the dusty wood flooring. He took off his hat, revealing a sweaty, but neatly combed head of hair black as crude oil. "Gentlemen," he said. "I understand that you three are the men in charge of things around here."

Smith, described in both myth and true accounts as dangerously temperamental, was almost always the spokesperson for the committee. He looked over his shoulder at the stranger but did not turn on his stool to face him. "Could be," he said. "What's your business?"

"Whatever you're selling out of that black bag we don't want," Gotley added, hooking one thumb on the strap of his bib overalls.

"I see," Huxley said. "Then we've already struck on an agreement. Because I'm not selling anything out of this." He held up his attaché and tapped it with his hand. "But you're right. I am selling something." The three committee members looked at each other smartly as Huxley continued. "What I'm selling is life itself. The element that transforms common dirt into a beautiful red rose, the one thing that keeps us all from turning to dust and blowing a way." Huxley paused for effect. Smith, Morton, and Gotley listened but did not move. "I'm selling water, gentlemen, acres and acres of water."

The men, at the mention of the word water, were instantly aware of their parched throats. Smith turned on his stool, which gave permission for Morton to do the same. Smith placed his straw cowboy hat with its dark band of clotted sweat on his head. "There ain't no doubt, Mr . . . ." Smith looked at Huxley square in the eyes. "What did you say your name was?"

"Claude W. Huxley." He held out his hand but Smith didn't accept.

"Like I was saying, Mr. Huxley. There ain't no doubt we could use water around these parts. But if you're talking about some scheme to pipe it here, or setting up a drilling operation, we don't got the time, the money, nor the interest."

"You misunderstand," Huxley said. He stepped closer to the group and set his hat on the railing. Out on the street and beyond, Mudlick baked under the unprecedented January heat. Main Street fuzzed and wavered in the sun's coppery refractions. A bony-hipped dog staggered into view finding refuge in the narrow shade of a young pepper tree.

At the wide doorway of the Hay and Feed, a few men gathered to listen to the conversation. As Huxley took note of them, Smith turned and sent them away with a single "Git."

Huxley unclasped his attaché. "This is not for sale. These are samples," he said, pausing for effect, then producing three dark brown glass flasks sealed with cork and hardened bee's wax. He handed one each to the men.

"Now that's more like it," Gotley said.

Smith shot him a look to keep him quiet. "We can't be drinking in the middle of the afternoon, Mr. Huxley."

"Church folk would have a fit if they saw the committee liquored up," Morton offered.

Smith shook his head and held out his unopened flask. "Can't accept it."

"Again, you misunderstand me, gentlemen. It's not liquor you hold in your hands. It's water. A sample, in fact, of the acres of water I've brought to Amarillo, Cheyenne, and Albuquerque."

Smith was the first to break off the wax and pull the cork from his flask. He smelled the bottled and put it to his lips, the neck partially hidden by his brush-like salt and pepper moustache. The other two men followed, not allowing a single drop to escape their lips.

"That's water alright," Gotley said, sounding almost disappointed.

Smith tapped the brown flask on his knee but didn't say anything. He took a second drink and swished the water around his mouth as if testing it for some flaw.

"Sweet," Morton breathed out after a long swig.

"That's because it never sat in some muddy old well," Huxley said. "That water came straight out of the air." He leaned back on the railing, retrieving his hat, which he used to fan his face, the forefinger and thumb of his unoccupied hand pressing the sweat from his thin moustache. "I'm a bona fide Rainmaker, gentlemen. And you just drank the proof."

Though the committee was suspicious, they allowed Huxley to give his entire spiel uninterrupted. First, from his attaché, he produced official-looking recommendations and several yellowed news clippings—HUXLEY DELIVERS 5 INCHES, RAINMAKER FILLS RESERVOIR, which he allowed the men to look at as he spoke. He said he'd come to Mudlick to do for the town what he'd done for these other places, bring rain. For $2,000 and $250 an inch, he promised to fill up Mudlick Lake—after so long without rain, it had become a grassy plain with a shallow pond—and any wells and reservoirs within four miles. "I'd like to make it further out," he said, "but my techniques right now limit me to a very specific area. Every drop of rain I produce will fall right here in Mudlick." Most importantly and convincingly, Huxley insisted he not be given a dime until he delivered rain in the quantities promised. Anything short of his guarantee, he told the committee, was free rain.

Two days after his meeting with the committee, Huxley had erected a narrow platform thirty-five feet up in the three-pronged crown of a large sycamore growing near a dry, stone-filled, creek bed a mile and a half outside of town. Huxley cut down all the branches higher than his platform and walled himself in with four wide sections of canvas tarp. In order to get up or down, he climbed a makeshift ladder built out of strips of wood pegged every two feet up the side of the tree.

On the morning of the third day, Mudlick was as hot and dry as the day before, and perfectly windless. The only difference was the bluing sky lanced with a single white column rising so high it seemed to terminate in a pinpoint. Its source was Huxley's platform. Too white for smoke, too permanent for steam, the column was watched all day from the corners of the eyes of the outwardly suspicious but secretly hopeful townspeople. When the breezes came, as they usually did in the late afternoon, the white line rising into the fiercely hot blue sky did not bend so much as bleed sideways in soft streaks as if the hand of God had raked his fingers through it.

People with the luxury of time, which was much of Mudlick—what crops there were had withered or were so minimal as to not need much tending, and livestock had been reduced, in most cases, to the fewest possible animals—these people rode their horses out to see Huxley in his sycamore. Even Jarvis Smith made time from his dairy to see what the man he'd hired was up to. Like Wisemen following the North Star, Huxley's curious visitors needed only follow the plume rising from the narrow ravine called Bobcat Canyon. Which is exactly what Smith did when he saddled up.

"Huxley," Smith called out as he rode up. A pair of men in worn square-toed boots sat below the sycamore drinking from a water bag. Smith recognized them as the Burton cousins, two young men who were on the verge of losing the small hay farm built by their families. Any decent rain, to them, and soon, would make the difference. "Huxley," Smith called out again to the canvas-covered square above him where it wasn't hard to discern the sound of steady bubbling. "Jarvis Smith here."

Huxley hung his chin over the top of the canvas side. "Sorry for the delay. People've been troubling me all day." The Burton cousins looked toward Huxley's voice, clearly upset that Smith had gotten an answer when they hadn't.

"Folks kind of want to know what you're doin' up there," Smith said.

"Tell them I'm making rain."

Smith looked at the sky above and at the surrounding distinctly brown foothills. Not a cloud to be seen, nothing except Huxley's column of whatever and the sudden gray-brown flutter of a Scrub Jay that skimmed across Smith's vision. "Don't look like rain to me," he said.

Huxley climbed down the tree, his white undershirt soaked with sweat. He looked up at Smith, who remained on his horse. "Pardon my appearance," he said, dabbing himself with a dirty rag. "It's hot work up there."

"I expect." Smith's horse jostled slightly beneath him. "But it don't look like you've conjured up much but a bit of smoke and sweat."

"It's a process. I haven't chanted yet."

At that, the Burtons looked at Smith and shook their heads. They stood up, grumbling and brushing off the seats of their pants. "Got to head back," the older Burton said, exiting the fog of dust encircling him and his brother.

Smith slid off his horse and looked Huxley in the eyes. It must have been an intimidating view for Huxley. Smith was thick-boned, stood well over six feet, and used every bit of this bulk in all his dealings. "When it was scientific-sounding," Huxley said, "the committee thought we'd take a chance on you. But folks won't hold much stock in the idea of chanting."

"I don't need their confidence," Huxley said. "All I need is payment in full when I deliver, which will be soon if I get back up there."

Smith looked at the Burton cousins, who still appeared to be skeptical. At least they'd seen someone from the committee doing his job. "Git up there," he said.

Huxley scrambled up his ladder that ran like an exterior spine along the trunk of the sycamore. Half way to the top, he stopped and looked at Smith who had returned to his horse. "If it helps, instead of chanting, call it praying."

"We already done prayed a hole in the sky and ain't got a drop of water to show for it." Smith straightened his horse to head back. He examined the dry creek and the partially exposed roots of Huxley's sycamore emerging from the bank. He called back up to the rain-maker who had already disappeared beyond the canvas walls of his platform. "Mr. Huxley, if we get a gully whomper like you promise, I wouldn't stay perched up in that tree very long."

On the fifth day of Huxley's presence in Mudlick, in the lavender shades of twilight, the wind picked up and the sky began to cloud. The full moon dimmed and dimmed behind the thickening cover. By midnight there was a full-fledged storm at work, the kind, even in rainy years, Mudlick seldom, if ever experienced. Residents woke to claps of thunder and heavy winds that pelted the walls of their homes with debris. It rained all night and all the next day, and the next, each hour worse than the previous. It poured like it never had before. Maloney's Creek overflowed its banks, filling the lake so fast it was triple its normal size. The small valley where Jarvis Smith ran his dairy was flooded side to side. The roof of his barn collapsed on his breed stock and forced their heads under the water. When it was clear nothing could be salvaged, Smith got on his horse and rode through the downpour into town where he found Thomas Morton standing mud-soaked and a bit dazed on the dock of the Hay and Feed. "My place is flooded up to the rafters," he told Smith, speaking loud enough to be heard over the rain.

"My house went down the river yesterday. I won't have anything left after all this," Smith said, looking out on the town. Visibility was terrible but the pair knew the lower half of Mudlick and well into the valley was underwater. Even the railroad trestle, Mudlick's artery to commerce, had washed out. Later, it would be reported, bloated cattle from Mudlick were found floating in Mission Bay. Nearly fifty people lost their lives, ten percent of the town's population. Only the part where Smith and Morton stood, near where the lodge had once been, was slightly elevated, and thus saved for now.

"Do you think that Huxley is still at it out there?" Morton asked. He squinted on the chance he might be able to make out some sign of the man they'd hired to bring rain.

"I suppose I ought to ride out and get him to stop if he ain't already."

"You can't get out there in this."

"I'm here, ain't I? I'll ride along the hillsides." Smith took off his hat and tapped on the rain-darkened wood railing. "The committee got us into this fix, and I'm head of the committee. I have to go if it's the last thing I do for this town."

"You're the head of the committee?" Morton asked. There had never been an official distinction between the members.

Smith tapped on his hat and looked solidly at Morton in reply.

Near the end of his life, Morton recalled that wet day standing on the loading dock where they'd held so many meetings, where they'd made the one decision he regretted for the rest of his life. Morton talked about the committee as if they were soldiers and he sometimes wondered aloud, even though he was there, wondered how it was possible that all that suffering had gone on. There was something hardier about folks then, he'd say, and the further away we get from that time it's harder to believe they existed. People forget. But Morton remembered Jarvis Smith riding off on his horse to stop Huxley and the rain, and save whatever was left of the town. To his dying day, Morton talked about watching Smith ride down Main Street, his horse and body fading in the rain, everything except for his hat, which Morton said he could make out for a long, long time, as if Smith had been a ghost all along.

19

For Ivy, the campaign had gotten off to a good start. She impressed the members of the Republican Women's club and you couldn't go anywhere in Mudlick without seeing her green and white signs. She recognized, perhaps as Dogg hadn't, that despite all her meddling fundraising for "good causes," people still didn't know her and the election allowed her to make a first impression with most of the voters. While all of Mudlick knew him from his commercials and his accomplishments in tennis, only the younger people of Mudlick knew Ivy—Poor Ivy. Everyone else's opinion, she clearly understood, was up for grabs.

The morning of Ivy's first big event, a hot dog giveaway in the Safeway parking lot, she was anything but jubilant. As she, Ryan and Thatch prepared the stand Ivy had gotten donated for the day—complete with soda dispenser and hot dog steamer—she had to take frequent breaks to dry heave into the juniper bushes. "I've got to take a walk," is all she told her friends, but that small group knew, of course, *why* she didn't feel well.

A few blocks into her walk, one arm across her abdomen, Ivy ran into Mrs. Doggins and two others beneath the shade of a blighted Fruitless Mulberry growing near the street. Ivy smoothed her denim skirt as she came face to face with Dogg's mother and Amelia Jenks and her daughter, Casandra. "Hello Mrs. Doggins," Ivy said.

"Judy, dear. Call me Judy," Mrs. Doggins replied in her quiet voice. She extended her hand with its French tipped nails. "Of course you know Amelia and Casandra." Mrs. Jenks nodded her greeting without smiling, though she was happy to see Ivy. As usual, Mrs. Jenks looked tired, dark circles under her eyes, a constellation of tiny pimples across her wide, shiny forehead. She held tightly to her four-year-old daughter's hand. It would have been hard not to know of this family. Cassandra was born six weeks premature, her heart outside her body, kidneys poorly developed, and, as they later discovered, a host of other medical problems that cost the family all their savings and a second mortgage. For her most recent surgery, in at least a dozen businesses around town, it was Ivy who placed hand-made donation coffee cans with Cassandra's face on them. Not to mention the door-to-door campaign Ivy arranged with some of the same kids she rounded up for her campaign. And for what? She didn't know the Jenks family personally.

(Charity begins at your boot straps.) - The Committee

"Hello," Ivy said to Casandra, who wrinkled her nose and hid behind her mother, her rubbery arm a bluish pink worm wrapped around Mrs. Jenks' leg.

Mrs. Jenks suddenly brightened. "She's doing much better. You really helped." Casandra peeked from behind her mother's leg and offered a half smile. "I hear you're running against Judy's son," Mrs. Jenks said.

"Or he's running against me."

"Well, that's just terrific. I haven't really been paying attention. Cassandra goes in for another operation in a week."

Mrs. Doggins crossed her arms and shook her head slowly. "You really are an inspiration. I don't know how you hold up."

"We give all our problems to God." Mrs. Jenks shrugged, placing a hand on her daughter's too-small head. "Our whole church has been praying for him to help this little girl of ours." To see Cassandra then, with her thin-boned marionette stature, wispy blonde hair, and near lipless mouth that always seemed curved downward in displeasure, it was hard to know whether God was doing her any favors or not.

"Maybe," Ivy said, "after I win the election, we can have a big fundraiser for your family."

Cassandra came out from behind her mother. "That would be very sweet," Mrs. Jenks said, to which Mrs. Doggins agreed.

"We're having a hot dog give away at Safeway today. You should come."

The four were quiet for a moment, the light sifting through the mulberry speckling their faces. "I'm just headed up to see Fern," Ivy said, finally. "Then I have to get back."

"That's where I'm headed too, actually," Mrs. Doggins said, "I just took a little detour with Amelia and Cassandra. At that, the group dispersed, Mrs. Jenks and Cassandra going one way, Ivy and Mrs. Doggins the other, the sick mulberry suddenly wracked by fighting jays.

(Support the local library but monitor librarians.)
- The Committee

As they walked toward the Colton house, Mrs. Doggins tucked her bobbing hair behind her ears and adjusted her pastel blue collar. Besides Dogg, she and Ivy had another connection. For a few years Mrs. Doggins volunteered at the library twice a week. For some reason, all the resentment Ivy held toward Dogg never got transferred to his mother. Instead, Ivy sought Mrs. Doggins out to talk about books like *Charlotte's Web* and the *Encyclopedia Brown* series.

"It's really sweet what you did for Cassandra," Mrs. Doggins said.

Ivy shrugged. "It wasn't just me. A bunch of people helped."

"No, really Ivy. This town has no idea how incredible you are." Mrs. Doggins stood still and put her hand on Ivy's shoulder. "I keep my ears open. If there's something goodhearted going on in Mudlick, half the time you're behind it."

"You should be my campaign manager." Ivy winked and the pair started their walk again.

"It's true, though, Ivy. I hope you recognize that about yourself. You're like the thread in the sewing machine, the stitching no one notices is holding everything together."

"Mrs. Doggins, that's nice to hear, but you're exaggerating."

"You'll never hear it from a more reliable source than your opponent's mother." This was a comment about which the committee still wonders if Mrs. Doggins was giving Dogg, her own son, some bad advice just to help out Ivy.

"Speaking of which, how's *your* mom?" Mrs. Doggins asked, patting her face lightly with a tissue. It was another warm day in Mudlick and the textured air felt almost like dry cornhusks running against the skin.

"Working a lot. And Grandma takes up most of her time. She's staying with us now. Alzheimer's." They were in sight of Ms. Colton's property, the backyard side with ivy-covered brick walls and a partial view of an enormous glassy-white greenhouse that looked like a cocoon laid on its side.

"And how is the campaign?" Mrs. Doggins stopped and placed her hand on Ivy's shoulder. "You seemed a little angry the other day at the meeting."

Ivy rolled her eyes, and continued walking as if she was about to explain something Mrs. Doggins should already know. "Your son is exasperating."

"He's a good boy, Ivy."

"That's easy when you're privileged and good looking."

Mrs. Doggins didn't answer. They were at the very corner of the Colton property; a green and orange jumble of late-blooming nasturtium grew below the wrought iron fence. Inside, the wide lawn surrounding the house had taken on its summer grayness. "Did you see the paper today?" Mrs. Doggins said as Fern came into sight. "They're having a contest: *What would Fern say if she could talk?* They're going to publish one a day for the summer on their website."

"How about, 'Vote for Ivy Simmons'"

Mrs. Doggins laughed. "I hope she's a non-partisan plant."

"Are you kidding? I have the topiary vote all locked up." As they reached the front of the yard where Fern stood, arm still raised, this time with an apple in her hand, Ms. Colton, resembling a large blue pear in her denim jumpsuit, tottered out. She waved at Ivy and Mrs. Doggins and replaced the apple with a pink striped Hula Hoop which rocked in Fern's loose grasp.

They watched Ms. Colton return to her house and Mrs. Doggins leaned on the fat, shedding trunk of a eucalyptus tree. Everything about her had an elegance, the way her short hair bobbed softly above her shoulders, the way, leaning on the tree, her body seemed like one clean line. "She's a cute little girl. She kind of reminds me of you when you were her age."

"Maybe the green part." Ivy said. "But I've never been cute."

"Don't talk like that."

"Mrs. Doggins," Ivy said sternly, "Judy." A narrow shred of bark fluttered between them, catching the light like a descending strobe. "That is precisely why I'm in this election. I'm running *against* cute. And cute with money at that."

"You make it sound like a moral failing because Jimmy was born into good circumstances. But it wasn't always like that for our family. I didn't have money growing up, you know."

"But you were pretty, right? You had choices?"

"I suppose." Mrs. Doggins, a former Ms. El Cajon who rode with her court of princesses in the annual Mother Goose Parade, shifted off the trunk of the tree and walked closer to the fence to look at Fern, who, for all the world, seemed as if she might at any minute place the Hula Hoop around her waist and start twirling her hips.

(Steer children toward wholesome activities like volunteer garbage pickups.) - The Committee

"You know I adore you, Ivy. But I'm not sure it's a healthy thing to seek the responsibility you're after just because you don't feel rich and pretty."

"You don't get it. I like the way I look just fine. I like my birth-marks and my hair that won't do anything. I like that fact that nothing in the magazines fits me. I don't care about being rich or pretty. I just don't want to be ignored because I'm not." Ivy joined Mrs. Doggins at the fence.

"So are you running against Jimmy or against what you think he stands for? They're two different things."

Ivy paused, grinding a heel into the ground as if she were crushing a bug. "I'm running because the only time I ever feel like I have a chance is when I'm in charge."

Mrs. Doggins turned and put one hand on Ivy's shoulder, the other on her cheek. "Just so you know, Jimmy's coming around to some of the same conclusions. It's true that this town loves him, but he's really trying to do this on his own. He won't take any money from his father and you saw what he did to his hair."

Ivy's face briefly shone with a positive response, but just as quickly tightened as she clutched at her abdomen, stumbled toward the eucalyptus, and launched into her final dry heave episode of the morning.

"Oh, dear," Mrs. Doggins said in recognition.

20

After Ivy's intentions became clear at the Republican Women's club luncheon buffet, the committee thought it best to monitor her campaign whenever possible. We made sure that at least one of us would be at her hot dog give away the whole time, which meant taking shifts so we didn't look conspicuous. Though we were a lot less nervous when we heard that Dogg was planning a free dance in the open-air pavilion over-looking the lake. Two thousand "Disco with Dogg" flyers were being distributed even as Ivy gave out her first hot dog.

By noon, Ivy's stand was up and running at the far edge of the Safeway parking lot. No one who went to the store or drove by could miss the green and white double braid of balloons that arched over the whole operation. On the street side was a sign painted on a sheet of plywood in large black letters: FREE LUNCH! Vote for Ivy Simmons! On the store side, rather than a sign, Thatch and Raul stood at each entrance handing out "coupons" for a complimentary hot dog and soda.

It was committee member Jasper Carson who wanted more than just sitting in the car, watching teenagers give out hot dogs and cups of soda, so he actually talked to Ivy. Jasper, the only military veteran on the committee—he was allowed to join us mostly because he could help us get use of the V.F.W. Hall cheaply—Jasper was often impossibly confrontational, a loose cannon amongst us, and not our brightest member. He once theorized, in all sincerity, that clocks, like toilets, ran backward in Australia. And it was Jasper that yelled at a Girl Scout troop for blocking the sidewalk during their cookie sale. In the Marines he'd learned the way to win was with overwhelming force.

Short, but a serious body builder, Jasper was fond of wearing tank tops and bike shorts everywhere he went. The day of Ivy's hot dog give away, he rode up on a motorcycle, his orangish, thoroughly shaved skin gleaming in the sun where it wasn't covered by shiny black spandex. "I'll take me a couple of them hot dogs," Jasper said, checking his thin, crew cut hair with a flat hand.

"Aren't you on the committee?" Ivy poked at the brim of her green cap embroidered with her campaign slogan.

"Sure am, little lady. I just can't make it to all the meetings. I hear you're being kind of harsh on some of our plans."

Ivy dropped the hot dog she held back into the steamer and turned to face Jasper again. He stood, like always, arms bent at his sides as if he had guns holstered and ready to be drawn.

"Somehow I don't think it's appropriate for you to be approaching me about the campaign," Ivy said, retrieving the hot dog and placing it in a bun without bothering to shake off the excess water.

Jasper wasn't used to being challenged, especially by women. And now he had two to deal with since Pat Hunter walked up holding out a coupon in her frail, shaking hand. "I'm just saying," Jasper said, "that we're trying to do good things and you should consider that."

Mrs. Hunter held up a quivering digit and interrupted in her aged voice "A hot dog and Coca Cola, please,"

Ivy took her coupon. "Yes Ma'am," she said, and then turning to Jasper. "As for you, consider that some of the 'good things' the committee tries to do are only good for the committee."

(**Trust your community leaders.**) - The Committee

"Oh," Mrs. Hunter said, looking at Jasper carefully with her foggy gray eyes. "Are you on the committee?"

"I am, Mrs. Hunter."

"My late husband was a member for a while a long time back."
Avon Hunter, who was much older than his wife, had spent three
years on the committee before his first heart attack forced him to
slow down. Years later, after he died, Mrs. Hunter seemed to stop in
time. So, as she stood before Jasper, she wore the same avocado and
yellow polyester dress we'd been familiar with for years, along with
the clip-on pineapple earrings she only wore with that outfit. And
her sandy colored wig, once full and round, had collected in rowed
mats allowing the brown mesh to show through like crop rows.

Rather than responding, Jasper shoved the remainder of his hot
dog in his mouth, cheeks bulging. Ivy came to his rescue by setting
Mrs. Hunter's hot dog and soda in front of her. "Remember to vote
for Ivy Simmons."

"Such a Pretty name." Mrs. Hunter was somber. "My husband
had a sister named Ivy. But they're both gone now."

"It's sad when you lose people you love."

Mrs. Hunter brightened. "That's just what Fern told me."

"Fern?" Jasper coughed in mid-swallow.

"Oh, yes. Such a pleasant little girl. I don't know what took Ms.
Colton so long to share her with us. We had a nice long talk today."

Jasper rolled his eyes. He wasn't the smoothest guy in that kind
of situation, more of an enforcer than charmer. "What else did she
tell you? Stock advice? Lottery numbers?"

"Oh, no dear. Nothing like that. We just chatted about my late
husband. The weather being so warm. She talks to a lot of people."

Just as Jasper was about to probe further, Ivy stopped him
by tapping on the counter. "You should eat your hot dog before
it gets cold."

Mrs. Hunter smiled and took her soda and hot dog and walked
back through the parking lot toward her car. At the same time, near
Thatch at the store entrance, Amelia Jenks stood with her daughter
Cassandra, who, at her mother's side, looked bleached and diminutive
as an old lawn ornament. The three of them waved in Ivy's direction.

"They go to my church," Jasper said. "That's one sick little girl. We must've prayed for that family a thousand times."

"*You*, go to church?" Ivy said.

"I've accepted Jesus Christ as my personal lord and savior. Have you?"

But before Ivy responded, events were unfolding in the parking lot that would come as close as anyone could expect to proving that God does answer prayers. Mrs. Hunter sat in her dusty Lincoln Continental eating the hot dog meant to sway her vote. She took two bites and wrapped the rest in a napkin for later. Her car groaned to life with a cloud of blue smoke that rolled up and across the parking lot like an escaped spirit. Mrs. Jenks and Cassandra finished their conversation with Thatch and started walking, hot dog coupons in hand, toward Ivy, Jasper, and the stand with its arch of green and white balloons that excited Cassandra so much she pulled away from her Mother's hand and started running, finger pointed skyward. Mrs. Hunter took a sip of her soda, tossed the remainder out the window, and put her car into what she thought was reverse. Instead, her car lurched forward, bumping an empty grocery cart, sending it flying forward as she corrected her mistake and backed away. Mrs. Jenks couldn't yell fast enough as she saw the rammed cart barreling toward her daughter.

(Dress children well in case of hospitalization.) – The Committee

There are plenty of surprising, random things witnesses recalled about that moment, Casandra's untied left shoe, the sudden and inexplicable smell of bacon, the case of beer left beneath a cart by Trevor Dale, Mrs. Jenks wide open arms and shriek that cut across the parking lot as if it were the demarcation between Heaven and Hell. We like to think that Cassandra's last thoughts were of the balloons waving back and forth across a blue sky, that she didn't even feel the cart strike her squarely in the temple, making her drop lifelessly to the asphalt as easy as if she'd been a rag doll. We like to think that God has a reason for things, as the pastor said at Cassandra's funeral. And maybe, after all those years of prayer, after all of that little girl's illnesses, God couldn't see that family suffer any more and he sent them a solution.

21

None of us knew a whole lot about Ms. Colton, even though she'd lived for all those years in that same house built by her father. She always kept to herself, though if she saw you in the store, she'd smile and say hello as she pushed her cart along, and she sent a sizeable spray of pink roses to Cassandra Jenk's funeral. (That day, Fern held a small black wreath and she told Martin Kaze that she was sad her friend died.) In town, Ms. Colton almost always wore a knee-length denim skirt and light blue cotton blouse buttoned up to the neck like some sort of stocky Old West nun. And never any makeup on her reddish, freckled skin that made her cropped white hair seem even whiter. No makeup, that is, except for the dark maroon lipstick that thickened her narrow lips, so that when her mouth was closed, combined with its rays of freckles and wrinkles, it looked as if a small oval mollusk had attached itself just below her nose.

Once, a few years before she brought out Fern, she saved Bobby Krupp from choking on a nectarine pit in the produce department. Just grabbed him around the waist and made it pop right out. Janice Krupp isn't exactly known for her child rearing skills, and, if truth be told, letting Bobby eat that nectarine in the first place was just the same as stealing. The committee pretty much all agreed on that. But, none of us said so to the man from *The Weekly Chaparral*. Some people just don't know how to raise their children right and you can't help them when they won't listen.

Another thing about Ms. Colton was that she's never been married, and we're pretty sure she hasn't been on a date in fifty years. It was just her and her housekeeper, Viola Thomas—who represented a third of our African American population—just her and Viola all these years. The two of them alone in that big house but for a couple times a month when two blue vans pull into the long red-brick Colton driveway and a dozen or so African-American children pile out, each excitedly hugging Viola and Ms. Colton.

What the committee knows, we learn from rare encounters. Leroy and Ellen Zalinski, the pastor who presided over Cassandra's funeral, went to dinner with Ms. Colton a couple days after the services—her treat. She said she was celebrating her birthday and that Viola was visiting a sick cousin in Los Angeles. Ms. Colton had Alaskan Salmon with some of that fancy mustard on the side. Pastor Zalinkski had shrimp and his wife had a Greek Salad because she's awfully allergic to shellfish. One time someone forgot to tell her there was crab in the potato salad and she blew up like a giant lumpy raspberry.

"So how old are you?" Pastor Zalinski asked between shrimps.

Mrs. Zalinski blushed and slapped him on the shoulder. "Now Leroy, you don't go and ask a woman such things." But she was glad he asked and both of them gave Ms. Colton the chance to answer.

"Old enough to celebrate," is all Ms. Colton said. For the evening, she'd pinned a gold, ruby-eyed squid broach to her blue blouse. In her later years, Ms. Colton had become quite an adventurer. The squid, she explained to the Zalinskis, was in honor of her trip to the Sea of Cortez where, after becoming one of the oldest women at her school to become SCUBA certified, she did a night dive to get a glimpse at the aggressive beauty of the Humboldt Squid. "If my sleeves weren't so long," she told the Zalinskis, "I'd show you the scar on the arm where a three-footer took a nip right through my wetsuit." She paused and stared off before coming back. "Beautiful things."

As the evening progressed, and any mention of Cassandra had long since stopped, the three began talking about her topiaries. She'd been doing it a long time, starting out with shapes like hearts and such and then moving onto more complicated forms. We all remember the day the welders arrived and started making a ruckus in her back yard, putting up the frame for her outsized greenhouse. You can't see anything but the top of it from the road, but, judging by the height, it's big enough for a whale. "If you think Fern is great," Ms. Colton said as she scraped her plate clean. "I've got something even better in the works."

22

If there was a better topiary in Abigail Colton's massive green-house, the people of Mudlick didn't seem to be anticipating it. Fern captured our imagination. It had been just a couple weeks since we first saw her out in the yard, and even Ms. Colton had to admit that Fern started to mature a bit. Her dress was more distinct, variegated leaves growing like a sundress. And somehow her eyes started to come out distinctly and pretty lips too, though some said it was her teeth that showed and not her lips. And all that time she had that one hand up in the air.

The day after Cassandra died, Fern held a book, though none of us could quite make out the title. It was orange with black lettering, kind of like a library book. Mrs. Bowles, the librarian, said there wasn't anything checked out to Ms. Colton for almost a year and that one was called *Monsters of the Deep Sea* and she'd returned it right on time. "Not much of a reader if you ask me," Mrs. Bowles said, and she explained how that book was mostly pictures with some captions. "And," she added, "we weren't too happy about the potting soil between some of the pages."

On a hunch, Mrs. Peck asked if it was possible a book had been checked out in the name of Fern Colton and Mrs. Bowles looked but came up empty. So, Fern stood there practically the whole day holding that book, Collie laying in the shade of her body. But Greter Johnson, eighteen that year and going off to college on a track scholarship, Greter got the idea to get some binoculars and so we found out just exactly what Fern was reading—*The Art of Self Defense.* Now we couldn't imagine why a girl of her age would read such a book and some of us thought, briefly, that maybe we ought to say something of the sort to Ms. Colton. Why scare children about the world? But that idea was shot down because you can't interfere in people's business.

(Report suspicious behavior.) - The Committee

What was certain was that people were paying attention to every little detail about Fern. In the *Chaparral Weekly's* website, the front page was a full screen photo of Fern with a cartoon bubble leading from her mouth. The announcement they ran for suggestions as to what Fern might say received two hundred entries. The first one posted: *"Photosynthesis isn't as easy as it looks."*

People were so interested in Fern that some even consulted Mrs. Hunter—Mr. and Mrs. Jenks prayed on it and insisted no charges be filed against their daughter's oblivious killer—some consulted Mrs. Hunter to see if Fern was saying anything new. Among other things, we learned that Fern liked Vic Damone, wouldn't touch vegetables, and was very adamant that children hold their parent's hand while crossing streets or parking lots.

There was also considerable groundswell for Fern to make a special public appearance. Every year, we have a little Founders Day Parade downtown and it gets quite a crowd. Most years our grand marshal is someone who's done something special since the last parade. One year Mr. Phillips was chosen because he grew a three-pound tomato and another year, and this is the truth, Becky Parker set the United States record for points in Archery. And even though she hadn't lived in Mudlick, her Grandmother got her to be in the parade. So the year Fern came along, it was pretty unanimous that she ought to be our grand marshal. With that beautiful green hand of hers, we all agreed, at least, she had the parade wave down pretty good.

23

The day of "Disco with Dogg," the committee held an emergency meeting at the home of Ruby and Flack Jones. Jacob Alter had heard something and wanted us gathered so we could hear it, too. The Jones' living room was the only place we could agree to on such short notice. When their son moved, Ruby and Flack knocked out the wall to his bedroom, doubling the size of their front room. The walls were dark with wood paneling trimmed at the top with strips of gold-flecked mirrors. Ruby had envisioned the space as a place to throw smart cocktail parties. She'd reupholstered her flat-cushioned, sixties style furniture in charcoal fabric with white and maroon throw pillows that matched the carpet.

(Ice must never be higher than the edge of the glass. And only round, never square.) - The Committee

When we arrived, an array of store bought cookies lay neatly spread on the tinted glass coffee table. Ruby and Flack were eager for guests and even dressed up for the occasion, she in a black silk blouse and red leatherette cocktail pants with matching high-heeled sandals, he, still covering up his tattoos, in blue silk and freshly ironed and creased black jeans. "God Bless them for trying," Lucille Otto whispered before speaking up.

"Might I ask what all this is about?" Lucille asked as we settled in on the uncomfortably firm furniture.

(Moustaches make a lip reader's job difficult.) - The Committee

Jacob Alter crossed his legs and put his arms behind his head. He was growing a moustache and it was coming out redder than his hair had ever been. "I've heard from a pretty reliable source that Ivy Simmons didn't tell us something very important about her candidacy." All of us, as if on cue, leaned in to hear what Jacob was about to say.

"The thing is," Jacob said. "I've heard that Ivy is pregnant."

Flack laughed and Ruby stopped swirling her drink. "Are you sure?" she asked.

Jacob pulled a pack of cigarettes from his pocket and tapped out one of the slim white sticks. He put it to his lips but did not light it. It was an experiment on his part with quitting. "I think so," he said, the cigarette waving between his lips as he spoke.

"Who's the father?" Flack asked, lighting one of his own cigarettes.

"That is a mystery for now."

Ruby sat and crossed her legs, lighting a cigarette as well. Though the three of them rarely smoked around other committee members, when cloistered together, they could fill an ashtray in short order. "It won't do to have our next Junior Mr. Mayor walking around with a baby in her arms."

"Ms. Junior Mr. Mayor," Jacob corrected.

Flack blew a wave of smoke into the air above him. "Don't matter. It won't get that far anyways. She'll have to pull out."

"That's right," his wife agreed. She stood and walked to the sliding glass doors. In the dark, their pool glowed like a giant, radiated lima bean. Ruby slid the door open, the singed smell of chlorine and oleander riding in with the dry air.

"I'm not so sure we can stop her. There isn't really anything that covers this." Jacob laid a copy of the "Rules of Conduct" on the table, pointing at his proof with a thick-nailed index finger. People can say a lot of things but there's no arguing with something put down on paper.

"Well, we have to talk to her," Ruby said, exhaling smoke through the screen door. "Convince her it won't be good for the town."

"What if she's gets an abortion?" Jacob wondered out loud.

Ruby put her hand to her temples. She hated the word. She knew the value of life, confronted it head on, she thought. Once, over the Rockies during a flight to Minneapolis to visit her sister, she'd seen the seatbelt light go on during some turbulence. The boy across the aisle, who was maybe six, lay curled up and sleeping on his side across two seats. She'd thought to wake his drowsing parents so they could secure him. But it had been a blessing for the entire cabin when, after a half hour of the boy yelling questions about the plane and loudly imitating the voice of the muscle-bound action figure held in front of his face—"Stratoliths unite!—after all this, when his mother winked at Ruby and called to her son as she held out a small white pill—"Take your *vitamin*, Stephen"—it seemed that the jet's slight bumpiness hardly warranted the risk of rousing the sedated child.

Ruby said nothing to the parents and did not call a flight attendant, a decision which worked out fine until the plane dropped a thousand feet and the child, in Ruby's slow motion memory, as if levitated, rose from the seat still in his fetal position, and floated into the aisle—one tennis shoe missing, dirty socks, page boy haircut in a spray, Mickey Mouse shirt with red sleeves—floated across, over, between several seats before the plane recovered and he ended up lumped and unconscious at the feet of an elderly couple. On the ground, after an emergency landing in Denver, the boy was bleeding from one ear when the EMT's rushed the plane. Though she inquired, Ruby never heard what happened to the boy after she saw his tennis-shoed foot disappear down the aisle.

(Restrain children at all times.) - The Committee

"The other thing," Jacob said, "is that I took the liberty of asking Ivy to meet us here at 9 P.M."

Half of Ruby's face reflected the pool's green light as she nodded and looked outside. It was just a half-hour until 9. "You boys go to Dogg's dance," Ruby said. "I think I should talk to Ivy alone."

When Ivy arrived, Ruby was netting toad and June Bug carcasses from the pool. The invasion of the latter was nearly over though a few latecomers still thumped about in our near barren fruit trees. At the sound of the doorbell, Ruby called to her guest from the side gate, only, as Ivy stepped in to the jade light of the backyard, Ruby saw that she wasn't alone. Thatch had come with her. Both of them were dressed in black sweat suits. Ivy's hair was pulled back tightly, and in the light, Thatch's razor straight part made it look as if he had a green racing stripe running through his scalp.

"You two look like cat burglars," Ruby said, returning to the task of netting bugs from the pool. She wanted the moment to seem as relaxed and casual as possible. "Have a seat." In some sense, she wished they were adults so she could offer them a drink. It was a perfect night for martinis.

Though her hair was impossibly black and she had no grandchildren, or even children of her own, Ruby thought of herself as Mudlick's wisest senior citizen. She often volunteered to do things for the committee that called on persuasion. Though we almost always assented—it's the unfortunate nature of our position in town that we often find ourselves delivering unwanted news—we let Ruby speak for us often not because, as she conjured in her head, that she was grandmotherly, but because she wasn't subtle. "It's getting around that you're pregnant," Ruby said.

Ivy and Thatch had taken seats on two plastic deck chairs. Neither of them flinched at the revelation. "I guessed it would," Ivy said, crossing her legs calmly.

"So it's true."

"Geez, I'm not sure this is any of your business." Thatch's defense was earnest but hardly intimidating. It merely touched Ruby as if it were a half-inflated balloon at the end of a dull party.

"The committee runs this election. Anything to do with it is our business. And in this case, we have Ivy's best interest at heart."

Ivy raised an eyebrow. "How do you figure?"

"It's going to get around fast, dear." Ruby stroked the surface of the pool with the net a final time, emptying the contents beneath

a row of tall white oleander. She wanted to tell them Ivy *had* to quit
but she held back. "I know you really wanted to do this, Ivy. But a
girl in your condition is going to have a lot of things to think about
other than being Junior Mr. Mayor. And people can be awfully
mean. The committee thinks you should consider withdrawing for
your own welfare and the town's." She was trying not to sound
wish washy. As all of us on the committee know, confidence is the
only substitute for reason.

**(Prevent toads from clogging your filter by poisoning
them in the yard.)** - The Committee

Ivy stood and walked along the lip of the pool, her dark sweat suit
an automatic silhouette against the green water. She stood directly in
front of Ruby. "Do you know why we're wearing these?" She plucked
at her shirt sleeve. "Stealth. Thatch and I planned to sneak to the edge
of the pavilion and check out Jimmy's dance. But just before we came
here we realized that this is not *Mission Impossible*."

"Not quite sure what you mean by telling me that, dear." Ruby
clutched the pole sure as Moses with his staff that turned into a serpent.

Ivy returned to Thatch, waving at him to stand. When they were
side by side, looking at Ruby still holding her long net, it was if they
were two minor super heroes in jogging outfits. "I'm in, Mrs. Jones.
If people bring up the fact I'm pregnant, I'll have to deal with it. But
I'm going to win this election."

Ruby set down her net. Normally, she would have appreciated the
fact that this girl in front of her was being tough. But she only admired
moxy tempered by civic-mindedness. The image of a pregnant teenage
candidate on the six o'clock news was too much for her. And if the
committee ever wavered about which candidate it hoped would win,
out of that single moment, it was clear that it had to be Jimmy Doggins.

Suddenly, music rolled across town, Alicia Bridges' four cornered
voice singing, "I Love the Night Life," the first song from Disco with
Dogg in the Park. "You can run for Junior Mr. Mayor if you want,"
Ruby warned. "But I know this town pretty well. It's going to get ugly."

24

It was an innocent enough conversation at the time. MJ Maxler was bike riding with his young son Charles through the park the very evening of "Disco with Dogg." Mr. Maxler was a tall, handsome, well-to-do, former triathlete with 20/10 vision, raising his son in the spirit of his own wealth and vitality. On this occasion, they were stretching out their time before Mr. Maxler had to return Charles to their mother. The divorce had been long and bitter, with the former Mrs. Maxler, now Scotta Lundgren, threatening to take the boy back to Denmark. That attempt had been staved off, but now, Mr. Maxler was left just two weekends a year with Charles, who with his bike helmet, looked not unlike a thin-legged mushroom on his small bicycle.

Dogg was supervising the final touches on the outdoor pavilion where his dance would take place in just hours. The Maxlers watched his work for a while before Dogg noticed them, surprised at how elaborate the sound and lighting was going to be. To Mr. Maxler, the huge black speakers on the pavilion stage looked as if Dogg was planning on broadcasting music all the way to the coast.

Dogg, not yet in the elaborate outfit he planned for the dance, jogged over to his small audience, tapping Charles on the helmet with his knuckles. "What's up Coconut?" he said to his young friend. He knew Charles from the previous year's Peewee Sports camp.

"Man, he's going home tonight to see Mom," Mr. Maxler said, answering for his son.

Dogg nodded, apparently remembering the public arguments the Maxler's had in front of Charles and the other children on the tennis courts.

Without missing a beat, Charles smiled and took on an excited look. "Watch this, Dogg." He rode off to a flat, straight part of the asphalt, where he got up some steam and popped a series of feeble but earnest wheelies.

"Hey man," Mr. Maxler said, "I never thanked you for helping him out last summer. His mother and I were really going at it. He needed that camp."

"I just put a racket and ball in his hand."

"Man, you gave him a hero while we were making fools out of ourselves."

"Hero, Mr. Maxler? I don't think so. Just a friend." Dogg waved at Charles who was still riding his bike and showing off to the extent he could.

Mr. Maxler sighed in a kind of forecast of the frustration of the coming years of weekend visits and split summer vacations. "They make you feel like the only thing you can do is scoop your kid up and disappear to Mexico." Mr. Maxler noticed Dogg's worried look. "Don't fret, man. I'm not kidnapping my son. That's practically what his mother wanted to do. I'm just saying, this whole custody thing makes you feel like the only solution is a run for the border. Man, I definitely married the wrong woman."

(On taco night, do not offer diced meats. Use authentic ground beef.) - The Committee

"Do you think she married the wrong man?"

Mr. Maxler thought for a moment. "I guess so. There are the relationships you choose and the ones you settle for. I think both of us settled. We looked good together. And, well, the physical part at first was excellent. But there was a woman before Scotta I should have paid more attention to and I let her go for stupid reasons."

Dogg was silent.

"Hey man, I only wanted thank you for helping out Charles. He needed a role model right about then. But, hey, I shouldn't be laying all this on you before your big night." The two of them looked at the silent pavilion, which in the late afternoon, seemed strangely barren.

"Trust me," Dogg said, "With all the lights, you won't recognize it tonight."

"Man, you must be excited."

Dogg looked directly at Mr. Maxler. "To be honest, right now I feel like I'd be better off running for the border . . . " and then with a wink, " . . . man."

25

Everyone who might have complained about the music being too loud attended Dogg's disco party. If ever we needed proof this town loved Dogg, that night was it. He was just one of those people who could make you feel good just by being around. By 11, the concrete dance floor was full and people were dancing in the dirt; and on top of picnic benches. The outdoor wood-slat pavilion was outfitted complete with multi-color beat-matching lights and two full-size disco balls carbonating the darkness with specks of glimmer that floated like bubbles over the sweating dancers, the surrounding pepper trees, and the black surface of Mudlick Lake. There hadn't been so many people attending a dance in town since the 1954 rodeo when an impromptu promenade broke out in the arena after the last bull ride and people came down out of the stands to square dance in the dirt.

(Use Calico sparingly.) - The Committee

Among the gathered, most of whom had attempted some sort of retro look, Dogg gleamed with his freshly shaven head and all white ensemble: long sleeve silk shirt with a wide-open butterfly collar, tight-crotched slacks, and platform shoes. He danced through the crowd as if he'd been transported from 1978, Travoltaesque in the way a space cleared around him as he circulated. Dogg randomly pulled women to him, spun them, displaying a talent for disco style dancing no one could have guessed, except his mother who had forced him into six years of private dance lessons. Miss Penelope Calveaux would have been both startled and proud. Wherever he got them, Dogg had the moves, dropping into the splits then sliding upward as if pulled by a rope, his bellbottoms following every move with their own motions. The only thing moving across the dance floor more quickly than Dogg was the rumor that Ivy was pregnant.

Gavin Han—famous in town for being the high school's only Chinese wrestler, and for developing an eating disorder trying to make weight—waded onto the dance floor during "Turn the Beat Around" to find Dogg. It had been Gavin who supplied the paper with Fern's website quote for the day—"I'm a Disco Diva!"—which he thought was perfect for the green girl with her hand pointed upward in a suspended dance move. Gavin found Dogg near the opposite edge, dancing with Maria Rivera and her mother. They were teaching him a few new steps. Maria wore a bright red dress, and when she spun close into Dogg, the two of them looked like a large twirling peppermint stick.

Gavin waved Dogg to the edge of the dance floor. "You're going to be the next Mayor."

"Thanks," Dogg said.

Gavin pulled his friend farther away from the music. "I thought you should know, they're saying Ivy got pregnant from one of the teachers at school."

(Pregnancy is a blessing based on community standards.)
Dogg was stoic. "Wait here," he said, tapping Gavin   - The Committee
on his plump chest.

Gavin watched as Dogg waded through the dancing crowd up to the stage where the DJ stood rolling his head to the beat coming from his black earphones. Dogg tapped the man on the shoulder and gestured broadly as he spoke. It was a brief and desperate looking conversation. The man checked his watch and pointed to it with a question but Dogg shook his head, mouthing the word "now" several times. The DJ patted him on the back like they were old friends and nodded.

Even after Gavin watched his friend leave the DJ and disappear behind the portable black curtain backing the low, narrow stage, he stayed where Dogg told him. More than even a successful wrestler, it seemed sometimes that Gavin wanted to be Dogg, to own his thin body and Caucasian features. It was no accident that Gavin had chosen to wear all white that night, though he had to settle for tennis shoes, bleached denim pants, and the cotton long sleeve shirt he'd worn to his Uncle's funeral. It was a dismal imitation of his hero, but if people thought of him in the same breath as Dogg, he was happy.

The DJ faded out of Van McCoy singing "The Hustle" and lights dimmed, giving way to 5 lengths of blacklights. The dance floor oohed and ahhed as everyone inspected the brightness of one another's teeth, constellations of lint and dandruff on the lapels of polyester leisure suits, and the ladies shoes that seemed hollow and moving on their own. The speakers rattled with a drum and a narrow spotlight shot to the back of the dance floor onto Dogg's shiny face as Andy Gibb's falsetto began "I Just Want to be Your Everything," Dogg lip synching as he moved forward in the crowd, holding a mic to his mouth, almost believable when after a couple minutes the first verse rolled out.

For so long
You and me been finding each other for so long
And the feeling that I feel for you is more then strong, girl
Take it from me
If you give a little more then you're asking for
Your love will turn the key

As he sang, Dogg shook men's hands and touched ladies' cheeks. He emoted to the lyrics as if they were his own and this was a spot on a TV talent show. Even with his shaved head and disco costume, Dogg easily managed the charismatic magic that never seemed to leave him. People pressed forward on the dance floor to be closer to him, slowing his progress. By the time he got to the final line, "Cause I'd do anything to be your everything," Dogg had reached the stage.

He raised his hands at the fade of the song, and the gathered applauded as if he were the singer himself.

"I just want to be your everything," Dogg boomed in his own voice over the loudspeakers. Once again, everyone cheered, some of the younger ones woof-woofing in reference to their host's name. He wiped his sweating, shaved head with a towel and continued. "I've been thinking about what the Junior Mr. Mayor elections mean this year. In the past, it's mostly been ceremonial, dedicating a new store, planting a tree. But I'm not about that this year."

Someone in the crowd yelled an amen, and brief laughter rolled forward. Dogg fixed his collar as the crowd quieted. He walked across the short stage and before he continued, milked the pause for all the expectation he could draw out. "And some people always want to talk about what's wrong with Mudlick. But I'm not about that either." Dogg bent down and picked up a stack of narrow flyers which he started tossing to the crowd, handing half of them down to be passed around. It was a schedule of campaign events, including, among other things, a charity fishing derby at the reservoir and a free movie at the Mudlick theatre which had been converted into a church. "Here's what I say." Dogg pointed to his left as the spotlight clicked off and a banner, white on a dark background, unfurled from above, the lettering electric under the blacklights. Almost simultaneously the crowd read Dogg's campaign motto aloud: "Let's have *FUN!!*"

A cheer went up and Dogg started the chant of his own slogan until everyone pumped the phrase into the air and out over the entirety of Mudlick. There couldn't have been a person in town who didn't feel the rumble of those collected voices. As he chanted, Dogg jumped into the crowd with his mike and yelled "Vote for Jimmy Doggins and keep on dancing!" A set of spotlights hit the stage where men in Village People costumes started their own lip-synching to "Macho Man." Dogg waded through the hyped-up crowd singing to what he hoped would become his anthem throughout the campaign. He popped out near the edge where Gavin stood. After a last few congratulations he freed himself to talk.

Gavin followed Dogg as he walked by. "What's up?"

Dogg stopped far enough away so that the music wouldn't rattle against their skin. From there it was still loud, but not overwhelming. The dancers inside the large round gazebo looked like freed carousel animals under the spinning lavender glow of the blacklights. Dogg leaned on the edge of a concrete picnic bench, a pair of sleeping Mallards complained at the disruption as they moved away in darkness. "Listen Gavin, you've got to get the word out that this pregnancy thing with Ivy can't be part of the campaign."

(Campaigns fail, not on what's said, but on what's witheld.)
- The Committee

"But why?" Gavin shook his head. He and a few of Dogg's buddies were helping Dogg with putting up posters around town and such and it seemed to Gavin like talking up the Ivy thing would be the best thing that could happen. "No one's going to vote for a teenage prego. Her campaign is dead."

Dogg stood up straight and held Gavin by the shoulders, looking him directly in the eyes. "I don't want to win that way. It's dirty."

Gavin recognized something different in Dogg's eyes, something dark and angry. "Maybe, but it sounds like she's getting a rawer deal from whoever the dude is."

Dogg didn't hesitate in his response. "I'm sure he has his reasons. Maybe he's an asshole and she's better off without him. Or maybe he's just afraid of the whole situation. Like about what his family is going to say, or how he'll afford it."

"Yeah. A real pussy."

"You're probably right."

Gavin waited for Dogg to say more, but nothing. "Well, anyway," Gavin finally said, looking back at the dancing, "you put on a cool party."

But Dogg didn't seem in the mood for compliments. He shrugged and crossed his arms over his chest, examining his disco creation. "I don't know why I can't stop doing stuff like this. I want to be known as more than a party."

26

Viola's great-grandchildren prevailed on her and Ms. Colton to buy a voice activated audio system instead of the record player/radio console that they'd used for forty years. Some of the committee members visiting Fern—web-phrase for the day emphasizing her raised hand: "Look! Up in the sky! It's a bird! It's a plane"—saw a delivery truck pull into the long brick driveway. The driver was Ben Vole, which interested the committee since, in our long memory, no one from Mudlick had been inside the Colton home. But there Ben was in coveralls, unloading the various boxes of an entire entertainment center, though that wouldn't be known until later. Dolly after dolly went into the home, Ben like a little blue ant busily going back and forth. And then, when the committee saw there was one box left and they expected him to come out for it, he did not. No sign of Ben.

They waited, pretending to pay attention to Fern, but trying to plumb some sort of movement from beyond the white lace curtains in the front windows. Invariably, and though they'd seen her dozens of times already, Fern naturally distracted them. Her dark green leaf-skin contrasted with the whitish glare from the grass. A sparrow landed on her outstretched hand and she seemed to regard it as calmly as St. Francis. It dove down to her feet where several other sparrows swooped in and joined it, pecking the ground before simultaneously scattering off. "I have no enemies," she was saying.

All of the committee kept an eye on the delivery truck, waiting for Ben to come out. They tried to turn their attentions back to the yard, which was always offering something new. A weeping willow planted five years earlier had finally matured to the point where it was pruned in an even plane at the bottom. It swayed in the warm breeze as neatly as a pleated knee-length skirt. Someone remarked how they missed the peacocks that used to roam the grounds and even the neighborhood. But then it was remembered the committee had rid of them because of their noise. And we agreed it was a good thing we had.

Ten minutes passed and still no Ben. Fifteen and no Ben. What had they done with him? A recent broadcast of *Arsenic and Old Lace* was on Dillard Phipps' mind. Finally he asked out loud the question the other two thinking. "What do you suppose he's doing in there?"

Gloria Valdez, so frequently at Dillard's side those days, rubbed his old shoulder. He was twenty years her senior, white haired with two old-school hearing aids plugged into his ears. "Maybe she's conked him on the head," Gloria laughed.

Lucille Otto, who had, in younger days, herself dated Dillard, and who was mildly protective of him even still, hmmphed at Gloria's attentions. "These rich people think they can get away with anything," she said. "That Ms. Colton's had it easy all her life."

She stepped opposite of Gloria and brushed some imaginary lint from Dillard's shoulder.

Sometime later, Ben revealed he'd been inside and saw Gloria and Lucille hovering about Dillard as if he were a matinee idol. From behind, it almost appeared as if Fern were waving at them. Ben stood in a large hexagon front room the color of Key Lime pie and though he could hear no air conditioner, the house was at least twenty degrees cooler than outside. Ms. Colton had gone to the kitchen to make iced tea that she insisted he have after making a special delivery of her entertainment center. The proof of his efforts lay stacked in the room in boxes of all shapes and sizes, most of the thinly padded, light green furniture having been already moved to one side. On the walls, in addition to a faded, color military photo of Ms. Colton's deceased brother, were large and small paintings of sheep in various locales and seasons, on a snow-covered farm near a not quite covered yellow haystack, walking through a misty valley at dawn, freshly sheared and grazing on the side of bright green hillside. The paintings of horses were almost all of wind-swept Mustangs overlooking red valleys from high atop rocky me-sas. In the corners of these paintings were the names Farquharson, Wieghorst, and Remington, names that meant little to Ben at the time. "They were just pretty pictures," he said later. "Farm animals and nature stuff."

Though he heard the crack of ice trays and looked forward to a cool drink, Ben could easily have left right then and been a happy man. He felt uncomfortable around the wealthy, suddenly self-con-scious about his thick, dirty hands and sweat-matted hair cut in a style he'd had since he was twelve. But, he'd requested the deliv-ery assignment, actually bought lunch for his supervisor to get it. Ever since he was a boy he had walked by the Colton property and wondered what might be inside the big house. At different times he imagined heaps of gold and jewels, cobweb filled corridors, and the ghosts of matronly ladies walking up and down wide staircases. What he got was a cool green room and a very polite old woman who walked, mostly, by rocking side to side.

(Green as a wall color indicates laxness.) - The Committee

Ms. Colton returned to the room. The elastic band of her denim skirt stretched to its limit above a waistline that existed in theory only. "Now here we are. Some of Viola's famous raspberry tea," she said, motioning Ben to sit down on a long, thin settee scrunched against the other furniture. Ms. Colton placed their glasses in front of them on the box containing the stereo. She sat next to Ben and smoothed her short, side-parted, firmly set hair that was the whitish blue of shadows on snow, a frame for a fair and freckled face that had seen a lot of sun over the years. "We so seldom have guests anymore, except Viola's great-grandchildren."

Ben took a drink of his tea. Condensation had already soaked into the cardboard, leaving a mark that reminded him of a one-eared Mickey Mouse. "When I was a kid I always thought you people had all kinds of fancy parties."

"Oh no, dear. When I was young, of course, Daddy tried. But it was so hard in those days to get people to come out this far. Everyone thought we were fighting off Indians and coyotes."

"Some people still think we're hayseeds out here." Ben set down his tea and looked around the calm green room, at what he figured was "art" and what he figured people like the Colton's expected compliments for. "I was looking at your paintings. Nice."

"Most of them were Daddy's. Do you know Olaf Wieghorst?" She pointed to a large painting where three horses, two brown, one black, stood in front of a Thunderhead heavy sky. "He used to paint nearby."

(Clown paintings are said to indicate poor taste, but not if you paint them yourself.) - The Committee

Ben listened as Ms. Colton pointed out different paintings around the room. The last time he'd been this close to art was when his daughter, along with other children, showed their paintings at the library, a show Ivy had helped to arrange with the First Grade. Ben's daughter had painted a smiling white delivery van with a happy Sun shining down on it, a smudge of a face crammed into the driver's side window.

Ms. Colton noted the Farquharson that still bore damage from the fire at Grand Mudlick Lodge, and the Remington her father had specifically commissioned. Ben watched her small wrinkled mouth as she spoke, the maroon lipstick caked at the corners, the way the skin on the inside of her lips kind of adhered and pulled apart with each syllable. Every painting had a story, like the Farquharson, "Left Behind," brought over from England that was the last painting Joseph Colton ever purchased. Her father prized it because of its depiction of a fat gray sheep walking out of a thicket into an open valley. On the horizon sits an enormous orange sun silhouetting a flock of sheep with their shepherd. "Daddy and I used to speculate whether that shepherd was returning for the sheep or leaving without knowing it was missing."

Ben finished his tea, the freed ice clinking at the bottom of the glass. He nodded toward the window and perfectly framed view of Fern in the yard. "I bet most folks in town would say that's the prettiest picture right there."

Ms. Colton laughed. "They *have* taken to her, haven't they? There's three visitors out there right now."

"Everybody thinks she's just about the most perfect little girl in the world."

Ben and Ms. Colton turned as they heard the rumble of Viola's beige, 1972 Cadillac roll into the driveway. She walked into the house with a bag of groceries tucked to one side. Viola was small, with peppery hair that softly rippled up and away from her face. She wore a loose blue skirt suit that accented skin the color and texture of a perfect Bosc pear. "It's a hot one out there today," she said looking around the room at the boxes. "And some mess in here."

Ben stood as Viola passed him going toward the kitchen. She didn't even acknowledge his presence. "You've got some of them committee members out there visiting your daughter," she called as she went out of the room.

"Fern," Ms. Colton said to Ben, almost giggling. "You'll have to excuse Viola. She's not very fond of strangers." She smiled and a web of lines asserted themselves in her mature face. "Mudlick wasn't very nice to Viola when she first moved out here. You'd think people had never seen a brown-skinned person."

The reaction to Viola's arrival in Mudlick wasn't our proudest moment. For a while, from Ike to L.B.J. the town became a minor den of Ku Klux Klan activity. A young man by the name of Lee Short drifted into Mudlick and quickly let it be known he hated Mexicans, Indians, and Blacks. Like his name, Lee lacked height, but he'd been gifted with terrific strength. He won the bail tossing contest four years in a row, beating men half again his size.

(Racism, like obesity, is an unattractive quality.)
                                                     - The Committee

Despite his loud mouth and ill manners, he managed to get quite
a bit of work at the local ranches and farms. And in that time, somehow Lee's bad mouth gathered enough support for a KKK chapter.
Nobody paid much attention to any of them, nor to the burning
cross we'd sometimes see up on Garrison Hill. There wasn't reason
to then. The Indians pretty much stayed on the reservation and what
Mexicans that came into town quickly left after they found that all
the jobs they sought were taken by local men and high school boys.

Viola's arrival in town was conspicuous. Even the most liberal of
Mudlick citizens took note. There had never been an African-American living in town and rarely even one passing through. That first
February day Ms. Colton, then with long black hair and cherry red
lipstick, drove Viola all around town in her convertible Oldsmobile.
They wore matching white blouses with pastel sweaters over their
shoulders, Viola in blue, Ms. Colton in peach. And when they had
pie together at the café it was clear something had to be done. That
night the committee met and agreed that someone should warn Ms.
Colton that it wasn't a good idea for her to be flitting about with her
maid all over town. "It just ain't safe," is how Martin Forbes quoted
himself after ten minutes of standing at the Colton door trying to
make Ms. Colton understand.

Though Viola never did anything alone in town, grocery shop,
pick up laundry, that was the extent of Ms. Colton's sensitivity to the
situation. The two of them carried on as if nothing was the matter,
even eating out together. The whole time, of course, it was all anyone could do to keep Lee Short—"We got one nigger too many in
Mudlick"—from hurling bricks at the Colton house, which in those
days wasn't surrounded by so much as a wood fence.

On a Saturday night, after a typically long stint at the far end
of Mudlick Inn's bar, drinking bourbon and water, and after letting
everyone know who cared to listen to his various and convoluted ra-
tionales, that Viola was taking work away from him, Lee Short, hair
slicked back with petroleum jelly, fresh jeans and going-out cowboy
boots, weaved from the bar to do something about the injustice of

having a black woman in his town.

Somehow, Lee got hold of a can of gasoline and in near pitch black he poured a cross on the Colton lawn. In his unsteady condition, some of the gasoline spilled onto his pants leg and shirt. When he took out his lighter to ignite the soaked grass, flame not only shot across the lawn, it went up his body as well. It must have taken him a few seconds to register he was on fire because when Ms. Colton and Viola woke to the yelling and looked out their upstairs window, Lee was thoroughly ablaze, his greased hair acting like a candle wick. He ran around the yard in arm-flapping circles, screaming not next to a well-executed cross, but a wobbly, flaming "X."

When Lee came to, the first thing he must have seen was Viola's face as she stood above him holding the wet blanket she'd tossed over him as if netting a wild animal. Ms. Colton followed up with a hose, and between the two of them, Lee Short was extinguished.

Ten minutes after she'd come in with groceries, Viola stepped into the room with a pitcher of iced tea and refilled Ben's glass. She poured one for herself and offered Ms. Colton some, who waved it off. "I can't take all the caffeine," she said. Viola didn't say a word, walking to the window and plucking at a few dead leaves from a spider plant.

"So," Ben began, raising his full glass in a gesture of thanks, "exactly how many years have you worked here?"

Viola shot Ms. Colton a look but said nothing at first. She set down her glass and took off her jacket, revealing a loose white cotton blouse with slightly padded shoulders. "This town," she said shaking her head. "I've never worked for Ms. Colton." She turned her attention and body away from Ben. "You know, Abigail, they're *talking* about that girl, Ivy, too."

We would have preferred to go on thinking of Viola as Ms. Colton's employee, because what were the alternatives?

Eager to change the subject from whatever nerve he'd struck, Ben chimed in. "They're saying she's pregnant."

"Oh dear," Ms. Colton said.

Viola gestured toward Ben as if she'd made her point. "These people are going to turn her life into a mess. I've been in that little girl's position. It's bad enough without having a bunch of people you don't know nosing in."

"I know her," Ben said. "Well, kind of. I think she did that painting thing for my daughter's class at the library. I wouldn't worry if people get a little upset about her pregnancy. It'll die down."

"After they tear her apart. Abigail, we should do something."

"What?"

Viola looked out the window where Fern stood in the yard. "Distract them. Bring out the monster."

"Viola, dear, I could bring him out, but for the last time, he isn't a monster." Ms. Colton shook her head and smiled as if this was a soft dispute they'd had more than once.

27

There are rare summers, when conditions are just right, that we feel lifted to the coast, and we'll get a mist in the morning as if Mudlick itself were built inside a cloud. It was one of these mornings where our future Junior Mr. Mayor saw fit to meet up with the opposition. We frown upon Junior Mr. Mayor candidates fraternizing outside of official events, but, unfortunately, we can't control as much as we'd like. Just after dawn, Ivy, Thatch, and Dogg met in front of the Colton house, and not by accident. If we'd known, we'd have put a stop to it, though later we did put our foot down about keeping our candidates apart.

What we've learned is that the candidates decided they needed their own ground rules, as if the tried and true rules the committee laid out for them weren't good enough. Thatch acted as a moderator, of sorts, with Fern, glistening from the mist, the silent witness from the center of Abigail Colton's yard. Thatch, loyal campaigner, wore his green and white "Ivy for Junior Mr. Mayor" t-shirt beneath a matching green windbreaker, a small camera hanging around his neck. He, like everyone else, was not immune to wanting a few photos of Fern. "I'm thinking," he said, "that you two ought to come to some sort of agreement about how to keep people from getting all stirred up."

Dogg, on his way to practice, spun a racket in his hand. "I'm not the one," he said, responding to Thatch but looking at Ivy, "who seems to want a neon sign pointing at them all the time."

"You were born with a neon sign in your mouth," Ivy said. Her hair lay wet and flat against her head. At her feet sat a small box of campaign flyers destined for car windshields.

Thatch crossed his arms and leaned against the Colton fence. "Geez. The point, you two, is that we can make this a campaign or fight. Which do you want?"

"What's the difference?" Ivy said.

"Dignity, for one thing," Thatch answered, feeling just a little uncomfortable in the position of teacher, and probably because he himself would prove to have very little dignity of his own.

Dogg shook his head, looking at his racket, running a finger along the damp curve of its head. "I don't want to fight you, Ivy. I can't."

"You use that phrase a lot," she said.

The three spoke for a half hour about how the campaigns would proceed. They would be aggressive but not personal. They would each go all out to win, but not at the expense of ruining the other. Though Mudlick may be up in arms, they agreed not to be pulled into the fray. The pair were so immersed, Thatch was able to step away to record the moment in a series of three photographs which ended up in that awful black photo album foisted on us. In the photos, Fern stands behind the wrought iron fence bathed in hazy light, positioned almost as if she were an umpire at a tennis match. In the first photo, Ivy in her typical jeans and t-shirt gestures wide and upward with Dogg wearing a kind of pinched expression; in the next, Dogg responds with his own gesture, tennis racket clenched between his bare knees, hands clasped together as if he were pleading, or holding a sledge hammer; finally, the two of them leaning in toward each other, as if caught in a whisper, Fern almost seeming to lean in herself, as well she should, since it would turn out that the elections held as much at stake for her as for anyone.

"Your situation," Dogg said, "shouldn't be what this campaign's about. And I promise that I won't let myself get dragged into the mud."

Ivy picked up her box of windshield flyers leaving behind a ghost-square of semi-dryness. "It seems like we have an agreement," she said. "But I'd point out, Jimmy, that you're just the same as half the people in this town. It's small comfort to hear you say that my pregnancy might somehow drag you down. But you hold on tight to Charlene. She'll keep you above it. Pretty will save you. It will save us all."

(Signage on telephone poles indicate a lower class town.)
- The Committee

Dogg reached out and took Ivy's hand, and held it firmly between both of his as if sealing a contract. She didn't resist. "There has to be a way to keep this from getting bad between us."

"Jimmy, there are people who are going to try to make sure it gets bad between me and an entire town. And that means you, too."

Had one of the committee been there, we might have told these kids they were missing the point. We would've said that Ivy's public display of her lapse of judgment, her pregnancy, was practically an invitation for tension and division. That her first act as Ms. Junior Mr. Mayor would be to split our town into factions. We would have pointed right over their shoulders to Fern who represented so many of the values the town needed, and wanted to get back to. We would have looked Ivy straight in the eyes and told her to ask herself if she were running for Junior Mr. Mayor against Fern, did she seriously think she'd have even a remote chance of winning?

28

On the same morning Ivy and Thatch met with Dogg, they stood at the corner of Pepper and Main watching car after car run over one of her green and white signs. The lower portion was torn on one side, so that the slogan read "Pride Progress and –reservation." There were pulled-down signs like this all over town. They'd been able to rescue a few, but gave up once they saw how extensive the vandalism was, the ground littered as if overnight it hailed green and white cardboard. Now their recovery operations were focused merely on image. Ivy didn't want people seeing her tattered name in the streets.

"It's only paper," Ivy said, "not the whole campaign. It's all up on the internet. They can't tear that down." She wiped sweat from her forearms as she stared at the sign. "But I'm clearly running against more than just Jimmy." The wet overcast had burned away and the mid-morning sun angled in on her face, making her squint. The air felt especially hot because the town had just completed tearing up and replacing the asphalt on Pepper and Main, their surfaces still unlined and nearly pristinely black.

Thatch ran a finger along the part in his hair as if he were reading Braille. "Ivy, I hardly ever doubt you, but geez, as your friend, I guess I should at least ask if you're really up to this."

"To be honest, I won't know until the vote." There was a break in traffic and Ivy ran into the road to retrieve her sign. She folded it neatly, tucking it under her arm.

"It's starting to feel like the villagers are gathering with torches and pitchforks."

Ivy rolled her eyes.

"All I know is that you've done so much for this town and people seem to have forgotten that."

"The campaign just started. Don't be so pessimistic."

"If they knew you like I do they'd want to keep you around forever."

"You've got to calm down," Ivy said. "Let's go get a soda. Mom's treat."

Witherspoon's Liquor Store was famous for two things. It was located in the old train depot, complete with two Grizzly heads carved from marble and guarding the small arched entryway. The other notable feature of the liquor store was the short, assertive woman with the thick braid of hair running down her back past her tailbone. Ivy's mother had worked for the Witherspoon family for twenty years and after the parental namesakes died, the children allowed Gwen Simmons to run the store. Under her stewardship, Witherspoon's had become increasingly profitable, due, in part, to the fact that people just liked to visit with Gwen.

(Beware of liquor, tattoos, and smiles in one place.)

When Ivy and Thatch walked into the store, her   - The Committee
mother was at the counter talking with Morey Franklin, a gray, elephant-skinned ditch digger who looked twenty years older than the fifty he actually was. Besides his wrinkled exterior, Morey is famous for having run a backhoe into the water main which drowned a beagle chained to a tree in the adjacent yard.

"There's my baby," Gwen said, hearing her daughter clunking ice from the soda fountain dispenser. "She's a little politician these days."

Morey winked. "You can say that again." The implication was clear. He'd heard the rumors too.

Gwen's mood turned instantly. "You old bastard. That's my

daughter you're talking about." She pointed toward the door and Morey scooped the beer and cigarettes he'd purchased off the counter and left. Gwen watched him all the way, not letting her finger with its definite direction fall until he was gone. "I'm sorry he was so stupid, Baby," Gwen called to her daughter.

Ivy, followed by Thatch, walked to the register with their drinks. "I deal with it all the time."

"Hello, Ms. Simmons," Thatch offered from the ground where he'd bent to tie his shoe.

Gwen looked over the counter at him. She was always baffled at how her daughter had become such good friends with, as she had put it to Ivy, "a pale, knobby kneed, geek." She ran a finger across the new pooka shell necklace given to her by a secret admirer. "You got a boyfriend yet, Thatch?"

"Mom!" Ivy reprimanded

Thatch, rolling his eyes, took little offense. This was how Gwen was with nearly everyone. And in this case, it was a routine the three of them had worked out, Gwen's accusation, Ivy's outrage, and Thatch's calm, non-committal reply. "Ms. Simmons, even if I wanted one, you already have all the good men in town."

Gwen looked again to her daughter, putting her hand to her cheek. "You feeling okay this morning?"

"A little queasy, but we had a lot of work to do."

"I heard that Disco thing went over big. And I saw your signs on the way to work. Bastards. Picked up a few."

Thatch took a first drink of his soda and let out a pleased sigh. "Style vs. Substance, Ms. Simmons."

Gwen pulled her long rope of hair over her shoulder and inspected its end, reclipping the horse-shaped barrette that held the braid together. "Let's Have Fun. Is that his slogan?"

Ivy frowned. "It got around that fast?"

"Baby, I hate to be the one to point this out, but come here." She led Ivy and Thatch into the back room that once served as part of the ticket office during Mudlick's train days. From a barred window, they saw the freeway and a tall white billboard with Dogg's slogan in black lettering and a bright yellow Happy Face next to it.

"Geez, he must be using his dad's money," Thatch said.

"No," Ivy said. "He's using his college money."

"How can we compete with that?"

Gwen poked her daughter in the ribs. "How about if you changed your slogan to 'Let's Have a Baby!'"

Ivy offered a reluctant smile as a shadow crossed the doorway.

"Customer," Gwen said, leaving her daughter and Thatch to the view of Dogg's new sign. The Happy Face stared back at them, the familiar smile and button eyes all a taunt.

Near the center of the storeroom, a cardboard display for Wright's Lager—"Got the Wright Stuff?"—lay against a support column. In it, a thin, tan woman in a white bikini wraps her arms around an aluminum mirror that the customer sees his reflection in. Ivy stood in front of the display and inspected the wavy version of herself. She wore a pink t-shirt that showed every line in her bra and the distinct fold where her jeans waist bit into her flesh. She looked at Thatch who had one eyebrow raised at his friend. "What if," she said, "it was a campaign about style *and* substance?"

(Hairstyle is a window to the soul.) - The Committee

"We can't compete with Dogg on style." Thatch stood next to Ivy, examining the way his legs stuck out of his shorts like sticks. "I look like Pinocchio. No wonder I'm bad at P.E."

"I'm never going to be a model," Ivy said. "But maybe I could get a haircut, you know. A few new clothes."

"Pretty will save you? Pretty will save us all?" Thatch offered, recalling Ivy's own words from earlier that morning. "None of that is going to change the fact you're pregnant."

Ivy raised her hand, cutting Thatch off. She pointed toward the doorway leading back into the main part of the liquor store. Her mother was beginning to talk more and more loudly.

"It's not that big a deal, Harv," Gwen said. "She's my daughter and I'm going to support whatever decision she makes."

"I was just saying," the man weakly countered.

"You were just saying something about which you know squat." Gwen was going to have a lot of conversations like that, because at that moment in time there were only two things in Mudlick anyone wanted to talk about, Ivy and Fern.

Thatch leaned closer to Ivy, "What decision?"

"Are you dense? I have to decide whether or not I'm having this baby."

Thatch gave a long look in the mirror at his parted hair while the cardboard woman leered at him. "Oh. I assumed you would."

"I'm not sure," Ivy paused and stepped away from the mirror, turning for a last look. She walked back to the window with Thatch where they had a clear view of Dogg's billboard. The white background glared in the sun. "I'm not sure," Ivy continued, "that I want to take care of something before I know how to take care of myself."

Thatch put his arm around his friend. She'd not confided in him as to who the father was and he had no good guesses. There were the dates with college boys of course, but she'd always claimed it was their minds she valued. And there was the hint that she'd have to move away from Mudlick to be with the father. "It stinks that this guy isn't helping you."

"I told him not to," Ivy said without hesitation. "I don't want to feel like someone's noose."

"Then I suppose you're doing the thinking for three now," Thatch said.

Ivy took a deep breath and let it out slowly. "Sometimes I feel like I'm doing the thinking for an entire town."

29

Though Ivy was grappling with a life changing event, the committee took note right away that just two days after the Disco, and the news of her pregnancy, she was sporting an entirely new hair style, short on the sides and back, a loose perm on the top, highlighted with blonde and strawberry. It didn't turn her into a beauty, but it was an improvement. Mary Falco, longtime employee at Kay's Ladies Shoppe—"Fashion for the Average Gal"—called one of the committee members and reported that Ivy purchased three sundresses—lily pad green, sunset pink, and duckling yellow—and brought in a pair of new off-white sandals to make sure they matched.

Ivy stood in front of the same grocery store where she'd had her hot dog giveaway, reintroducing herself, shaking as many hands as she could. Her white shoulders looked strong and thick under the narrow straps of her dress. And while she greeted people with one hand, she passed out leaflets with the other. On one side was her green and white slogan, on the other, something new, a list of campaign promises of sorts, a contract, as its first line indicated.

Contract With Mudlick

1. Ivy Simmons will organize the largest Spring Cleanup beautification campaign the town has ever seen.
2. Ivy Simmons will organize fundraising events to construct and supply a technology center for Mudlick Elementary.
3. Ivy Simmons will promote the Historical Society's efforts to

identify and preserve the town's heritage, architectural, botanical, and otherwise.

4. Ivy Simmons will fight those who encourage national chains and franchises locating in Mudlick at the expense of independent businesses.

5. Ivy Simmons will speak up for any Mudlick citizen whose personal liberty and freedom are being challenged.

The committee could endorse most of the list, of course, though we didn't appreciate the last two items. The final one, we felt, was a slap at us for making an issue out of her pregnancy, which, the committee, as guardians of the town's welfare, felt was within our rights. It's not as if she was deciding what to do with Easter chicks that had gotten too big. Sure, we made a few mistakes that summer, but it wasn't really we who started the fuss. There were a number of occasions where citizens complained about Ivy's condition and basically wanted us to openly strategize against her, which of course we refused; openly, that is.

Then again, it seemed as if Ivy was going out of her way to taunt *us*, as if we were her campaign opponents instead of Dogg. The fourth of her contract items also rubbed us the wrong way. In order to remake Mudlick, of course the committee was going to have to attract businesses with national recognition. Places people stopping off of the highway would feel instantly comfortable in, where they know exactly what the food will look and taste like or the kind of clothes hanging on the rack and products on the shelves. People want that.

The same morning Ivy was handing out her contract, Thatch was across town doing something very unrelated to the campaign—making up P.E. credits in summer school. He had wanted to be with Ivy to see how people would react to new her look. They had mildly argued over whether she was violating her principles by making cosmetic changes to her appearance. But when she stood in front of the mirror for the first time, complete with new hair and new dress, even they were surprised at the difference.

But Thatch wouldn't get to see the initial surprise on people's faces because he'd failed a semester of Physical Education. An Honor student generally recognized as the smartest kid at Mudlick High School, Thatch refused to dress for swim for the inaugural semester of the school's new swimming pool. His position was uncharacteristically firm and unmoving. "I'm not interested in walking around half naked with a bunch of people I don't know," he told Ms. Derk, one of the P.E. instructors and an alternate Shot Putter for the Olympics.

The day of Ivy's new look, Thatch wanted to help her but instead waited near the Tennis courts for Ms. Derk, who consented to let him make up the missed credits with regularly scheduled, three hour P.E. sessions over the summer. To her surprise, he was a good tennis player, very good. By then no one remembered it, Thatch beat Dogg in three straight tournaments when they were nine and ten. But around then Thatch had to make a decision whether he was going to put more time into tennis or computers—"You were born with a racket in your hand," his disappointed father told him, "and it got eaten up by a mouse."

The jade oval that was the football field where the Mudlick Crayfish had ten consecutive losing seasons lay behind a chain link fence just a few yards away from Thatch. At one end, two tall sprinkler heads spat water over the field in perfect circles, rattling back like machine guns at the end of each cycle. In a couple weeks, dozens of boys would be on the field for summer practice, grunting and bruising, trying to get Coach Hauser to notice them.

Closer to Thatch, an abnormally large flock of blackbirds sat perched along the chain link fence dividing the track from the High Jump area. In the sun, they looked like shiny funeral ribbons, all except one bird which caught Thatch's attention immediately. Nearly in the center of their row, a yellow parakeet sat perfectly still as if movement might give away the fact it was not a blackbird. Thatch moved slowly along the fence to get a closer look. The birds were

fifteen feet away, chattering softly and apparently confident this boy
approaching them wouldn't fly over the fence and attack. The parakeet, a fluorescent banana, turned on his segment of fence to face
Thatch. They regarded each other quietly for a moment when suddenly the flock bolted into the air in a flurry of beating wings, the
parakeet a yellow star in their center as they flew off in quirky undu-
lations, landing on the other side of the field.

(Exterminate excess bird population by mixing rice with seed.)

Thatch sunk down, racket falling to one side. The   - The Committee
asphalt was already hot and he felt the intensity on his bare legs. He
put his hands in his face and began to cry. The parakeet had presented itself quite unexpectedly, and the feathered metaphor which
life had just waved in his face was not lost on him. Instead, he'd felt
more and more surrounded and more and more different, increasingly, it seemed, out of control. Though he couldn't tell anyone at
the time, he didn't want to take swim because he was afraid that the
sight of a class full of boys in trunks would give him an erection. Not
that anything even close ever happened, but the fear was enough. It
was all he could do to get out of the locker room each day.

And the committee doesn't want to romanticize all this because
certainly Thatch had a problem that might have been fixed with some
counseling. Nevertheless, this is what he was going through and exactly how he told it to us later. Even the part about how his sense of
isolation was increasing because for months he'd been "going with"
someone who was moving away. He joined Ivy's campaign mostly
out of loyalty, but also out of self-interest. He needed something to
keep his mind off the fact that the only person who even remotely
understood what he was going through would be gone soon. It was
love, he was sure, a desperate ache he could not turn off. They'd met
through an app, and then at a run-down arcade, Thatch laughing at
the young man's horribly inaccurate shooting. All it had taken was
thirty seconds to show him how to aim at the video screen and they
connected. After that, never talking at school, they met late at night,
snuck into the park or took a drive into the hills, always parking in a

different place. Though their situation didn't allow them to be seen in public, nor for Thatch to mention even to Ivy what was happening, their intimacy didn't feel cloistered at all. It was a big bright open place in Thatch's heart and now, as he sat crying, knees up around his face, he felt an unmistakable dimming and constriction. He recognized that narrow place, had been there, and wasn't sure if he could go back.

30

"Did you and Ivy ever?" Dogg couldn't say the words. It was the first time he'd actually gotten that far asking Mumford about what happened with Ivy.

"Shit," Mumford said, drawing out the word in an almost Southern way. Dogg was driving him to the airport. It was going to be a short trip to the university for an orientation, and then back. With an hour to kill, they bought sunflower seeds and sodas and parked near the harbor. "Why the hell do you want to go and mention that, Bro?"

"Don't get defensive. I was just curious." It was a natural question to ask. In the past year Mumford had spent a fair amount of time with Ivy getting tutored in English to keep his grades up for a baseball scholarship.

"I've been with lots of girls. And they always come back for more."

Dogg nodded. In front of them, the smooth harbor was spiked with sailboats. There seemed hardly any wind at all, yet the craft were moving briskly across the water.

"But did you?"

"The only thing I got off Ivy was a B+ in English. And I was thankful for that." Mumford cracked a seed and removed the shell halves with his fingers as he read the suspicion in Dogg's face. "Really, man. And it isn't my kid either, if that's what you're thinking."

"Have you seen her?"

"Ivy?"

"I heard she changed her look." Dogg casually popped a handful of seeds in his mouth, pouching them in one cheek while cracking them open and spitting them out with only his tongue and teeth.

Mumford laughed. "Saw her at the store, Bro. She cut her hair and got new clothes. She looks good," he paused, as if he didn't want to sound committed to that statement, "for Ivy."

The two looked at each other, Dogg shaking his head. "Don't talk like that, man. It's disrespectful."

"What is it with you and that chick? It's like half of you wants to beat her in this campaign and the other half wants to protect her."

"I told you before. I just wanted to prove I could do something on my own. But it got all serious and I don't want Ivy getting hurt. I know I can win, but sometimes it feels like it's not worth it if Ivy gets leveled."

Mumford took a long drag of soda through the straw. His father was a county sheriff and had told his son dozens of times that most of the problems he encountered cropped up because people were stupid and they didn't keep to themselves. Mumford nodded, acknowledging the presence of his father's words. "Ivy Simmons' problem is that she let her personal business get out."

"No," Dogg said. "Ivy's problem is that she's a good person." He stood and walked to the harbor's edge where the dark green water sloshed against the concrete edge. A dead seagull rocked just below the surface, its wings half opened. Dogg took a deep breath before he spoke. "I want to be a good person, too."

(Bury dead fish and small animals deep in flowerbeds for increased bloom yield.) - The Committee

"Damn, Bro. You're already a good guy. You have a hot girlfriend. You play the hell out of tennis. What more do you want?"

"Every good thing I do feels like a calculation. It's like, I think, what's this going to do for me? Sometimes I feel like I'm turning into my dad. He makes all these donations because he knows in the end it won't cost him anything and he still gets all the good will. With Ivy, it's natural and it's sacrifice. That's why she gets hurt all the time, because she has a big heart." Dogg paused and squinted as if considering his next words. "In fact, sometimes I think I'd like to be with someone like Ivy rather than Charlene."

Mumford was stunned. "Bro, you don't really mean that or you would have made that choice. You can have anyone you want. A lot of us would love to be in your shoes." He stood and joined his friend near the water, putting his hand on Dogg's shoulder. "And for the record, you're a good person because you act on your conscience. That's just you. People are born who they are."

Dogg smiled, looking unconvinced. "I guess. But in a way that makes me feel worse."

"Why?"

"Because I was born as a rich kid. Because Charlene looks good next to me and its easy and I just let it happen. Because I can't think of another reason I'm going out with her. Because I run from anything that even closely resembles the kind of problems Ivy's having." Dogg paused and looked at Mumford as if he were considering a confidence. "There's a huge difference between what I want and what I have."

31

(A rose by any other name is better.) - The Committee

Enough people were interested in the possibility of changing Mudlick's name to Valhalla West that the committee felt compelled to hold a public meeting to discuss the matter. The firehouse conference room was filled with concerned citizens, among them the Belmont sisters who organize all the potlucks at the First Baptist church, Chester Godfrey, descendant of Maxwell Godfrey, the man who built Mudlick's original filling station, and Belle Manning, who ran a hat blocking shop downtown for twenty-five years. These people and about fifty others gathered to discuss the town name situation.

Lucille Otto, always good at such proceedings, sat in front of the gathered at a small desk, a glass of water stationed to one side of her note pad. Her eyeglasses hung around her neck and she kept her hands clasped and resting on the table. When it appeared that everyone who was going to arrive had arrived, she rapped a bony knuckle on the table and cleared her throat. She repeated this three times until the room filled with shushing.

Lucille set her glasses on the end of her nose and looked at her notes. "We're here," she began, "to discuss the possibility of elevating Mudlick's image through a name change.

Before she could finish, Maxwell stood up. "I'm sorry to interrupt," he said. "I don't know about the rest of you, but I'm more interested in what the committee intends on doing about this Ivy girl possibly being our next Junior Mr. Mayor."

There was a surprising amount of support for Maxwell's outburst, as if Ivy's situation was what was truly on everyone's minds. Lucille, rarely one to get flustered, raised a silencing hand. She thought perhaps if the group got this topic out of the way quickly they could move on to the scheduled business. "First," she said firmly, "let's dispel the rumors. Ivy Simmons has confirmed to the committee that she is indeed pregnant." At this announcement, a general chatter rose and fell like a gust striking a pile of leaves. Lucille continued. "As you know we have never had a pregnant Junior Mr. Mayor but in reviewing the rules and procedures, the committee has found nothing to keep Ms. Simmons from running."

"Two for the price of one!" Maxwell yelled out. Once again the room fluttered with sound, giggling and outright laughter.

(Yellowed teeth may be bleached.)   - The Committee

Kelvin Thomas rose, resting one hand, as usual, on his large stomach. With the other, he scratched at his thin white beard. "The young woman should be made to resign," he said.

Lucille slid her glasses off her nose. "Resign from what exactly? A campaign? This is part of the problem."

A slim, pinkish hand went up in the back, Mary Coster's, a weary forty-five year old Catholic with twelve children. "I believe in the miracle of life. I believe this girl should have her baby. But she's young still and I don't like her being a role model for my children. It's all just so inappropriate." Though everyone agreed and nodded as she spoke, no one missed the irony that Mary's oldest son was in jail for auto theft, her middle daughter had been caught drinking from a silver flask in the girls' restroom at the high school, and Skateboard Charlie, the most recent of her kids to become a teenager, was a recognized menace to pedestrians on the streets and sidewalks of Mudlick.

"Point of order." Vida Clark, in a blue suit, was leaning with her shoulder against a butcher paper mural of Mudlick's agricultural history recently installed by the Fourth Grade. "Might I remind everyone," Mrs. Clark said, "we're here to discuss changing the town. I've seen too many of these meetings degenerate."

There was a general disapproval of Mrs. Clark's position, and it was more than clear that she was outnumbered. "If we proceed down this path," she continued, "I'd like to go on record as saying that Ivy Simmons made Cole Junior's last months so much happier than his father and I could have alone. And I bet at one time or another Ivy's touched everyone in this town in some way, whether you know it or not."

"That's not the point," Mary Coster replied wearily. "No good deed conceals a sinful one."

Vida remained planted at the wall, slowly shaking her head.

"This won't be the most popular statement made this morning," Catherine Oaks began, as she put her thick brown hair in a ponytail, "but I have to say, for my part, it's not the sin, but the spectacle of an unwed mother that I don't want representing Mudlick. I mean, giving the key to the town to a dignitary with one hand while she holds her baby with the other? In all honesty, my concerns would be answered if she decided *not* to have this child."

At that the room erupted into a series of angry variants of "I never." Though, as the committee would learn later, half the people in that room had come to the same conclusion as Catherine Oaks, none were brave enough to back her up. She was used to going out on a limb by herself and had twice attempted to unionize the department store where she worked for seven years.

Lucille drank from her water glass slowly, as if tolerating the outburst. When she set the glass down she surveyed the angry room and rapped her knuckle on the table once again, this time standing. "We do not have the power," she began to no effect. She restarted, louder, both hands planted on the sides of the table. The group settled. "We do not have the power to send Ivy Simmons off to some clinic. The best we can do is make firm recommendations to save her from public humiliation."

"Excuse me," a voice came from the back of the room. It was Abigail Colton standing in the doorway. She looked as if she'd come straight from the garden, her hands black with soil and little smudges on her cheeks and nose. "Sorry I'm late, but I just heard the circus was in town and I had to come see. I thought you all were meeting about the town name."

Lucille sat down, waving Ms. Colton inside. "We are about to get to that. But one of our citizens expressed some concern about the Junior Mr. Mayor election so we're having a very frank discussion on the matter of Ivy Simmons. Naturally, there are passions that surface. People are trying to decide what's best for the girl."

"I doubt that," Ms. Colton said, wiping her hands on the back of her denim overalls. She walked into the room, into the center of the other attendees. "Has anyone here thought that what might be best for *the girl* is to let her make decisions about her life without an entire town butting in? Has anyone considered that she has a mother she might be talking to?"

"With all due respect, Abigail," Dillard Phipps said, running his thumbs along the inside of his suspenders, "That young woman made her business our business when she decided to flaunt her immorality." For this there was a mumbling of agreement.

(Feel free to speak up when you know we're right.)
                                                    - The Committee
"And," Catherine Oaks added, "I'm not so sure you'd have the same opinion if Fern was the one that was pregnant."

"A topiary, pregnant?" Ms. Colton rolled her eyes. "I'm outnumbered here. I figured I would be. But just for the record, I want to say this. Ivy Simmons is making a decision for herself, for whoever the father is, and for the fetus. It's not going to help her one bit to hear what an entire town has to say." Ms. Colton walked back to the door where she'd come in. She turned and faced the group. "Leave her alone." There was a hint of threat in her voice, though she had no power in Mudlick. The sound of door closing behind her was clipped and certain.

"Well," Lucille said, "there's one in every crowd. Back to the matters at hand. Any final comments or suggestions before we talk about Valhalla West?"

"What if you just tell her," Betsy Cochran said, "it's okay to run, but people aren't going to vote for her because of her condition. Tell her Jimmy Doggins is going to win in a landslide. Maybe she won't want to go through with it." Betsy had some experience in sidestepping humiliation. She successfully served the entirety of her community service sentence outside Mudlick.

"It's the best thing for that child she's carrying," Catherine Oaks added.

Lucille fussed with her collar, and folded her hands in front of her as a half-hour worth of comments poured forth. Most of them were simple statements of embarrassment that an unmarried mother might represent Mudlick. From the more compassionate sector, there were calls for the formation of an advisory committee to assist Ivy in her decision. But the majority nixed that idea because they wanted no part in anything that might result in aborting a child. "They can think things," someone said of the baby in the womb. Despite the minor disagreements, it wasn't hard for the committee to detect a consensus that Ivy would be a great detriment to the town and to our children. The only dissent had come from Abigail Colton and she had harmlessly walked out the door.

When it appeared that everyone had their say, Lucille stood and walked from behind her desk, hands clasped in back of her. Her long, pleated blue skirt accordioned as she paced slowly to the back of the room where the campaign posters stuck brightly on the wall. She stood beneath them, partly obscuring Ivy's green and white slogan. "It's not the Junior Mr. Mayor election that's at stake here. That will survive. This is about the honor and dignity of Mudlick. About its vitality. And Mudlick is not merely a place. It's people. You people. I believe I speak for the committee when I say it's clear you need to vote your conscience and ask other people to do the same. The committee can listen, but it must be publicly neutral." Lucille raised her arms above her head and smiled without showing any teeth. "We have the Founders Day parade coming up and the election not far off. You need to do everything to make the right candidate win. Mobilize."

"Lucille Otto for Junior Mr. Mayor," someone cried out, which received a wave of laughter.

Lucille offered a rare, toothy smile and spoke again. "We came here to decide what to do about changing our town name. And what I hear is a surprising amount of pride and unity that will serve us all well. As for Ivy, I'm sure that debate will continue and many of you will find ways to get her ear. Even I have my own opinions about precisely what she should do, but I won't let that distract me from the campaign. I hope it doesn't distract you either."

The committee intended a spirited debate about changing our town's name but an hour later there was little decided about Valhalla West. The only comment of substance came when Marsha Bakerton, just back from a visit to Missouri, suggested the alternate name of Lake of the Ozark's West which is clearly not as evocative as the Valhalla West.

Though the meeting didn't center around what we'd hope, we didn't look a gift horse in the mouth, because the unintended consequences worked in our favor. When they left that meeting everyone knew they had a serious job to do. There were now three campaigns. Dogg's, Ivy's, and the underground one against her, the one that would donate cash to her opponent's campaign, cheer at his events, and whisper his name in every available ear. Ivy didn't have a chance.

32

It wasn't a quiet summer.

"Watch this," Jasper Carson said, tapping his phone. The committee had gathered to debrief on the meeting. Jasper ran in just as we were beginning. "Trust me," he continued, "this is un—fucking believable." He checked a flexed a bicep in the wall mirror. "A little trouble for Ivy and our Junior Mr. Mayor."

And suddenly it dawned us. We were about to see the very thing that would embarrass us to no end. Maybe we didn't put two and two together as quickly as we should, but there it was, we were about to see video evidence of Ivy and Dogg in the all-together. The whole Junior Mr. Mayor election was about to come crashing down around us.

"We should've known," Gloria Valdez said, exasperated. "Walking out on the Brownies was a sign."

Lucille, ramrod straight as if bracing herself for a head on collision, cleared her throat. "Even if someone came and told us, would any one of us have believed *that* could be with Jimmy Doggins?"

Everyone on the committee agreed that it would have been a joke. We waited. Jasper's video began mostly in blackness, though one could tell the video was shot through a thick cover of leaves. There was a small source of concentrated light that blinked as foliage waved in front of it. We heard a whispered voice. "I'm acquiring the target now," it said. "I'll be close to the perps soon but I have to be slow. Stealth. Stealth. Stealth."

"That's me talking," Jasper said, pausing the video. "I was out in the bamboo stands with my camera two nights ago. This shit is good. And there's a full moon, so the light gets a little better." He hit play, jabbing the remote toward the monitor as if it were a sword.

(Appropriate behavior renders surveillance unnecessary.)
- The Committee

The darkness continued for minutes, Jasper slowly moving through the bamboo, then stopping, the light becoming more distinct. There were definitely two people coming into view. Jasper paused the tape again and the committee sighed. "Dammit all, Jasper," Dillard Phipps said, "Just let us see the proof. We've all got other things to do today. Namely, picking two new candidates."

Jasper didn't respond. He tucked in his already too-tight shirt and walked around the room shutting the shades of the historical society meeting. "It's easier to see with the room darkened," he finally said, hitting play again.

"This is Jasper Carson," the video said as it made one last slow move through the dark bamboo. "I can't talk anymore or I'll spook the perps." The camera continued moving until it arrived nearly parallel to the light source, a pocket flashlight we guessed. That and the moonlight allowed a fairly distinct view of two pair of jean-clad legs. All of us guessed what was coming.

"No," Gloria Valdez said, standing. "I don't want to watch this garbage." She pretty much spoke for all of us at that moment. Jasper was useful to have around when we needed an imposing figure so we put up with some of his stupid stunts, though none of us cared to stoop this low.

The screen stood on pause as Jasper's face tightened. "Whether you watch it or not, what's on this video might change the Junior Mr. Mayor election."

Lucille grabbed Gloria's hand. "It's going to be Ivy," she said, somewhat resigned. "Maybe we should watch. Just for verification."

Jasper complied, smiling and rubbing one hand over his abdominal muscles as he turned up the volume and continued.

"Yes," a young male voice said tenderly. It sounded like Dogg, but we couldn't be sure. "I love you. You fucking know that. This is all bad timing. But I can't ruin my future, can I?" Poor Ivy, all of us thought. She was getting the same line a million other single mothers had fallen for. "I love you but ...." We didn't want her to win, but none of us wanted her to be abandoned.

"This just sucks," the other voice said, a *male* voice, higher pitched than the first. We gasped. Dogg with another man!?

(Think of Spencer Tracy, Katherine Hepburn, and Princess Diana.) - The Committee

"I told you this was good shit," Jasper said. "Just wait til you see who it is." He paused the video and we signaled our irritation with groans. "You people give me a lot of crap for carrying this camera around but it's going to pay off now and I'd like a little more respect." He gritted his teeth with a wink and flexed in an Incredible Hulk pose. "Now let's see what we have here."

The camera moved through the bamboo again as the couple spoke in intimate muffles. Jasper was clearly moving up a small rise above the two young men because the perspective began to change. Suddenly, the view was nearly unobstructed. "I was fifteen feet away," Jasper said. "They never heard a thing. Coulda closed into ten I bet."

The moon and the flashlight offered just enough illumination. One of the boys wore a baseball cap, his face deeply shadowed by the bill, one of his big, thick legs moving to curl over the skinnier boy. This smaller one turned on his back, facing the moonlight and we all saw it was Thatch.

"That's the little guy that's helping Ivy," Jasper said. But we couldn't see Thatch long because the larger boy leaned over him, enveloped him and they began to kiss.

"Okay, Jasper," Gloria said, standing and shutting off the video, leaving the monitor in blue again. "We get the point." She adjusted her pink scarf in a gesture toward exiting.

"I don't think you do." Jasper tapped fast forward on the remote. "You'll probably want to know who the other guy is. But this part is a little graphic."

Dillard Phipps slapped his palms on the table. "What difference does it make who the hell it is?"

Jasper stopped the video. "Now these boys are fully engaged," he said, making quotation signs for the last word. He hit play, and indeed, the two young men were naked, mercifully shadowed in the right places, the larger boy sitting atop Thatch, his broad back and shoulders facing the camera, moving up and down. Jasper laughed. "You'd think the little guy would be on the bottom. But he's a pretty big boy. If you know what I mean."

If ever the committee were to admit to a low moment, that had to be it, all of us allowing ourselves to get involved with Jasper's prurient hobby. But involved we were, however temporarily. No one felt good about it, but we were so concerned with the image and success of the Junior Mr. Mayor race, not to mention the welfare of Mudlick's itself, that it took a bit for us to come to our senses. Well-intended people will have clouded judgment now and then. We're just fortunate it's such a rarity for the committee.

When we had enough and were about to shut Jasper and the video down, the larger boy, hat on backward turned, his face instantly recognizable in the white moonlight—that broad cow nose, the heavy brow line. Mumford. Our Junior Mr. Mayor. "Bingo," Jasper said, turning off the video and pointing at the screen as if he were a hunting dog in front of a covey of quail. "And they do it a couple times more."

A general murmur rose among us about how we were going to handle the situation. Should we talk to these boys? Get them counseling? Go to their parents? Lucille Otto tapped on the table. She looked at us over the top of her glasses perched precariously close to the tip of her bird-like nose. "Needless to say, this could prove to be quite embarrassing to all parties involved. Mumford is going away to school soon, so he'll not likely be a liability for the committee or the Junior Mr. Mayor program." Lucille slid her glasses closer to her once famously periwinkle blue eyes. "Therefore, I motion, that we simply pretend that this video does not exist."

Jasper looked like he was about to burst. "What? This is the nail in the coffin if we spread it around that not only is Ivy pregnant, she's hanging around with a little homo whose having sex in the bushes."

"It's unseemly, Jasper," Gloria said.

"It's necessary."

Dillard Phipps ran an index finger over his eyebrows. "This all sounds like a house of cards bound to collapse on its own and I prefer that the committee isn't anywhere near when it does. And besides, is there anyone in this room who isn't just all out relieved it didn't turn out to be Ivy and Dogg?"

33

The day after we saw Mumford and Thatch having sex on that video Karen Everhardt shot her boyfriend in the face, killed him. It was all practically anyone could talk about during Dogg's fishing derby at the reservoir. Karen had taken shooting lessons at the range. It was her boyfriend, Lance Calder, in fact, who bought her the gun. From what she told police, she was playing quick-draw, thinking the firearm wasn't loaded, and the last thing she saw was Lance's head snap back at the sound of the gun.

The committee got to see some of the police photos through Carr Johnson, who works for the Sheriff's department. Of course, we didn't see the more gruesome photos, but we did see Lance spread out backward, laying there in his blue boxer shorts, the fat tip of his penis staring back at us. These pictures they take aren't as clear as the ones you see on television. They're kind of dull and greenish. But still, we saw Lance with that odd hole through the bridge of his nose, and a surprising lack of blood. Karen couldn't have gotten off a better shot if she intended it.

(Body hair may become public knowledge. Groom.)
- The Committee

Now, it's sad any time something like that happens, but if the truth be told, most of us thought that Karen might actually be better off without the Calder boy. He changed her in so many ways we didn't approve of. When she was a little girl, she rode the lead pony in the Founder's Day parade. A sweet little thing, she sat straight in the saddle with matching red boots and red vest. But by her early twenties Lance and she got a bit wild. They began attending the Unitarian church in El Cajon and paid for matching star tattoos on the small of their backs, each centered with the other's name. Though no one would wish what happened on poor Karen, shooting her boyfriend in the face like that, it just seemed like the best thing for her in the long run. After a period of grief which no one would deny her, hopefully she would take this new opportunity to fit in again.

As news of Karen's accident gurgled through the early morning crowd at the fishing derby, Dogg made his announcements. Behind him, the sun had yet to come up and a pink light hovered above the hills. "The proceeds from today's derby," Dogg began, "will not go to my campaign, but to the New Hope Center for single mothers." For obvious reasons, there was a tittering in the crowd, but if Dogg intended a slight at Ivy, he didn't show it. He stood confidently in front of a giant yellow smiley face, his baseball cap on backward, shorts revealing small knees and strong calves, and a campaign t-shirt that said, simply, "vote for me." Dogg continued. "I'd also like to thank my father for donating a brand-new Ford S Series pickup as today's grand prize." He pointed to his left where a set of lights blinked on, revealing the shiny black vehicle. The crowd oohed and the derby was on.

We've had a few derbies up at the reservoir over the years but none with quite the local interest as this. It's famous for its large-mouth bass, so lots of professionals always show up, but this time everyone in town brought a pole, not that they were likely to win with a few worms in a Styrofoam container, fishing from shore at that. Local professionals (and only local), seeing as how the cash wasn't all that big, launched their bass boats into the water like it was a business. And if you never seen one, there's nothing so unlikely to be on the water than one of those boats they fish from —it's like they set an engine on a raft with two nailed-down bar stools to sit on.

But maybe the biggest surprise was entrant number 234, Ivy Simmons. She too was wearing a baseball cap, green, with her ponytail pulled through the back. She wore hiking boots and cut off jeans. In one hand she held a large red tackle box, in the other, her pole. Those that were standing nearby saw Dogg talk to her. "Didn't expect to see you here," he said. Sunlight winked over the hillside and into his face.

Ivy leaned her pole on her chest, patted Dogg's shoulder and looked straight into his eyes, "It's a good cause." She patted her belly. "And a better investment." With that, she walked down to the edge of the water and along the shore until she disappeared into the tangled brush. And there was more than one person who watched her and were certain that Ivy Simmons was coming back later with some fish, a lot of fish.

Dogg had a boat of sorts, too. He was friends with the reservoir Ranger, Roxanne Patterson and she agreed to ride around the lake with him just to monitor things. Roxanne had only been out of high school two years. She was a top swimmer, broad shouldered with red hair kept in a buzz-cut. She was recruited like crazy, but when her mother got cancer, she set all that aside and started community college and managed A's even as Mrs. Patterson lost her hair and thinned to nothing. She'd worked at the reservoir every season since she was sixteen. But this was the first year she was in charge. Around mid-morning Roxanne brought the boat to a halt near the far-end of the reservoir. She and Dogg watched one of the anglers near the shore reeling in a fish.

Roxanne put a pair of binoculars up to her eyes as the man lifted his catch out of the water. "Poor thing. It's missing part of its tail," she said. She handed the binoculars to Dogg. "Three pounds, maybe four, I guess."

Dogg took a look and nodded. Water sloshed against the outside of the aluminum boat. "This is going to turn out great, Roxanne. I hope it'll help get people's minds off Karen Everhardt."

(Fishing with worms is not murder.) - The Committee

"Well, hon, you've created some excitement. Did you see Fern this morning? They say Ms. Colton put a fishing pole in her hand." Unlike Roxanne, we hadn't seen Fern, but we'd all been reading the daily web quotes attributed to Fern, and the web-quote of that day was, "Gone Fishing!" On that note, the committee was surprised that Colton was supporting Dogg.

"It's nice to see everyone get into it."

Roxanne shook her head. "I even saw Ivy showed up. She's got a lot of nerve, don't you think? She works with what she's got, and nerve she's got." Roxanne ran a flat hand across her blowing hair. "But there's no way she can win this thing. Why bother?"

"She doesn't believe in fate, I guess." Dogg got quiet and leaned forward staring off past Roxanne's shoulder. "And wouldn't that be an awful thing, anyway? If we gave into fate?"

"But we can't just throw common sense out the window."

"You're right. And common sense tells me the truth is that Ivy is a better candidate for Junior Mr. Mayor than I am. And the only reason she doesn't have a chance at winning is because the town won't give her one." Dogg looked out at the water for a moment. "Don't you think it's kind of weird how people think they know me and Ivy even though most of them haven't met either of us?"

Roxanne shook her head in humored frustration and prepared to start the boat motor. "Hon, you are what you put out there. And from what it sounds like, Ivy's been putting it out."

"The only difference between Ivy's sex life and mine is that mine's invisible because I can't get pregnant."

Roxanne looked Dogg directly in the eyes. "I'm a woman," she said. "I understand the politics *and* the biology. But the fact Ivy doesn't have a chance is because she got knocked up and she didn't keep it to herself. It's a cinch for you and you should be glad for that."

"It's not a cinch. For Ivy's sake, she needs to be beaten by a better candidate, not a more fortunate one. And that means I have to be that candidate. But I just keep giving everyone Fun Dogg."

Roxanne shook her head. She was one of those voters Dogg both needed and apparently dreaded. "Well, Fun Dogg, this derby is for a pretty good cause and either way, I'm voting for you. Let's go weigh some fish."

"Maybe. But I can't help thinking that I'm going to have to do something pretty big to force people to make a real choice. And then the whole town is going to be sorry."

"Hon, you don't have to feel bad because you're about to trounce Ivy in some stupid election." With that, Roxanne started the motor, pointing the boat in the direction of the way-off dock.

The weigh-in took place in the early afternoon on a stage decked out with red, white, and blue bunting. The lake itself was a big indigo crescent in the background. One by one Dogg called up the entrants who had fish to weigh. Anyone under 15 who caught a fish got a one-pound chocolate bar. Obviously this was a bit different than a regular tournament. In Dogg's vision, all fish would be weighed, regardless of kind. The bass and catfish fisherman had the advantage of larger one-time catches whereas those after pan fish could make up in numbers what they couldn't match in individual size.

There were some surprises, such as Derek Kennebeck's four-pound channel cat and Melissa Gardener's one pound seven-ounce crappie, her first fish ever. Then there were those local professionals, the real competition, vying for the truck. When these heavy hitters came up, Dogg put on as much show as he could. "Now the great Garson Everett," he said of a guy who's been on about every TV fishing show. Dogg continued, "The Legend of Lures, the Bishop of Bait moves into the lead with four bass at fifteen pounds five ounces total." Most of the crowd, even those who weren't fishing and those well out of the prizes stayed to watch the totals. Garson's held up until an unknown fisherman stepped up with his catch. He wore a red baseball cap pushed low over his eyes shadowing a pepper-gray beard. "Martin Keenan," Dogg introduced looking at the registration card. "Fisherman of mystery hailing from Escondido, California weighs in four bass at sixteen pounds, eight and three quarter ounces.

Of all the surprises that afternoon, the second biggest was Ivy Simmons pushing through the crowd with a dusty stringer full of Bluegill. She'd turned her green hat around backward, her cheeks, nose, and forehead pink from the sun. "Don't give out the prizes yet, Jimmy Doggins," she said marching up to the podium, fish in one hand, red tackle box and pole in the other. "I've hiked a half hour to get these fish weighed."

Small as they were individually, it was an impressive stringer of fish. Jimmy smiled. "Ivy Simmons, Politician with a Pole, The Heroine with a Hook!" The crowd pressed forward slightly as Ivy's fish were weighed. "Fifteen pounds, one and one half ounces," Jimmy announced. "Third place so far." And that's where she stayed, even after the final two fishermen weighed their catches.

Except, there was one more surprise in store for us. "Hold up a sec," a voice called out. It was Roxanne. She took the stage and asked Martin Keenan to open the cooler where he kept his fish. She looked inside and pulled out the stringer of bass. "Just as I thought." She turned to the crowd. "When Jimmy and I were out on the lake, we saw this fish right here get caught." She pointed to a bass with a damaged tail. "It was a three or four pound fish then and suddenly its part of a sixteen pound catch?" She pinched the fish's belly and shot Martin Keenan a look. "Feels a bit lumpy in there. You using this fish as a place to keep your sinkers?"

It took the crowd a second to grasp what was going on, that this man had weighted his fish. He snatched his catch back from Roxanne, though she was bigger than him and any one of us would have bet on her in a fight. "I withdraw my catch," he said, dropping the fish back into his cooler and scowling all the way through the crowd in the direction of the parking lot.

(Seal fish parts in plastic sandwich bag, enclosed in foil, placed in a paper bag. Discard.) - The Committee

Dogg didn't let any time pass before speaking up. "Which means, that Garson Everett takes First Place!"

"And," Ivy chimed in from just below as she ascended the platform, "Ivy Simmons takes Second Place." There was a surprising amount of applause, a dangerous amount as far as the committee was concerned.

Dogg shook Garson's hand and gave him an oversized novelty key for the truck as a few people took pictures. The applause continued as Dogg walked over to Ivy and removed her cap, replacing it bill forward. He winked at her. "I hope you like Second Place."

34

The picture in the paper of the fishing derby featured not the winner, but Dogg replacing Ivy's hat on her head. "Candidates Fish for Charity," read the headline above an article which briefly mentioned the suspected lead-stuffed fish, and mostly talked about how Ivy nearly stole the show. Though it was Dogg's event, somehow Ivy managed to get a majority of the publicity out of it. The committee was not happy and though we convened at the Historical Society on Monday officially to talk about final preparations for the Founder's Day Parade, Dogg's campaign was definitely not going as we planned. We were smart enough to know a lot of that applause at the fishing derby was for Ivy and that our sure thing in Dogg wasn't so sure if he was going to continue to be as gracious.

It's not that we had anything personal against Ivy even with her troubles. Some have even suggested, outrageously we might add, that there was something malicious about how we dealt with Ivy's run for Junior Mr. Mayor. But the committee is not malicious. Never has been. We just think ahead. We think about our town and the consequences of the decisions made on its behalf. In this case we had a rooting interest in Dogg's success because Ivy's pregnancy presented too many potential embarrassments. And it's not as if Dogg was some urchin we pulled off the street and dressed up in a tuxedo. Even at his young age he was a Mudlick celebrity, a hero.

Despite our frustrations over Dogg's kindness toward Ivy, the worst news at our meeting, however, was not related to Dogg or Ivy.

Gloria Valdez read from a brief letter sent to the committee. It had arrived in a light blue envelope monogrammed on the flap with an elegant AC and read:

> I regret to inform the organizers of the Founders Day Parade that my little girl topiary will not be able to appear as Grand Marshal.
>
> Yours,
> Abigail Colton

Dillard Phipps rapped a bandaged knuckle on the table. He'd cut the back of his hand cleaning the grass out of his lawn mower. He pointed to a yellowed photograph on the wall of Joseph Colton. "That man produced a willful child. I can't believe I cared for her once. What kind of woman wouldn't let a little girl experience the chance of a lifetime—to be Grand Marshall in a parade!?"

We all agreed it was a shame that Abigail Colton would keep Fern away from a town that had virtually adopted her. And it wasn't lost on any of us that maybe it was Abigail's way of getting back at us because she'd never enjoyed such popularity in town. But what could she expect coming from a family like hers, from a father who single-handedly sealed Mudlick's fate as a small town when he failed to rebuild the lodge after it burned? And here the committee was all these years later trying to repair the damage he'd done and there's Abigail Colton standing right in our way.

When we were all in a fit, Lucille Otto put her hand on Dillard's and held out her other to make sure we were silent. "Why don't we make Jimmy Doggins the Grand Marshall?" At that, she tugged gently at the starched white collar of her blouse, bringing her clasped hands down to the table. The idea behind her suggestion wasn't unprecedented. We'd honored sports heroes before and here was a way we could legitimately promote Dogg the athlete without mentioning Dogg the candidate.

(Warning. Catch is a game for back yards only.) - The Committee

It didn't take long for the committee to decide on precisely the course of action Lucille suggested. We'd ask Dogg to be our Grand Marshall, but not as a candidate for Junior Mr. Mayor. Instead, we'd offer him the opportunity for his accomplishments in tennis. It was an honor long overdue, in any case, we decided. In a year Dogg would be off to college and Mudlick wouldn't have the chance to say thank you to its favorite son.

35

The morning of the parade, before the sun rose, it was unusually hot and the air smelled like gasoline. Even though everyone knew that by noon, when the parade was over, we'd all be sunburned and sweaty, most of us were excited by the day ahead. All the entrants, the Boy and Girl scouts, Mudlick High's Marching Crayfish band already squawking and thumping in preparation, Mudlick Children's Dance Troupe, the fire truck and police car, dozens of horse groups, all of them gathered at the staging area to find their places. The Grand Marshal's car, a red Thunderbird convertible secured for Dogg was placed between the Marine Honor Guard and the V.F.W. marching band. Ivy's position was assigned between Claudius the Unicycle Clown and the Shriner's mini-cars. Though we didn't request it, Ivy's location was chosen partly because the primary organizer, Vera Dalton, was a Dogg supporter and partly because the vehicle Ivy chose to ride in was a dented, blue, 1974 Ford pickup looped with green and white crepe paper that looked as if wouldn't last the length of the of the parade route.

Vera was sensitive to aesthetics, as her twenty years of parade organizing attested to. She viewed parade preparation like stringing beads and, in her mind, she saw each parade like a new piece of jewelry. No single entrant mattered more than the whole. And in all the time she'd run the parade, it'd gone off without a hitch. This record was especially pleasing to Vera the year she lost her right leg. She'd come home in the late afternoon with several flats of African Daisies in the trunk of her car and was in a hurry to plant them before evening arrived. When she got out to open her garage door, the car **(Garden fanaticism and driving don't mix.)** - The Committee rolled forward and crushed the one leg she wasn't able to get out of the way. Still, she managed to work the parade that year from a wheelchair as her amputated leg healed, warming the stub with a crocheted tea cozy.

The only glitch in the dim light of morning was when the Grand Marshal banners were placed on the side of Dogg's car. Ivy stormed over from her pickup. She wore her hair pinned tight, with green and white boutonniere carnations making crowning the bun. "That isn't right," she yelled before she even got to the car where Dogg was trying out his ride. Like every year, the identity of the Grand Marshall was kept as a surprise, so it was news to everyone that he was star of the parade.

As usual, Vera was on the spot. She stood directly in front of the Thunderbird and Dogg, extending a large clipboard fluttering with paper. Even with a prosthetic leg and a stature that, on a good day, might reach five feet, Vera was imposing. "The Grand Marshal this year is Jimmy Doggins, local tennis hero, Ms. Simmons. What isn't right about that?"

Ivy halted a few feet from Vera. "He's also candidate Doggins and this shows a lot of favoritism."

Dogg stood up in the car. The blond stubble on his head glinted in the sunrise light. "I couldn't turn it down, Ivy. Would you?"

"Definitely. I have ethics."

"And it's unethical for me to ride in the same parade as you are?"

"You don't get it, Jimmy. I have to jump a million hurdles just to get people to listen to me. All you have to do is show up. You're this little jewel the committee owns and this car is the pretty case they're displaying you in."

Dogg looked startled and cowed. "Why does everything come down to what I have and what you don't, Ivy?"

"For the same reason you don't know the answer to that question."

Running a hand over his bristled head Dogg stared at the Thunderbird beneath him. "Tell you what," he said, "I'll take the banner and the truck and you take the car. Then I've done as much as I can. We're even."

"I'll take the car, but we're not close to being even."

Vera waved her arms. "No changes. Absolutely no changes."

Dogg jumped from the Thunderbird and patted Vera on the back, smiling. "Mrs. Dalton, I guess if you want a Grand Marshal this year, you're going to have to let me ride in the bed of that truck." He faced Ivy and took her hand, raising it to his lips and giving it a kiss that looked half serious and half courtly, and entirely unacceptable as far as the committee is concerned. "Will that satisfy you?"

Ivy nodded, almost shyly before catching herself. "For now," she said. She turned and headed back to the truck to get her things.

"I hope you know what you're doing, young man," Vera said.

"Mrs. Dalton," Dogg said quietly, "I never know what I'm doing with Ivy."

By 9 a.m. most of the committee found our places in the grandstands and none of us knew yet what went on a few hours earlier between Ivy and Dogg, though, as we took our seats, we did hear a disconcerting inkling about a kiss to the hand. Vera had decided she couldn't stand the distraction of an upset committee, but, to be honest, we *were* distracted by lesser things, unfortunately. Our duties for that day were to check on how the businesses were doing, shake hands, and listen to complaints about narrow roads or neighbors with olive trees that drop their unwanted fruit on the wrong side of the fence.

(Force trees to obey property lines.) - The Committee

The streets were lined with spectators, as they are every year, but with more people than usual, perhaps because we'd convinced a carnival to set up on the rodeo grounds, or maybe because Mudlick was just getting bigger, or, we hoped, because these people were be-ginning to realize that all the changes the committee was making and trying to make—like finally getting a specialty grocery store to come in—were good for us. As much as we all loved Safeway and Trent's Market, they just didn't carry everything we thought people needed. There are three kinds of mustard alone that Trent's doesn't have room for. So that good feeling is exactly what Ivy was trying to tear down, which annoyed us to no end, especially since she apparently wasn't able to keep her own business in order.

And if the truth be known, we're always the ones to start good things. In 1928 it was the committee that held the first Founders Day Parade with just one entrant, a hot air balloonist named Ar-ley King. Early in the morning he inflated his big gray balloon in the field where Holt's Ice Cream and Taco Bell are now. He put it up about fifty feet and thirteen people holding ropes walked him through town and all the way to Parker's Field where he gave rides for ten cents. Dillard Phipps was one of the first to go up. He was just a boy then and he always said it was one of the most depressing feelings he ever got, riding up in that balloon and for the first time seeing all at once how small and dusty Mudlick was, how our big lake didn't seem like much with all that empty land that stretched out around it. Right there is reason enough to want to change things.

So all those years later and the parade wasn't just one hot air balloon anymore. It was the real deal and a few thousand people showed up every year to see it. That morning as we waited under the already intense sun, children blew on their long plastic horns and vendors walked up and down the street selling miniature flags, cotton candy and giant, striped banana balloons. Everyone was fan-ning themselves with flyers or paper plates, whatever we could find. From the grandstand, we heard the parade begin up the street with Mudlick High School's marching band. Jasper Carson pointed out that they were playing a song by U2. Every year we ask them to start off the parade with something patriotic and every year they agree and then ignore us. The committee has requested that the high school talk to the Music teacher, Mr. Stroh, but to no avail. So, each year he walks by us next to the band, puffing on his asthma inhaler and smiling.

Despite not honoring our wishes with the music, the committee and Mudlick were awfully proud of the band. They won plenty of statewide awards and, that year when they **(Marching Band trophy memories last a lifetime.)** - The Committee paused in front of the grandstand playing "I Still Haven't Found What I'm Looking For," all we really noticed were the beautiful new red and white uniforms that all of Mudlick had paid for with thousands of dollars worth of magazine subscriptions and chocolate bar purchases. They never quite got over the hump to afford matching boots, but almost all of them managed perfectly white tennis shoes. All of them, actually, except Greg Johnson on the Snare drum. His family was so poor that even as a teenager making money at our McDonald's, his paycheck went to support the family. So, his marching tennis shoes were really a pair of black Chuck Taylor's slathered with white shoe polish.

There were two truly big shocks in the parade that morning, and one of them wasn't the fact that on the Mudlick Square Dancers' flatbed truck Glenda Feldman in her bluish calico dress and bright yellow petticoats wore stockings and see-through panties, each of her more aggressive turns advertising her bad choice. That was nothing to the committee compared to the fact that where we expected the Grand Marshal's red Thunderbird was a big blue truck blaring "Macho Man" from speakers mounted on its roof. In the back was fuzzily bald Jimmy Doggins sitting on bails of hay, waving to the crowd with a tennis racket. The sides of the truck did indeed have the Grand Marshal banners, but the whole effect looked slapped together. "Heavens," was all Lucille Otto managed in response to the sight. Still, as Dogg went by, people clapped to his theme music and chanted "Let's Have Fun," so the committee hoped that maybe he hadn't ruined his appearance. And for most people, in his tennis outfit that he'd cleverly embossed with a yellow smiley face, he still looked every bit the Jimmy Doggins people liked.

When Dogg stopped in front of us, Jacob Alter yelled to him, asking what happened with the Thunderbird. "Macho Man" all but drowned out their voices so Dogg shrugged and pointed with his racket before cupping his hands to his mouth and yelling back, "It's on its way."

Indeed, a half hour later, when we'd reviewed the KMVP Jamboree Van, the Princess Pony Club comprised of thirteen young girls in matching pink cowboy hats riding Shetland ponies, Kent the kitchen knife juggler, Orlando Rodriguez the trick roper on horseback, and all the other entrants that show up each year, indeed we did see the red Thunderbird. But what we heard before that was the crowd cheering louder than it had all morning. As the parade turned the corner, we saw why. There was the Thunderbird, its sides fluttering with green and white crepe paper and its back seat occupied by Ivy *and* Fern.

The loud cheers met Ivy's car all along the route as she rode toward us, Ivy with her new sundress look and carnationed hair waving to the crowd, and Fern, perfectly poised and balanced with her naturally outstretched arm looking just as eager, her surface glittering in the breeze. Just that morning, Fern's quote bubble on the newspaper website contained the phrase "I love a parade!" Next to it was a brief article under the headline "Colton Corrals Kid." It began, "Local celebrity Fern Colton is being kept from participating in the Founders Day Parade today by Abigail Colton. Ms. Colton of 2339 Colton Lane refused comment. Local citizen and committee member Lucille Otto expressed her disappointment. 'That little girl has become an important part of the community in a short amount of time. It's a shame Ms. Colton can't see past her own prejudices against the town to allow Fern to appear.'" After that, the article went on to recount the historical relationship of the Colton name to Mudlick, which we were all familiar with, and quite frankly, were tired of hearing.

The Thunderbird rolled to a brief stop in front of the grand-stand where its reception was polite but not nearly as raucous as on the street. Ivy put her arm around Fern and waved to us. "She's kind of pretty," Gloria Valdez found herself saying out loud.

In response, Ruby Jones leaned into her husband Flack, "Somebody better put their foot down or that could be our new Junior Mr. Mayor."

"I don't get it." Dillard Phipps was beside himself. "Why do you suppose Abigail Colton would let Fern run around with the likes of Ivy?"

(Be alert to secret agenda's. Check home fire alarms each Founders Day Parade.) - The Committee

"People," Lucille Otto warned from beneath her wide brimmed straw hat, "Let's not have this argument in public."

With that the committee waved politely, reluctantly, and Ivy nodded at us as if she knew she'd had a victory. Even the committee had to admit that sitting next to Fern, Ivy, with her look, did indeed take on some of her magic. And if we weren't the thinking types, we might have been taken in just like all those people on the parade route. But it's easy to look at two sweet girls in the back of a nice car. What the committee saw however, was what pregnant Ivy would look like in just months. How would the town embrace her then? In some ways, it could be argued we were protecting her from certain humiliation.

The Thunderbird started forward and the cheers for Fern began again, rolling like a wave away from us. Dogg had been one-upped and in a campaign like the one for Junior Mr. Mayor, you're only as strong as your last event.

We watched Ivy and shimmering Fern as they rode away. "Do you suppose that counts as her endorsement?" Gloria Valdez wondered out loud.

Dillard mopped his sweating forehead with a handkerchief and pushed the bush of white hair back off his face. "That little girl is being used as a tool. There should be a law against it." He continued running his handkerchief across the back of his neck. "I think it's time I go see Abigail alone. I guess forty years is enough time passed to have another chat. Only this time I'm not bringing flowers."

36

Of all the families in Mudlick that had any possibility of rivaling the Coltons, it was the Phipps, owners of a hardware store, lumberyard, and the grain and feed. Before there were any actual street blocks in Mudlick, the Phipps family built a large home about three blocks from the Coltons on what was then the edge of their property. Mr. Phipps, Dillard's grandfather, built his house on a hillock and in direct contrast to the Colton home, contracted a Spanish style ranch house complete with a tile roof and large oak doors for the front entrance brought up from a decaying Catholic church in Mexico.

The presence of these two families in their fine homes made that part of Mudlick what we still call the wealthier side. Now days though, while those two houses remain, there are lots of homes between them and it takes some imagination to understand how strange it was to people who happened into Mudlick in the old days to see this wood slat town with its two great houses, especially after the lodge burned.

When construction began on the Phipps house, Joseph Colton wound his way through his citrus grove, lemons and oranges mainly, the trees still only head high. Even in the May heat he wore a wool suit complete with tie and celluloid collar. He waved one arm at the builders and called out in his strange, gravelly voice. "McCaffery Phipps!"

Old Mr. Phipps, Dillard's grandfather, turned to the voice he surely recognized. "That you Joseph?" He wasn't nearly as formal as his neighbor, comfortable in Levis, suspenders, and the red cotton shirts he was famous for. McCaffery made his fortune in the West, first in Nevada silver mining, selling his share just before the vein gave out. Then he came to Mudlick as a businessman.

Joseph Colton waited as McCaffery made his way to the property line. He was slow, McCaffery was, hobbled slightly by an injury suffered as a very young Confederate soldier in the last days of the war. To steady himself, he used a brass-handled walking stick. Joseph Colton passed the time by looking at his thick shadow on the ground, then briefly at the sun. He checked the pocket watch connected to his vest by a gold fob. When McCaffery arrived in front of him, Colton spoke again. "I suppose we ought to talk about some sort of fence."

McCaffery scratched at the long white moustache that hid his upper lip and narrowed like icicles at the sides of his mouth. "You s'pose we need one, Joseph?"

"It might be for the better."

McCaffery laughed. "Afraid I might pinch a lemon or two?"

Colton, who often seemed confused by humor, tried to assuage McCaffery. "I assure you Mr. Phipps, I have no fear of you coming on to my property."

McCaffery nodded, a bit disappointed at the seriousness of his neighbor. He looked to the left and right of them. In the distant sky, three turkey vultures circled at the edge of the hills. Following an imaginary line back to the space between him and his neighbor, McCaffery made a furrow with his walking stick. "That about where you figure it?"

"We'll have the man out to check it of course. But that's about right." Colton put his hands to his waist uncomfortably, unsure of what to say next. "I didn't want to do it without talking to you first."

"You got manners all right," McCaffery said, smiling. "But I got one question still on my mind. What's this fence for exactly?"

Colton dropped his hands to his sides a bit exasperated, taking on the expression the town was familiar with, the one with the agitated eyes and tightened lips, the one he used whenever anyone in Mudlick seemed not to comprehend him. But McCaffery did not let him off the hook. He waited silently for an answer. "To keep things out, Mr. Phipps," Colton finally said.

McCaffery nodded as if Colton were making sense, pausing to look over his shoulder at the home site and then at the far off gleaming white house just over Joseph Colton's shoulder. "That's all well and good, Joseph," he said softly, "but I don't feel the need to keep you out. You're more than welcome to come sit a spell at my place anytime."

"I think it's for the best, Mr. Phipps." The truth was, and McCaffery knew it; Joseph Colton had no plans on making a house call on anyone in Mudlick.

McCaffery scratched at his moustache again. "You can have your fence Joseph, if that's what you want. And I'll help pay for it. But I'll tell you what else. We're going to put a gate right here where we're standing in case you change your mind. And," he winked, "in case I need a lemon or two."

Years later McCaffery said that he never could figure out why Joseph Colton approached him about building the fence. He had the right and more than enough money to do it himself. "I should've told him no," he told Dillard near the end of his life. "I think the man was looking for someone to tell him no."

37

Dillard Phipps never had children of his own and was the
last of his namesake. He inherited the house directly from his grandfather because Theodore Phipps, Dillard's father, died of tuberculo-
sis, leaving the family businesses in the hands of his wife and young
son, which they ran together until Dillard's mother passed away at
the age of 93.

Dillard went to see Abigail Colton the day after the parade to
see if he could talk some sense into her about allowing Fern's obvious endorsement of Ivy's candidacy. It was a Sunday morning. The
last of the June Bugs struggled dumbly in the trees, buzzing and
bumping without purpose. A cool breeze signaled our heat wave
was aborted, cool enough for Dillard to walk up Colton Lane in his
pressed white shirt, red bow tie, gray slacks and suspenders. Other
than the white hair and Santa Claus belly, he didn't look altogether
different than the last time he made this walk all those years back.
As promised, though, this time no flowers in his hand, no sweet peas
and daisies picked from his long dead mother's garden.

When Dillard arrived at her drive, Ms. Colton was already outside, weeding around the red and white hollyhocks in full bloom
that stood each summer as colorful, if stiff, sentries at the driveway
gate. Ms. Colton straightened and smiled upon noticing Dillard's
presence. She wore her usual denim outfit, dirty and grass-stained at
the knees and accented with a bright orange pair of gloves that she

removed immediately. "Dilly," she said smiling. "The last time we spoke you said I hadn't heard the last from you. I thought I had."

"Aw Abigail," Dillard offered in that boyish way of his. "We were just kids."

"Comparatively," Ms. Colton said, referring to the fact that they hadn't been all that young when Dillard finally got around to proposing and she finally got around to saying no and the town got to spend the following days saying I told you so and that a Colton wouldn't ever marry a Phipps and worse. But that morning, both of them white-headed and much rounder, Dillard and Ms. Colton recognized that whatever water once passed beneath their bridge was too far downstream to fuss over and so she walked him up the drive to the porch where they sat on the very swing in which they'd shared their one and only kiss.

(Do not brush or otherwise disrupt gums before kissing.)
- The Committee

"The view certainly has changed," Dillard said, looking beyond the wide, long yard to the other side of the road where open fields used to stretch all the way across the narrow valley. Now these fields each had at least one or two houses on them. As the pair surveyed their town, bells from the Catholic Church announced mass.

"Dilly," Ms. Colton said, "I suspect I know why you've come today and I think we should get it out in the air."

Dillard straightened his bow tie with one hand as the pair swung quietly. "First things first. All those years ago, Abigail, I was mad at you. I figured after three years you owed it to me to get married."

Ms. Colton turned slightly and raised a hand as if to begin a point but Dillard cut her off.

"But I ain't mad at you no more. You don't get as old as us without learning a few things. When I really look at it, we were never what you'd call romantic. We had that one awful kiss, and that was pretty much it."

"It was pretty awful," Ms. Colton laughed. The night they'd kissed, they sat on the porch swing, cooling down in the early morning hours after a dance at the V.F.W. hall. It was an evening when everyone was a bit overheated because the punch was spiked with Mexican grain alcohol. When Ms. Colton and Dillard leaned into each other to kiss, the swing came out from underneath them and sent them to the floor.

"But there were lots of fun times. We were friends and I forgot that, and I'm sorry," Dillard said.

Ms. Colton patted Dillard's age-spotted hand. "Yes, we were friends." They sat for an hour reminiscing, talking about all the changes in town since they were young, the torn down schoolhouse, the plant shop that used to be Gabe's Soda Shop, the cattle that sometimes wandered into the center of town. Finally, the two of them settled on the backside view of Fern between the two persimmon trees. She held an American flag. "That was quite a stunt you pulled with Fern yesterday," Dillard said, pointing at Fern.

"It wasn't a stunt. I'm voting for Ivy."

"Be that as it may, do you think it's a good idea associating your little girl with a young lady who's pregnant out of wedlock?" Dillard stood and put his hands in his pocket, leaning against a wood column.

"First off, *that* little girl is a plant, Dillard. And secondly, I'm not so sure you've changed at all. Ivy Simmons seems to be a perfectly fine young woman and why this town and that committee of yours is in her business baffles me."

(Strength of conviction creates reality.) - The Committee

"We have to look out for the town's image. And a single, pregnant girl is not exactly the role model we need these days. And as for Fern, all you need is love to make something whole. And this town loves her."

Ms. Colton stood, grabbing a stray orange bougainvillea branch and twining it back into the bush tied around the other porch column. "The committee has its purposes and I have mine. I guess we'll have to leave it at that."

"So there's no chance of you and Fern keeping out of this election?"

Ms. Colton put her hand on Dillard's shoulder. "If we're really friends again, Dilly, we're going to have to agree to disagree on this one. Besides, there's not much more I can do for Ivy. But I have bigger plans for 'Fern.'" Here she made quotation marks with her fingers. "It came to me last night."

The pair looked at Fern with her outstretched hand and the fluttering red, white and blue flag. A large yellow butterfly landed on the tip of the flagstick before flying toward the geranium bed. At that moment, Dillard understood what Mudlick saw in Fern, the simple, beautiful childhood we wished we had and that we wanted for our children.

"The town sure loves that little girl," Dillard said.

Ms. Colton clapped her hands together in a fisted prayer. "I'm counting on it."

38

Another unreported sighting revealed itself in the aftermath. However brief the encounter, the committee was not pleased to learn much too late from Nola Sprigs that she'd seen Ivy and Dogg "practically dining together." Nola is the nervous sort, and when she came to us, she couldn't keep from biting her eyeglass frames as she spoke. She told us that she was eating a bowl of Chili at The Country Cupboard when she noticed that Dogg was sitting directly across from her in the dining room. She explained to us, in excruciating detail, that Dogg had not too long ago helped her change a tire. She told us how badly she'd wanted to go to Disco with Dogg just to see the guy she recognized from the television ads and newspapers, but that she couldn't dance and her dog had been sprayed by a skunk.

"And Jimmy Doggins is just minding his own business," she said, "eating the garlic bread, the kind without the cheese, which is the kind I like when I don't get the other kind. So he's eating and then the girl comes up." By girl, we divined, she meant Ivy because she described Ivy's new look, a light blue sundress and short hair. "And Dogg smiles and pats the place next to him all cozy like. But she doesn't sit down and I can't hear what they're saying except she picks up a piece of garlic bread and says something and then holds two fingers up and takes another piece. Which I understand because they're good, especially if you get the kind without cheese."

When you talk with Nola you have to just let her go or she gets distracted. Her father was a model plane enthusiast, and we theorize that while he'd taken precautions to keep his own nose away from the glue, poor Nola, nose height to the table, probably got a whiff or two too many. She gnawed on the edge of her glasses some more and continued.

(Reserve nervous habits for skittish nuns.) - The Committee

"And then she eats the bread and stays standing and they talk a bit and Dogg was doing a lot of nodding and not eating. And then at the end Ivy pulls out an envelope from her pocket like, card size, and hands it to him, which he reads and then gets a curious teary smile. But before he could say anything Ivy just finished the last pinch of the garlic bread and left."

Nola talks about how the entire time she ate her chili, and even through a bowl of vanilla ice cream, Dogg sat leaning on the table, chin propped in his hand, searching eyes focused on nothing. "It was the kind of look," she said, "like a lost boy at the store, and you just want to help him find his mom."

After the election was over, the last thing the committee wanted to hear were things like this where, had we known, we could have intervened. Ivy and Dogg were two people who did not need to be spending time together and the committee could have very easily have made sure they both understood that fact. As it was, whatever she said, Ivy had clearly gotten to Dogg, and maybe this small moment over chili and ice cream is a place we can point to as the place where the Junior Mr. Mayor election turned. It's certainly a moment we can use as a prime example of why the committee is so important. Because certain short-sighted people didn't think to talk to us, the entire election ran off the tracks.

39

The momentum in the campaign for Junior Mr. Mayor was definitely on Ivy's side. The paper displayed a quarter-page parade photograph of her and Fern in the Thunderbird and quoted several citizens as saying that if she had Fern's support, they'd have to give Ivy a second look. Dogg didn't get mentioned until halfway through the article and then, only in reference to the fact he seemed to be letting his hair grow back. On the website's quote bubble, Fern said not so cryptically "I know who I'm voting for!" We were outraged, of course, that the paper didn't also note that Fern wasn't of voting age.

But there was another item in the paper that caught Ivy and Thatch's attention as they sat in the lavender, fish tank light of her living room preparing for the final ten days of the campaign. On the second page, under Community Notes, a blurb appeared, stating, "an anonymous source has asserted he has a video tape of someone associated with Ivy Simmons' campaign having homosexual sex in a public place." Jasper had gone behind the rest of the committee's back.

"This is outrageous," Ivy yelled. "It's low."

Thatch remained quiet, scanning the newspaper again and running his fingers down the part in his hair. This was the moment he dreaded, the declaration the world always seemed to be pushing, or pulling him to make. "If it's true, Ivy," he said, hesitating, "it could be me." He had expected a look of shock but instead he was met with Ivy's nod and smile. "I'm sorry. I should have come out to you a long time ago."

(Immoral behavior is shaped like a boomerang.) - The Committee

"Thatchy," Ivy said, holding Thatch's hand, "you've told me every day since I've known you. But how would someone have a video of you in public?"

Thatch was comforted by Ivy's ease. He thought about Mumford and him, how careful they'd been to go to out-of-the-way places and always at night. "I'm not sure. But if it's the committee, I can't believe they're making an issue out of this. The other guy is Mumford."

Ivy looked suddenly less concerned. She pushed Thatch over on the couch. "Get out. You and Mr. Baseball?" She leaned back and stared at the cottage cheese ceiling with all its dullish flecks of gold. "So now they're running Jimmy Doggins against the Whore and the Homo."

"Geez. It's just a cheap ploy. Is it going to matter?"

"In this town? In Mudlick? It's going to matter all right."

Thatch stood and walked to the wall of fish tanks. He tapped on the one containing the brightly striped Oscar which immediately flashed to the top, prepared for a feeding. Thatch recalled a rare rainy day when he and Ivy plucked struggling earthworms from puddles and brought them home for the Oscar, dropping them into the water, each a temporary wriggling "S" before being gulped. "Maybe I ought to back off from the campaign."

Ivy tossed a pillow at Thatch. "No way. I need you." She pointed to her belly and smiled. "Still trying to figure this thing out."

"It's not only about you." Thatch continued to face the tanks, having moved his attention to the neon tetra dashing between the legs of a bubbling, rubber diver floating above a treasure chest. "I've got to think about Mumford, too. He's coming home tonight from visiting the college and this isn't going to be good for him." Thatch plopped down on the couch next to Ivy and flung his legs over her lap as he lay back. "We are just too messed up."

Ivy bristled and tossed Thatch's legs aside. "Don't even say that, even if you're kidding. This whole town wants me to think that way and I don't need you agreeing with them."

The front door opened along with a blast of bright light and Ivy's mother, stood framed in silhouette like the detached shadow of an angel. "You kids ought to be campaigning in weather like this."

"Something's come up," Ivy said.

Gwen walked into the room and winked at Thatch. "Got caught with your thingy out, didn't ya?"

Thatch blushed. He'd hoped it wouldn't have been so immediately obvious that he was one of the boys in the video. But he was relieved this news was going over as easy as it was, at least in the Simmons home. Which gives you some idea of just what the committee was dealing with. No rules. No boundaries. Just whatever goes!

(Extremism in defense of morality is no vice.) - The Committee

"How do you know it's not me," Ivy chimed in, knowing Thatch was often speechless in the face of personal embarrassment.

"On your dresser there's a little pink stick that you peed on that tells me the odds are against it."

The three laughed as Gwen sat down and propped her sandaled feet on the table, jeans rolled up to her calves. She waited for a comment. "Notice anything?" On her ankle was the dense bluish outline of a seahorse-like creature with the head of a Chinese dragon. Gwen lifted her leg and wriggled her foot. "Like it? Chuck'll fill in the colors next week."

Ivy looked at Thatch, "Okay, you were right. We are messed up." She turned to her mother. "*All* of us." This was Gwen's sixth tattoo, five of which were visible to anyone passing the Pink Ghetto on a day when Gwen washed her blue Barracuda in the parking lot wearing her denim bikini top and cut-offs.

"Mom," Ivy said, "love the tattoo, but Thatch and I have got something bigger to deal with right now with this whole gay thing."

Gwen set her feet on the floor and leaned toward the pair of teenagers asking for her advice, if not explicitly. The room gurgled with sound from the fish tanks, and from one of the bedrooms, a sudden rumble of snoring came from Gwen's mother. "Ivy, honey, and Thatch," Gwen began, "who are you right now?" It was clear neither of the teenagers understood her question so she repeated it. Again, blank faces without an answer, Thatch caressing his parted hair, Ivy staring at one of her campaign flyers on the coffee table. "You're a pregnant chick and fag, right?"

"Mom," Ivy yelled. Thatch sat up.

"Well?" Gwen continued. "Well?"

Thatch closed his eyes. The word fag grated on him, the sound of it, even the definition he'd looked up in the school library a dozen times as if it would miraculously change upon each new reading, British definition of cigarette, fagot, a bundle of sticks, both things to be burned, or the slang definition with its clinical estimation. He looked at Ivy's mother, realizing she wouldn't settle for silence. "I'm smart," Thatch said. "I'm not a leader. But I know better."

Gwen nodded and looked at her daughter.

Ivy's eyes closed to a slit as she thought hard. "I'm progressive with a sense of history."

Gwen shook her head. "You've already got my vote, baby. Tell me who you really are."

Ivy ran her fingers along the thin arm of the couch. "I *am* a leader," Ivy began. "I'm a problem solver."

Gwen leaned forward, clasping her hands in front of her mouth. "Thatch," she said, "maybe I'm a bitch for having this conversation in front of you and for putting this off." She looked at Ivy. "Are you a mother?" Ivy looked stunned, crossing her arms and staring at the ceiling. Gwen continued. "I mean, right now, are you a mother?"

Ivy touched one hand to her abdomen. "Not yet," she said quietly.

Gwen stood. "Then, that leaves you with some options, baby," she said, walking toward her own mother's bedroom. "You and I will sit down and have as long a talk as you want. Just you and me. I'm here for you." She turned, obviously thinking about the fact she still didn't know half the equation. Ivy had insisted on keeping much to herself, but, in the moment, Gwen figured her daughter's privacy was less important. "One thing I'll tell you right now," she called to Ivy over her shoulder, "look straight into your guy's eyes and just say what you need to. If he's worth anything, he'll get it." But about that conversation they had—maybe the most intimate and complex conversation a parent could have with child?—Ivy's mother had the gall to tell the committee it was none of our business, though she didn't say it that nicely, which tells you the caliber of woman she is.

As she left the room Gwen considered how rarely she'd thought about the duties of a mother. Talking with her daughter about pregnancy was an odd place to start. She thought about how, with her mother's Alzheimer's, she'd become a mother a second time, maybe a better one. People from all over town told her how much they admired her for taking care of her mom. She wanted to tell them that this person who slept in her apartment wasn't really her mother, though she once had been. The person she took care of was just a shell of the woman who raised her, as if a wax museum had delivered an eating, defecating, talking facsimile. And yet, there was love.

40

Guardian Angels Daycare shut down, as did Playmates Preschool because our children had suddenly come down with the most massive outbreak of Shigellosis ever recorded in the county. At the stores, there was a run on apple juice and electrolyte waters to keep the children hydrated, everything coming out nearly as liquid as when it went in. Our babies were drying up like prunes and not keeping quiet about it.

That first morning when hundreds of Mudlick parents stayed home to care for their ill children, the threat to Fern's life appeared. Perhaps fleeing the echoes of crying in their homes, dozens of people carrying babies in torso harnesses or pushing them in strollers gathered in front of Abigail Colton's black, wrought iron fence to see the emerging tragedy. The children cried, wailed with the discomfort of their affliction,

(Conceal seriously ill children. They dampen spirits.)
- The Committee

fouling the immediate air with their leaky, dirty diapers while the people of Mudlick themselves gasped at what was happening to Fern. She stood in her usual spot, hand still outstretched, on this day holding a tiny red-haired doll. She was as beautiful and optimistic as ever, not comprehending the approaching and certain doom a dozen or so yards behind her. From her green house, Abigail Colton had unleashed a fifteen-foot-long giant squid topiary, tentacles outstretched and hungry. It sat suspended above its planter outfitted with thick wheelbarrow tires. On its first morning out, it was gleaming with green wetness, as if it had just launched itself out of the ocean. But it was the tentacles that really put fear into everyone. The open jaws of a crocodile or lion can mean a lot of things, but that bunch of tentacles coming after Fern meant just one thing, hunger.

"This is outrageous," Bonnie Colgate said, bouncing her crying baby.

Carlyle Beth held his son Hunter's hand as the boy pointed an arm through the fence at the grotesque scene. "Snake," Hunter said, and then, grasping the back of his pants and looking up at his father, "Uh oh." The Beths weren't the smartest family in Mudlick. Carlyle had once paid for an "authentic" Van Gogh from a man selling his grandmother's estate out of a moving van.

Gloria Valdez was the first of the committee members to arrive. She'd gotten a call from a neighbor and headed over without fully dressing or finishing her breakfast, though she did find time to pick out a yellow scarf. When she saw the crowd from the car it wasn't immediately evident what was beyond them. She wondered why there were so many children present, thinking that maybe there was some sort of preschool field trip going on.

Bonnie Colgate with her sickly tea-colored hair stopped her before she got all the way through the crowd. "That poor little girl is going to die. We've got to do something."

Gloria pushed through to the fence and saw what others saw as she clutched at her scarf. Fern was in trouble. But why would Abigail Colton do this to such a fine young citizen of Mudlick, Gloria wondered. First forcing her to ride with Ivy Simmons in the parade and now purposely putting her under imminent attack from the huge green sea creature. Just that morning Gloria visited the web page dedicated to Fern in which she said, "Would you rather pick flowers or be one?"

The crowd surrounded Gloria, the reek of their children becoming more potent than the crying, and in Gloria's estimation, all of it a choral reaction to the giant squid about to devour Fern. Ellen Malfi stepped forward, frantic. "What are you people going to do about this?"

Gloria tried to remain calm. "I'll call the other members of the committee to see what action we can take."

"By then it might be too late," someone in the back yelled.

"We can't exactly rush the gates and kidnap Fern," Gloria said.

But that was precisely the plan Carlyle Beth hoped to hear. "Why not," he said, his son cramping at his feet. "Why can't we just get someone to march in there and take Fern somewhere where her welfare will be better served?"

"Or where can we get a harpoon?" Connie interrupted.

Gloria examined the crowd and the parents with their sick children. "What if," she said tentatively, "what if someone barged into your home and snatched one of your kids because it looked like you weren't taking good care of them?"

"But the squid," Connie yelled.

"Squid or not, the committee will want to find out from Ms. Colton just exactly how tight a leash she intends to keep on that thing."

Carlyle Beth threw up his hands, Hunter crying now and on his knees. "Bureaucracy. Look at Fern. She's bait. Worse, she's chum. Do we need to know more than that?"

Then a small, old sounding voice spoke up from the outside edge of the crowd. And it found just the right moment to be heard. "Excuse me, Excuse me." It was Pat Hunter, the woman who'd killed Cassandra Jenks in the parking lot. She weaved her way through the crowd, wearing a gray and blue polyester suit with blackberry earrings dangling from her sagging lobes, her nappy wig a bit off center. "I come here nearly every day and talk to Fern," she said. "And she just asked me what we're all doing here. I don't think she has any idea about that squid."

"Well don't tell her, for God's sake," Molly Urhausen said as loudly as she could from the center of the crowd. Her twin daughters Becky and Bethany, both exhausted with Shigellosis, sat in their dual stroller, sedated with bottles. The Urhausens were famously failed entrepreneurs in Mudlick, starting with Amway all the way up to borrowing two hundred thousand dollars to open a hot tub dealership.

"What should I tell her then? I can't just lie."

The crowd was surprisingly mute before Gloria Valdez spoke up, noting the look of hopelessness and fear on Pat Hunter's face. "For now, just tell her we were on a fieldtrip with the kids and leave it at that."

(Like spanking, lying to children in small amounts is a useful parental tool.)   - The Committee

By the time some of the committee met on the evening of the squid's first appearance, hundreds of people stopped by the Colton house. Angela Chang from Channel Eight came out from the city and did a feature on the eleven o'clock news about Fern. We watched it on Jacob Alter's wide screen television in the den he built with his father three weeks before he died of a massive stroke. In one news report, Lucille Otto, standing in front of the black fence wearing a pastel blue sweater over her shoulders and a pearl buttoned blouse speaks for the committee. "We simply want what's best for Fern," she began. "A community must have standards and allowing Abigail Colton to abuse Fern in blatant disregard for those of us who have come to adore her is simply immoral."

"Amen," Ruby Flack yelled, pointing at the television. "That's just the way to tell them."

Lucille, sitting in a stuffed leather rocker, smiled and continued to watch the news. She'd never seen herself on television and was surprised at how large she was on Jacob Alter's oak-flanked big-screen. More than that, she was interested in seeing what the committee thought about the rest of her comments where she gave a long list of Mudlick's accomplishments and its positive features. But that part wasn't included. Instead, a close up of Abigail Colton with her tight maroon lips and cropped white hair came on the screen. "Architeuthis dux stays," she said directly into the camera. When Angela Chang clearly didn't understand, Ms. Colton added, "The squid stays. And I don't really see why everyone is so concerned with how I ornament my yard."

Angela Chang asked Ms. Colton if she planned any harm toward Fern to which Ms. Colton replied. "No harm can come that a little fertilizer won't fix. And some of the people in this town are pretty good about spreading that around."

Jacob shut off his television and stood in front of it, the rest of us, Ruby, Flack, Gloria, Lucille, Jasper, and Dillard waited. "That woman just has no respect for life or anyone in this town," Jacob said. He'd gotten a haircut that afternoon and one of his sideburns was notably shorter than the other. "But I'm not so sure there's much we can do. It's her property and she is the one who raised Fern."

"All I'm saying, honey," Ruby offered, "is that if any one of us tortured a child on our front lawn, no one would put up with it." Her dangling bracelets pinged as she shook a finger to make her point.

Up to this moment Jasper had been quiet. He stood against the wall behind us. "The problem with you people," he said, "is that you don't think far enough ahead and you keep your guns in your holsters." He moved closer, his muscled thighs straining his black spandex shorts. "I give you that video and you don't want to do anything with it.

"You leaked it anyway," Gloria said. "None of us appreciates that."

Jasper snapped. "Listen, Missy. I've taken fire giving out food aid. I watched one of my buddies lose an arm taking a piss in a mine-field. I've seen what happens when you let your guard down. Self preservation is all about offense."

(Medicate and assimilate our veterans.) - The Committee

Gloria was silent. We'd heard this speech before. You can't argue with someone who's been in combat.

"That video is going to do us a lot of good," Jasper continued. "Look, people, we've been on the defense. And now Abigail Colton is thumbing her nose at us. What we need to do is take things into our own hands. Tonight I'm going over the Colton fence and I'm going to rescue that little girl."

The committee, of course, has never endorsed guerilla tactics, but in lots of ways Jasper was his own committee and there wasn't much we could do to keep him from going his own way, though we were all privately hopeful that he'd pull something off.

41

After three surgeries and under constant pain medication, Jasper Carson admitted not everything went as he planned that night. It was perfectly dark except for the dull yellow streetlight at the end of the block. The gate across the driveway was locked, and beyond it, the exterior of the Colton house faintly glowed, each window like a black eye. Jasper counted on his military training and believed his physical condition would be more than enough to get him through the task of rescuing Fern. But he didn't anticipate the true difficulty of scaling the Colton fence and clearing its spear-like top.

Without a ladder, Jasper improvised, upturning the neighbor's two metal trashcans, setting them bottom to bottom next to the fence. He straddled himself on the rim of the top trashcan as he took off his shirt and wrapped it around two of the spikes to at least keep the points from snagging him. Using his big arms to good purpose he pushed off from the trashcan holding the fence and stopping his body in the air, astride the fence, inches above like a gymnast on a Pommel horse, ending with an equally deft dismount on the yard side of the fence.

He half-expected to see or hear a barking dog. Where was Collie? But the only sound came from lethargic crickets and the sandpapery noise of distant traffic. Fern stood in front of him, her outstretched arm almost a plea for rescue, he thought. At the side was the squid which was even more menacing than in the daylight, because the darkness felt like the cover of deep water. The beast reached forward into the night air in Fern's direction and it made Jasper angry that the little girl was being sported with as some kind of sick lure at the end of Abigail Colton's fishing line.

Jasper approached Fern quietly but certainly, running shirtless and bent forward across the lawn. When he got to Fern, he discovered that her feet were anchored into the planter with hooked steel spikes. She was essentially a prisoner. He tried to pull at her restraints but they were sunk too deep. She was immoveable. He realized immediately he'd have to come back, that this trip would serve as reconnaissance. He looked up at Fern from where he knelt. Her face seemed to be taking in the stars. "I'm really sorry about all this little lady," he told her.

Aborting the effort for the night, he approached the gate across the driveway, assuming he could open it from the inside. But it was key-locked. Jasper ran along the fence line, through a rise of English ivy, to the spot where he'd climbed over. Besides the gate, he'd not made a plan on getting himself over the fence. First, he thought he might reach through the bars and maneuver the trashcans over the top. But one had fallen over on the initial push off and wasn't within grasp. He would have to summon all his strength and balance. He took off his shoes and tossed them over the fence so he could use his toes to grasp the bars as well as his hands and in precisely that way he climbed the fence until he reached the top where his shirt remained tied. But this time around he didn't have anything to push off from. He gripped a single bar as high as he could and elevated his legs first parallel then above him, twining his feet between two spikes to get the rest of his body up. At the top, and nearly horizontal, Jasper attempted to roll over the rest of the way, but a spike caught him at the ankle, sending his torso down, the spike first puncturing then ripping through his Achilles heel.

(Trash cans should be put away immediately after collection. Sprinkle with baking soda.)   - The Committee

The Devons remember waking to Jasper's scream, both of them at first thinking they had a shared nightmare. A block away, Garber Smith woke at the sound and grabbed the gun he kept under his late wife's pillow. But when the Devons awakened enough to investigate, Jasper was gone, having had the presence of mind to bear the pain, hop on one foot to his motorcycle, and take off to the emergency room.

The Devons saw their trashcans and retrieved them, thinking teenagers were up to a prank. Mrs. Devon squinted into the dark to see Fern. The squid had not yet attacked. "She's okay," her husband said and the two of them went back to bed.

Ms. Colton must have known something went on that night, though the Devons reported no lights coming on at her house. The next morning thunderheads over the desert to the east began forming in the gray-blue sky, Jasper Carson's shirt hung on a wire hanger from Ms. Colton's red, white, and blue mailbox, and the squid had moved five feet closer to Fern, its tentacles somehow looking more eager than they had just the day before.

42

Fern's fate was, obviously, the major concern of the town. She was our baby-down-a-well. But even so, the committee had other responsibilities, most pressing of which was making sure the election of the new Junior Mr. Mayor went smoothly, especially since this promised to bring out more voters than it ever had. As temporarily naïve as we were, at that time there was still so much we weren't told. Our network failed us, and so, though concerned, we still thought we could pull off a seamless election, including getting Dogg elected. We certainly knew he had the support because the committee took its own poll of two hundred people, not very scientific, admittedly, but still a bell weather. Out of two hundred people, 179 said they planned to vote, and of those two hundred 55 percent were voting for Jimmy Doggins, 35 percent for Ivy Simmons, and ten percent Undecided. Needless to say, the number pleased us. Despite Ivy's surprising resilience and Dogg's unwillingness to press his advantages, he still held a nearly insurmountable lead. It looked as if we wouldn't have to worry about a pregnant Ivy embarrassing Mudlick after all.

(Allegiance to principal always wins out. FDR over Hitler. Coke lovers over New Coke.) - The Committee

As is customary, the committee called its formal voting procedure meeting where Mumford, Dogg, and Ivy would be in attendance to receive instructions on how this very special, and tradition-bound procedure worked. Lucille Otto, Gloria Valdez, and Jacob Alter represented the committee, officiating in the meeting room of the Mudlick historical society, Dogg and Mumford sitting next to each other, both wearing baseball caps backward. Ivy sat opposite them, her hands folded on the table, a little pink blush dusted on her cheeks and a hint of mascara. Apparently she was keeping up her new look.

Mumford leaned back in his chair against the walls with a new display on the history of Native Americans in and around Mudlick. The centerpiece was a collection of multi-colored construction paper Indian headdresses arranged in concentric circles like a mum in rainbow colors. These were the same headdresses made by the Second Graders in summer school and which they wore in the Founder's Day parade. More than one headdress' paper feathers were flopped over with wear, or shiny in places where rips were repaired. Mumford fingered them as he spread out his arms. At first he wasn't coming to the meeting, told Gloria Valdez he was retiring early from his Junior Mr. Mayor Duties. But Jacob Alter had Dogg convince him to come.

Tapping her pencil on the table, Lucille looked around, counting us in her mind. "We're here," she began, "to make sure the balloting goes off without a hitch. As is the tradition, the outgoing Junior Mr. Mayor tabulates the votes in full view of the candidates. An odd way to run an election if you ask me, but that's the way it's done. We've found this prevents charges of favoritism." Ivy snorted and rolled her eyes but Lucille continued, clearing her throat. She pointed at Mumford with her pencil and took on an almost accusatory tone. "You. You are our current Junior Mr. Mayor. If you can manage to sound professional for a second, you will take the stage and announce to the town what the numbers are and who won."

Mumford let his chair fall forward. "Actually, I don't have to do anything if you're going to throw attitude."

Lucille sat up straight. She'd never liked Mumford as Junior Mr. Mayor, none of us did. He'd been adequate but not spectacular, had gotten by on his baseball credentials and semi-hero status. Mumford, Jacob Alter once said, was what the Mad Scientist created before he made Dogg, all the right parts but none of them fitting together correctly. Perhaps it was a result of Jasper's last combat speech, but Lucille looked over her glasses and in an uncharacteristic harsh flash which Jasper later approved with a "hell yeah," she said, "I'm sure Thatch Hutchison would want you to put your best foot forward."

"Or any other body part," Jacob Alter threw in.

"What the hell is that supposed to mean?" Mumford was visibly shaken. Ivy slapped her palm to her forehead and Dogg stared at him as if he didn't know what was going on.

Mumford stood to leave but Lucille raised her hand before he could take a step. "Young man. Sit. Although there is a member of the committee who would love nothing more to hold this over you, we don't plan to make an issue out of it. We just want you to perform your duties as required." Mumford sat down, clearly worried. It doesn't take much to cower a young man with his whole future ahead of him.

"What do you mean you don't want to make an issue out of this?" Ivy shook her head, almost vibrating. "It's already gotten out about Thatch. He's practically scared to death about leaving his house." Just that morning someone spray-painted the word "fag" on Thatch's driveway. Ivy looked at Mumford directly. "You could make a difference."

"Whoa," Dogg said, catching on. He took off his hat and set both hands on his stubbly head as he turned to Mumford. "You? You and Thatch Hutchison?"

Mumford offered a stunned shrug. This was the calamitous moment he had been trying to avoid since he took up with Thatch. Until this moment in the Mudlick Historical Society meeting room, no one knew and he had no idea how far this had spread. He thought about Thatch and how people kind of already suspected something about him. But this could ruin Mumford's college baseball hopes in Kentucky if it got to his coaches. He reached back and snagged a hand on one of the Indian headdresses, pulling one end of the display so that it flapped outward like a pink and purple dinosaur tail. Mumford said nothing but tears came to his eyes. "This fucking town sucks. All this shit wouldn't be if you just left people alone."

"Mr. Smith," Lucille said calmly, "this is not a meeting about your sexual deviancy. And for the record, most of us on the committee have done our best to keep private the video of you and Mr. Hutchison."

"There's a video?" Dogg interrupted. He obviously didn't read the paper. People like him get to live in their own worlds.

Lucille shook her head disapprovingly. "This conversation is unnecessary. An over eager citizen made a video and the committee has decided not to act on it for your reputation and ours."

(When the cat's out of the bag you may as well pet it.)
— The Committee

"My parents," Mumford said as if he was having a separate conversation in his head. Then, his tears began in earnest as he got up to leave. "This is so fucked up," he said, straightening his hat so the bill sat forward and low over his eyes. Then he looked at Dogg. "Hope you see what you're getting into, Bro." With that, he left, the Indian headdresses rattling as he slammed the door behind him.

"Excuse me," Ivy said to Lucille. "So it's okay to preserve yourselves but let it leak that somehow someone in my campaign is gay?"

Lucille was calm and direct, bringing her closed hands near her chest. "That was someone's overzealousness and not authorized. But let's not miss the point, Ms. Simmons and Mr. Doggins, and this is just between those of us in this room, that the Junior Mr. Mayor is supposed to be a model for the community and the moral standards exhibited by you two isn't exactly exemplary."

Ivy bristled and stared hotly at Dogg. "So you're assuming," Ivy said, clenching her teeth, "that Jimmy Doggins is morally impeccable?"

"Excuse me," Gloria Valdez offered quietly from the end of the table, "but I think that's right. Dogg is precisely the kind of young man that we want to represent Mudlick." She turned to Dogg for confirmation.

Dogg tried but could not manage a smile. "I want to be."

"Unbelievable," Ivy said. She crossed her arms and scanned the table, quickly staring down anyone who looked at her—all but Dogg who returned a look with a pained and apologetic expression. "Unbelievable," Ivy repeated.

The truth was we were not happy at all with how things turned out that summer. People weren't discussing what we wanted them to discuss. Instead of an alternate name for the town and some of the new businesses we were trying to attract, Mudlick was talking about a pregnant girl, gay teenagers, and a little girl about to be eaten by a giant squid.

"Alright" Lucille said firmly, "We'll have to finish this without Mr. Smith. I've let us get off track."

Ivy snorted again. "I'll say."

"At 2 p.m. the Saturday of the election, someone from the committee will hand Mr. Smith the sealed election box in front of all who attend. The three of you will go into the V.F.W. where you'll be uninterrupted while you tabulate the votes. As I said, Mumford will take the stage alone to announce the results, at which time you two should both take the stage." Lucille looked directly at Ivy. "The runner up will give a concession speech followed immediately by the new Junior Mr. Mayor's victory speech."

Dogg was shaking his head slowly and Ivy continued to glare at him. They had no idea how much restraint the committee had shown. We'd done our best to protect all concerned.

"Are there any questions?" Lucille asked.

"Just one," Ivy said. "I wonder if Jimmy would agree to a debate on KMVP radio the Friday before the election."

Dogg was not quick to respond, so Gloria Valdez spoke up. "We've never done that before."

"The committee doesn't have to do anything. Just me and Jimmy moderated by Mark Britten. And maybe some call-in questions."

"I don't see the problem with it," Jimmy said softly, almost as if he had an obligation to agree to it.

Jacob stood and walked the length of the table, ending up next to Lucille. "The committee doesn't recommend Hail Mary dramatics. Any last-minute thing could unfairly upset the results," he said.

Ivy had done better than any of us thought she would and, even though by our calculations Dogg was well ahead, we didn't put it past her to pull some stunt to make Dogg, the committee, or both look bad.

Lucille raised her right hand to indicate to Gloria she would handle this one. "We don't officially have a candidate, Ms. Simmons. But given your condition and the uncertainty of all that, it's true that we prefer a more stable office holder."

"So," Ivy said, "the debate?"

"No tricks?" Dogg leaned forward. His blue eyes had never looked more earnest. "No ringers. Just the issues?"

"Just the issues." As Ivy smiled Gloria and Lucille thought Dogg had just made the biggest mistake of his campaign.

43

(Confide in us as you would a friend.)
- The Committee

For obvious reasons Mumford was reluctant to tell us what happened after he left the meeting. But this much he did tell the committee. He sat in his truck outside the home where he'd lived his entire life. What would he tell his parents? He thought about a lot of things, mostly about Thatch and what lay ahead of him at school in Kentucky. What he might have spent some time considering, we thought, was how his carelessness had jeopardized the Junior Mr. Mayor position, but of course he didn't.

Mumford's forehead was resting against the steering wheel when he heard tapping on the passenger window. It was Dogg. The two young men sat in the cab for a while without talking. Finally, Dogg cleared his throat and put his hand on Mumford's shoulder. "I just want you to know," he said, "the only thing that sucks about this is that you didn't tell me a long time ago."

"You keep it secret," Mumford said, "because you're ashamed and you hope it's going to make life easier." He looked at Dogg. "But I'm thinking now that shame is something that starts on the outside. It isn't real and maybe you don't have to give into it."

Dogg sighed. "Makes sense."

"Like I'm sitting here looking at you sitting in my truck and I'm thinking it sucks that you could actually lose some votes if people saw you with me. But then I realize, Bro, it's just stupid to give a shit about any of it. It's like you and that rich kid image stuff. Why do you spend so much time worrying about that?"

"Believe me, Mum," Dogg said, "if we're talking about giving up shame, money is the least of my worries. I can see it, though, the things I want most in life. It's within reach but somehow my feet feel glued to the floor."

"I know how it feels," Mumford said, looking in the rearview mirror as he fixed his baseball cap over his eyes, "'cause I have to cut this double-life shit out. Take those last few steps. People can either like the real me or go to hell."

The committee thinks this must have been the moment when Dogg made his most serious decision about the campaign and perhaps about his life. "When I let people see the real James Andrew Doggins," he said, "they might be telling *me* to go to hell."

44

No one knew when she arrived, but at morning's first light, Pat Hunter stationed herself in front of Abigail Colton's house in a green lawn chair. She wore a wide-brimmed yellow hat tied under her chin, the white cord tipped with a male and female pair of Mallard ducks. Pat kept her hands in her lap and watched Fern as if waiting for her to wake up. Some people in their old age regain the innocence lost after childhood. Pat Hunter was certainly one of those. Her account of her experience is both dear and compelling. It's a testament to the power of belief, of how something that cannot be true becomes true.

Pat watched the Colton yard as the light grew stronger, the pink sky over the foothills whitening and Redwing Blackbirds trilling from the reeds near the not-too-distant lake. This new light brought Abigail Colton into the yard where she turned on the hose to wet the still-shadowed giant squid, the ends of its tentacles just ten or so feet away from Fern. Abigail Colton sprayed the beast as if she were hosing down a benign old circus elephant. But it was a sea monster obviously bent on snatching Fern, a fate she had no idea was ahead of her. The website that day had Fern asking, "Does anyone smell sushi?" And because of that, the committee feared Abigail Colton's sadistic bent might catch on.

(Your sixth sense begins in the heart and leeches into the brain.) - The Committee

Ms. Colton dragged the hose a bit further and gently soaked Fern from head to toe, running the water along her young arm up to the empty palm that just the day before held a dark-skinned doll. The two women, Pat and Ms. Colton, regarded one another briefly as Fern got her bath. Pat never had anything against Ms. Colton but this thing with Fern upset her. She wanted to yell at Ms. Colton, call her a murderer, but silently remained in her lawn chair.

When Ms. Colton finished her watering, Pat stood up and situated her face between two bars of the fence, the front of her hat bent upward taco-like. "You're all prettied up now," she said to Fern who was still dripping wet from her shower. "You cold?"

"It's not too bad, Mrs. Hunter," Fern said. "I'll be dry here pretty soon."

Pat looked again at the monster threatening Fern, thinking how certain the outcome of their meeting would be. She remembered watching a documentary in which a little girl in one of those South American countries, she couldn't recall which, was covered to the neck in water and debris after a mudslide. The girl had short curly brown hair and a surprisingly quick smile despite her circumstances. Rescuers discovered in short order there was no way to extract her. The video camera captured her last days, showed how rescue workers kept her hopeful even when they knew that without excavation equipment, the situation was hopeless. The whole time she managed to smile. The last shot of her, Pat remembered, was of her gray bent head after she succumbed to her situation. To the end, however, it seemed her powerless companions had helped her remain optimistic.

For this reason, Pat did not bring up the squid with Fern. "I just thought I'd come spend part of the day with you."

"That's kind of you. Lots of people come by but they don't stay long."

"What about Ms. Colton?"

Fern seemed almost stoic, her stance rigid. "She doesn't say a word to me."

"Well, Sweety," Pat said pressing her face even closer to the bars. "I'm sure she loves you. I do anyhow."

"I can tell."

Pat sat down again and adjusted her hat. "I'll be right here if you need me."

Just as she said this, Jodi Sierveld approached during her regular morning jog. She wore a black, full body Lycra running suit and a gray sweatband holding back magenta hair. A tiny light blinked at her left ankle on the same leg from which three years earlier she'd finally had her little toe removed. Jodi stopped and looked at the scene of Fern and the squid. "That doesn't look too promising."

(Joggers, don't be a road hazard like young bicyclists and livestock.) - The Committee

Pat turned and gave the best glare possible from beneath her sagging eyelids. "Shush. Fern will hear you."

It was too late. "What doesn't look too promising?" Fern asked.

"You see? She heard you."

Jodi stopped jogging and nodded as if she understood. "Right," she said. "Let's not upset anyone."

She enjoyed being Fern's translator and in turn, the town enjoyed the opportunity to talk back to Fern. And because she was such an emblem of all we thought was honest and pure, some had even sought out her advice on everything from horticulture to childcare. "Fern says hello and that you're pretty," Pat said.

"Thanks." Jodi started her legs pumping again. "I've got to run by here more often."

When Jodi left, Pat turned her attention back to Fern and to the evil thing bearing down on her. She tried to keep a smile on her face, hoping that something could be done before Fern was devoured.

45

Thatch met Ivy at the edge of Mudlick High after the final session of summer school. She stood waiting on the other side of the chain-linked fence in a pink sundress and white sandals, a black book bag at her side full of *Pride, Progress, and Preservation* flyers. The previous two days had proven difficult for Thatch. Though the committee hadn't officially sanctioned any release of the video, Jasper took it upon himself, even in his injured condition, and maybe especially so, to at least make part of the contents known. It didn't take long at all for word to get around about Thatch. The principal of the high school contacted his parents and suggested that maybe his senior year would be best spent in home schooling or in one of the county's high schools for troubled teens. For his own safety, of course.

Though Jasper was a bit underhanded, all this wasn't necessarily a bad thing in the mind of the committee. Every town has to be protective of its moral standards. And where Thatch and Ivy were concerned, the pair of them clearly didn't fit in with what was right for Mudlick.

"Rough day?" Ivy asked as Thatch plopped his tennis racket bag down next to him.

"The worst." Thatch touched Ivy's hand through the fence. "But it's not what people are saying to me. It's the fact they aren't saying anything at all."   Thatch noted that at the base of the fence, where one of the posts met the asphalt, a colony of red ants entered and exited from a narrow crack, all of them full of purpose.

Ivy walked the length of the fence toward the gate. Thatch followed, looking at the bulkiness of Ivy's campaign bag. "I'm not sure I'm going to be of much use to you now."

"Ridiculous," Ivy said as they reached the gate. "That's just what they want."

"It's only a few more days. You'll be better off."

Whether he understood it or not, Thatch was giving Ivy some good advice. If she had any chance at all against Dogg, Thatch's presence would merely come across as her support of immoral activity. And on that front, as far as the committee was concerned, with her own condition alone she was losing the battle.

"I have a surprise for you when we get home," Ivy said. She was about to reveal just how immoral she was.

Darren Parker saw them getting Slurpees at 7/11. Theresa Conner spotted them near the park and Journey Bascomb who had lived in her blue van with the painted Centaur since 1977 watched them pass her on the way to the subdivision where Thatch lived. His house was guarded by a plaster gnome in a red cap and green jacket whose faded blue eyes kept watch over a yellow lawn edged by dusty geraniums and a sprawling greenish gray clump of honeysuckle.

Ivy stopped Thatch before they went in the house. She looked up and down the street and apparently heard what she was hoping for. A thick, grumbling engine signaled it was headed their way. Mumford's Jacked-up red pickup with its too-wide tires rounded the corner. Thatch felt his chest tighten. He hadn't talked to Mumford since he returned from Kentucky. He understood why, though he was hurt. It was the sports thing, as Mumford explained to Thatch a hundred times. "They don't want fags in sports."

The truck pulled in front of Thatch's house and Mumford

opened the passenger door, waving Thatch in. "Go on," Ivy said, pushing her friend from behind. "You two should talk."

"Geez, what about you?" Thatch asked.

Ivy smiled and looked to each side of her, laughing. "Poor Ivy, alone again."

As Thatch got in the truck, Mumford looked at Ivy in her pink sundress revealing still-pale shoulders. She caught him the day after the meeting with the committee and asked him to talk to Thatch. Though he was hesitant, seeing Thatch by his side, smiling and near tears, he was glad he had come. Now, looking at Ivy, he tapped a finger to the bill of his red baseball cap in thanks. She fluttered her fingers in response, and then, on impulse, ran to the driver's side of the truck where she stood on the tire and planted one of her flyers on his windshield.

Mumford laughed. "I'm still a Dogg man."

"That's what they all say. But you haven't voted yet." Ivy backed from the truck and waved as Mumford drove Thatch away.

(The road to cultural instability is paved with the teenager's driver license.)   - The Committee

What we know is that Elaine Murrow, whose two-year-old Shawn was almost done with Shigellosis, we know she saw Mumford and Thatch stop for gas when she was walking Shawn in his stroller. And Kurt Levine is pretty sure he saw Mumford's truck go by his small engine repair shop out toward the edge of where Mudlick turns into chaparraled foothills. But after that, we never got Mumford or Thatch to say just exactly what they said to each other that day. As much as the committee heard from them about Ivy and Dogg, they wouldn't say a word about the afternoon Ivy got them together. "It's just nobody's business," Thatch said. We explained to him over and over such details are our business because the committee needs to know about these things in order to keep everything under control. But it was a no go, and in the end, maybe for the best, because like any thinking people, the committee assumed what went on between those two wasn't a whole lot of talking about how they might have a future. It doesn't take a fool to figure out what boys like to do, and we saw the video proof of so much potential going to waste.

46

Stowe Hanshaw had a surprise for Ivy and the whole town. And who would have thought it possible for one man to catch us off guard twice in his life? Just five years earlier, he'd received a kidney transplant from one of his twin daughters, Eileen. Just a year later, in a fluke fork lift accident, that same kidney was punctured and ruined. His second twin, Tasha, donated one of hers. But aside from that, the Hanshaws were a fairly unremarkable family, just the scrape-by kind of folks common to Mudlick.

For years he and Mrs. Hanshaw supplemented their income through a variety of this-and-that ventures, giving blood, medical trials, and renting special event signs mounted on trailers Stowe welded himself. It was one of these trailers, on his own accord, which he hauled around town on the afternoon before the radio debate. On it, in standard black, block capital letters it read: *IVY, Call 1-888-AM I PREG. Save your baby! Respect our town!*

(Fund the Tomb of the Unknown Baby.) - The Committee

No one had asked Stowe to tow around such a message, nor did he consult with anyone, but after several hours of driving he created enough interest that a crowd gathered in front of his sign at the entrance to the Pink Ghetto. Of course, on her way home, Ivy had the guts to stop and confront Stowe and those who'd gathered to support his cause.

Ivy, in new cut off overall's looked swelled and heated when she stomped into the ruckus and stood next to Stowe, a man who looked not unlike her father, moustache dipping past the edge of the mouth, sideburns shaped like wool boots framing a thin face. Ten years earlier, Stowe's wife, Renita, had been Ivy's Brownie troop leader.

"Is this," Ivy said defiantly, "is this all you've got?" The sun hung low in the sky, unobstructed and laser-like on the skin.

"Murderer!" someone yelled.

Ivy raised her hands, ready to respond. The agitated crowd yelled at her to not embarrass herself or Mudlick. As her mouth opened to fight back, a voice came from the back of the crowd.

"Leave her alone!" It was Dogg, straddling his bike. His racket hung at his back. No cape, no super hero powers, yet with all the same authority. Tan and with fresh blonde stubble glinting on his head like angry sparks, Dogg spoke firmly. "Leave her alone and leave here."

The crowd grumbled, not understanding his opposition. They were, after all, in his camp. They were, by all accounts, with the committee in understanding that Ivy was innately unfit to be Junior Mr. Mayor. Ivy had too many personal things she would have to figure out without the burden of representing an entire town.

But Ivy didn't accept Dogg's gesture. "Stay out of this, Jimmy," She said.

"No way," he said. "It's not right."

"It's *not* right. But it has nothing to do with you, either."

"It has everything to do with me." Dogg looked at the crowd, at Carmine O'Neil and Tom Omar, at Jansen Tompkins who'd brought his three-year-old daughter, Cornelia, she with the lazy violet eye, at Janice Gross, and Tanya Boggs whose bitter, but curiously pale orange marmalade, bleached almost, won honorable mention seven years in a row. Dogg looked at everyone. "I don't want a single vote from this crowd," he said.

"Too late," Ivy said. "These are your constituents. Deep thinkers all."

Stowe, who'd been standing off to the side ambled up next to Ivy as if he were the Sheriff in a Western, the voice of reason and sounding three cigarettes shy of a tracheotomy. "Now, little lady," he said, pulling at one side of his moustache, "these folks have a better idea of what you're facing than maybe even you do."

Ivy was puffed up, red-faced, as if she was prepared to take on the world. She stared at Dogg who remained on his bike at the edge of the crowd. "All I know is that you haven't done a thing that comes close to making me respect your point of view."

Stowe tossed his head back and looked down his nose with one eye as if spying Ivy through a gun sight. "Apparently you've never heard of freedom of speech. Me and these folks are just speaking up to help you make the right choice."

"Meaning, to help me make *your* choice."

"Meaning, that it's not too much to ask of someone to make a phone call." Stowe pointed to his sign. "Learn about your options."

"Options, huh?" Ivy wiped sweat from her forehead and smiled. "Okay," she said, "I'll do it. I'll call."

A cheer went up and the group congratulated each other with nods and smiles until Ivy regained their attention. "Like I said, I'll call. But I'd like someone here to just prepare me for what they're going to say."

Stowe locked his thumbs on the hip of his jeans, clearly not understanding. "What?"

"Let's start with the men. When you called, what kind of things did they tell you?"

Everyone stood silent, so silent they clearly heard the tinkling bell of the Kidson's Tabby as it walked along the top of a backyard fence. The bell was a compromise with the Kidson's neighbors, who were bird lovers and who had grown tired of seeing the cat gnawing on their feathered friends in the branches of their fig tree.

(Pickled figs keep indefinitely but no one wants them as a gift.)   - The Committee

Ivy put her hands on her hips. "How about the women? Has anyone here called that number?" When no one replied, she turned to Stowe, who had one hand working his chin.

"It's not the type of number most respectable folks ever have occasion to call."

"I don't know a single one of you people personally, yet somehow you think you know me well enough to tell me what's best for my future? Your idea of helping me is to make sure I think like you do. And you want to achieve that by telling me to listen to people you've never spoken to yourself?" Ivy turned her back and started walking toward her apartment building. After a few steps, she turned and spoke directly to Dogg. "They're all yours."

47

Jacob Alter heard it while he was assembling a grandfather clock kit in his garage which he planned to give his parents for their fiftieth anniversary—Mary Beth Alter would die two months short of that date after a slip in the tub, a broken hip and heart attack, though they're not sure which came first. Ruby and Flack Jones hosted a cocktail party to listen in, both of them dying their hair a new shade of black, Sable Crow, that Ruby found on an internet site based in New Mexico. Gloria Valdez was at their party, as was our retired teacher Audra Webster, and Emory Case, Dillard Phipps in a yellow bow tie, and Lucille Otto. Bernice Klein and some of the women's club put on their best costume jewelry and gathered in the meeting room behind the firehouse and listened in on a stereo set up by her seventeen-year-old grandson, Heath, who got Bernice to sign off on five of his 115 hours of community service sentence which he got for tagging "Eat Heath" all over town. It was two weeks before anyone got wise enough to realize it wasn't a candy bar but a real hoodlum. Amelia Jenks and her husband listened, too, their dead daughter Cassandra's last Christmas photo sitting next to the radio, the picture with her in an elf suit kissing Santa—Gary Honis— and cheating out like a little star so one and a half of her blue eyes showed to the camera. Jasper Carson dialed in from his car—with the torn Achilles heel the motorcycle was not an option—where he was staked out in front of the Colton house with his video camera to record the moment when Ms. Colton let that squid snatch Fern. And he said he could see through the window that Ms. Colton and Viola were sitting in front of their new entertainment center listening, too.

The whole of Mudlick, to put it short, was dialed into KMVP on Friday at 7 p.m. ready to hear Dogg and Ivy go at it. News had spread, of course, that the pair had already met that day courtesy of Stowe Hanshaw and his followers. That radio station hadn't gotten so many people listening at one time since Bert Stephens and Ward Finch replaced Saturday Night Hoe Down with Saturday Night Hop. It seemed like a big deal then, hearing electric guitars instead of fiddles. There were a lot of parents turning Chuck Berry and the Big Bopper off but more teenagers turning their dials to KMVP just to get in on what the rest of the country was already dancing to.

So when the sky was a crisp lavender and our streets and stores were nearly silent, except for Witherspoon's liquor, which was brisk with lottery business--103 million to a single winner--everyone with an ear to the radio, Mark Britten signed on after a lengthy car commercial ended with "We spell guarantee with a double "g!"

Inside the studio, Britten, a goatee wearing, bald, rail-thin man with a glutinous twang sat at the console with an aging, off-white against dark-green computer monitor in front of him listing caller names, occupations, and affiliations, if any. Ivy sat on his left, earphones clasped over hair conspicuously down in the old stringy way in which she'd begun the campaign. Dogg, too, wore earphones, his shorn head now filling in like a glittering yellow porcupine.

"The Biiiiiig Briiiiiiiiiiiiiiiiiitt," Britten shouted into the microphone, baritone enhanced. Before he got to the candidates, he gave us a brief update on the furniture scam which had taken us all for a ride. Authorities recovered an abandoned rental car where the only clues left behind were in the back seat, seventeen Bazooka gum comics, and a wadded-up counterfeit one-hundred-dollar bill, which, it turned out, had been used by and *made* by Colbert Stevens, but who had no connection to the scam himself.

When Britten finished the not-very-hopeful news he moved on to subject of the moment. "KMVP is bringing you the first ever radio debate between Junior Mr. Mayor contestants," he said.

"Caaaaaaaaaandidates," Ivy inserted, mocking Britt's style.

"And that young lady chomping at the bit is Ms. Ivy Simmons. Facing off with her tonight is Jimmy Doggins, Dogg to his friends and to those of us who've followed his magnificent tennis career. Understand you two got involved in a little dust up this afternoon? Whoa on that! But more importantly, any colleges lined up? And what's this about Ivy shouting down a group of concerned citizens? Whoa."

Dogg looked at Ivy and apologized with his eyes. "I was there. My opponent responded to their concerns in terms they could understand."

"By mocking Stowe Hanshaw, double kidney transplantee?!!" To this, Britten's assistant played the submarine alert sound. "Oh my!"

Dogg was diplomatic. "You asked about college. My parents and I are looking at my options. But I'd feel more comfortable if we kept this about the campaign."

"Alrighty then," Britten said with a smile in his voice. The committee was pleased to discover that it sounded as if he was going to be on Dogg's side. "So why don't I give each of you a few seconds to lay out your platforms."

Britten announced that the order had been decided by a flip of the coin before the broadcast. Ivy went first, her voice sounding surprisingly mature. She talked about how Mudlick had a unique identity in the county, about how the town had a chance to preserve its rural identity and not become just another strip mall suburb. She talked about how we could market ourselves the way Julian did, pre-fire, in the Laguna Mountains with its apple festival. "But how," she asked, "how can we market ourselves if we tear everything down and put up Burger Kings and 7/11s?"

(Franchise stores can afford to keep gum off the asphalt.)
- The Committee

Dogg jumped right in, saying that his slogan of "Let's Have Fun," was something Mudlick needed more than another historical marker. All those years of television commercials paid off because every inflection in his young voice was perfect. "We're all too serious," he said. "And quite frankly, if we're honest with ourselves, what is Mudlick anyway? It's a little town that almost was. We don't have any real claim to fame. Why not be realistic about that? Why not try to remake ourselves? Get some new energy?"

At Ruby's gathering, everyone tinked their glasses together. It was just what the committee wanted to hear from Dogg, though maybe he'd been a little rough on our historical importance. Ruby, sparkling in a beaded red blouse and black capri pants raised her glass in a silent toast as the debate continued with Mark Britten's first question.

"Let me get this straight, Jimmy . . . Dogg," Ivy said. "You're interested in making something new, but not projecting what the consequences might be?"

Dogg was silent.

"Whoa there, my boy," Britten quickly interjected. "Commercial radio here."

Dogg ummed and cleared his throat. "Of course I'm interested in consequences. That's why people trust me. They've seen my honesty on t.v. half my life."

Ivy pushed her arm across Britten's chest to arrest his next comment. "You mean," she said, "people should vote for you because you've been a car salesman?"

"Because," Dogg said, "I've been honest."

"What do you drive now, Jimmy?"

"A bike, mostly," he said quietly.

"I think we should get one thing out of the way," Britten said. "The nine hundred pound gorilla in the corner. Get away from all this technical stuff. Ivy, Mudlick wants to know what you plan to do about your baby."

Ivy interrupted sternly. "Fetus." You could hear her roll her eyes as she spoke. "And it's nobody's business. I haven't seen a single one of Mudlick's so-called leaders walking around with halos, so I'm sure I'll be in good company."

Jacob Alter nearly dropped his clock works. He didn't like the insinuation that Ivy was as moral as he. Worse, that the committee was as immoral as she. He looked out his open garage door where the entire world had taken on a post-twilight gray. There were no colors except what he saw inside in the artificial yellow light immediately surrounding him, the mahogany-stained pine clock housing to surround the brass face, and his own reddish hands. Here with his tools in a makeshift workshop he knew what was what. "That Ivy Simmons has a lot of nerve," he thought, "comparing us to her." After all, Jacob was a good Presbyterian, went to services every Sunday and mowed the church grounds the second Saturday of every month. Who knew if Ivy ever set foot in a church.

The question turned to Dogg, which he declined to answer at first. But Ivy interceded before Mark Britten moved on. "Oh no," she said, "I'm quite interested in hearing what Mr. Doggins has to say on the matter."

Everyone in town must have leaned toward their radios at that moment. "Well," Dogg began tentatively and we heard him take a drink. "I guess we'll all know soon enough what Ivy decides, whether she tells us or not. And I suppose she has chosen to be a public figure so it's fair of people to consider whether they want a pregnant Junior Mr. Mayor." Another pause and the sound of another drink.

"That young man has a good head on his shoulders," Dillard said, sitting between Gloria Valdez and Lucille Otto on Ruby's couch. All three of them held their second glasses of white wine. And if anyone had thought about it, they would have taken a picture of Lucille because it wasn't but every two or three years that she touched any form of alcohol. It was a welcome sign of confidence from our most conservative member.

"But," Dogg continued shakily, "To be fair, I've known Ivy for a long time. And man, let me tell you, she's a good person."

(Goodness is a seed planted by parents and covered in fertilizer by the community.) - The Committee

Mark Britten chuckled and looked at the two adversaries on opposite sides of the table. Dogg was staring into his lap and Ivy was near tears. "Dogg, my boy, someone needs to give you some pointers on debating."

Those of us who were listening couldn't see what was going on inside the studio, of course. We could only go by what we heard. And though it seemed that Dogg was willing to be a bit softer on Ivy than we would have hoped, we convinced ourselves that in the end it was a good tactical move. Better not to let Ivy score any sympathy points by becoming a victim.

Britten looked at the caller lineup on his monitor and saw something remarkable. Under "Subject" half of the callers wanted to talk about Fern. Not about changing Mudlick's name, or putting in a Walmart in the last big open field near town, nothing at all about Ivy, at least not at that moment. From the list of names, Britten smartly put on Pat Hunter first, though it took a few seconds to get her to turn down her radio so she wasn't confused by the delay.

"Good evening," she said in a voice that sounded weak and choppy, as if she was speaking through a fan. "I'd like to hear these young people talk about this very serious business of child abuse we've got over at Abigail Colton's place. Everyone says we can't do anything. I talk to that poor little girl every day and she doesn't have any notion of what that Abigail Colton is doing to her. Just today she was talking about looking forward to going back to school."

Britten interrupted, thanking Pat for her call and throwing the topic to Dogg.

"It does seem pretty masochistic," Dogg began.

"The word you mean is sadistic," Ivy said.

"I mean, Ivy, you've got this poor little girl playing on her lawn. And I don't know if you guys out there have driven by, but there's this big squid that looks like it's just about ready to slurp Fern up for dinner. And I guess we really ought to do something about it. At least show that we care. What other child would we allow to be treated like this?" Dogg's voice was getting deeper and more firm and it sounded as if he sensed a last-minute way to solidify some votes. "In fact," he continued, "I'm announcing a rally in front of the Colton house tomorrow morning before the polls open. 11 a.m. come with your signs and your voices. We'll meet at the empty lot on Manzanita Street and march."

Jasper Carson was pumping his fist in his car across from the Colton yard. At the same time, all the lights in the house were turned off one by one and Jasper guessed that Ms. Colton and Viola were so struck by Dogg's announcement that they didn't want to listen to the radio anymore.

Ivy's sigh was audible. "Oh God, Jimmy," she said. "Not you too? Sometimes I think there's something in the water that makes this town crazy. I want everyone who is even half listening to me to give me their undivided attention. Fern ... is ... a ... plant!"

If you listened close enough at the moment Ivy blasphemed the town's favorite daughter, you would have heard all of Mudlick gasp. You would have heard Pat Hunter fall to the floor dead of a heart attack not to be found until days later. You would have heard Jasper Carson drop his video camera out his car window and Flack Jones throw back a shot of whiskey. You would have heard Mary Costers and eleven of her twelve children booing the radio between bites of macaroni and cheese.

As outrageous as her comment was, the committee took some sort of comfort in knowing that it all but assured that Ivy wouldn't be elected and that in Dogg we would have someone more like-minded to supervise. Most of us were surprised that Ivy had given us this gift. She seemed savvier than to slip up in such an obvious way. And it was surprising that she just didn't get it. Fern didn't need a beating or functioning heart to be real. She was real because we'd given her a voice. She was real because everyone in town said she was.

Mark Britten didn't change the topic for the entire hour, allowing caller after caller to defend Fern and denounce Ivy, who, to her credit, never backed down once. She answered every caller with the same equal conviction, though you could hear in her voice a kind of realization that with each word she spoke she was pounding another nail in the coffin of her hopes of becoming Junior Mr. Mayor. And even if you were against her, it wasn't a little sad at the end to hear her wearied voice

"But don't you think," Dogg asked, sounding almost apologetic, giving Ivy one last chance to backtrack, "that we should intercede at all? Even if it means just having a conversation with Abigail Colton? Don't you think our rally tomorrow could help put this debate to rest?"

"The only person Abigail Colton should be discussing the fate of Fern with is her gardener. And if she has to take a lot of flack because he's not by her side, so be it. She's strong enough to go it alone."

What came next out of the mouth of Dogg none of us could have prepared for. Ruby was already re-filling Dillard, Gloria, and Lucille's glasses with white wine. Jacob Alter put the last screw into the grandfather clock his mother would never see. And the women's club was gathering their purses and slipping sweaters over their shoulders. "I just want to say," Dogg mumbled, "that maybe Ivy and I don't agree on a lot of things. But she just said something about Ms. Colton's gardener that made me think."

Britten interrupted. "I'm sorry to say our time is nearly over. You'll need to wrap it up."

"See," Dogg continued, "Ivy shouldn't be alone taking all this abuse. The guy who got her pregnant should be helping her. That is," he paused and the air seemed dead forever, "*I* should be helping her."

Dogg had come to that conclusion at the last few seconds of the hour allotted to the debate. Mark Britten signed off, stuttering the KMVP call letters he said a thousand times a day. Ivy and Dogg said nothing to each other, both staring into the wood grain veneer of the table that separated them. Ivy looked up finally, tucking her hair behind her ears. "I never would have told anyone," she said.

"I know," Dogg said, reaching across the table where his fingers barely touched the tip of Ivy's. "That's why I had to."

"I don't need to be rescued, Jimmy."

"No, you don't. We wouldn't be in this situation if you did. But I want to ask you something I should've asked from the start. What *do* you need?"

48

Mumford and Thatch waited outside KMPV. Like everyone, Dogg's revelation came as a complete surprise to them. They'd been listening to the radio in Mumford's truck doing lord knows what. That kind can't seem to keep their hands off one another. The committee, of course was in fits. How dare he. Any reasonable person, anyone with any sense knows that such things ought to be kept private, and had we time, we would've scheduled a town meeting to make just that point.

"Bro, what the hell?" Mumford said outside the station, shifting his baseball cap so the bill angled down the back of his neck. His "executive" look, he liked to tell us.

"Hell might be in store," Dogg said.

Ivy followed seconds later, smiling but a bit dazed. She hugged Thatch without speaking.

"This changes everything," Thatch said. For the first time in anyone's memory his hair wasn't parted, but instead, sat atop his head full and wavy, still neat, but not subdued. "Now there's an even playing field. Not only that, Ivy's at bat."

"Hold up," Mumford said, proving his partisanship. "I think Dogg just did a pretty cool thing. That'll get half the town voting for him right there."

Thatch Grimaced, squeezing Ivy's hand. "And half the town disillusioned that their golden boy has a lead center." Then began the pair's first argument, each of them insisting that Dogg's revelation put their candidate in the driver's seat. They explained to each other just exactly what the town was thinking, each offering opposite opinions about how the same group of people were making up their minds and how they would vote. Ivy and Dogg stood side-by-side listening, not invited into the conversation. And in a total lack of appreciation and understanding, the one thing the boys seemed to agree on was that the committee was interfering in a personal matter. But, as we would point out later, they neglected to consider that we only wanted what was best for Ivy and Mudlick, not to mention Dogg's future as a tennis player, nor how much time and attention they could give to the Junior Mr. Mayor position.

In any case, why shouldn't the committee offer up the benefit of its years of experience? Maybe not in the specifics of Ivy and Dogg's disastrous choices, but in general. If it hadn't been for the committee, Tonya Dory and her husband might have adopted that little Chinese baby. And the Contreras sisters might've made the mistake of selling their property to the Jehovah's Witnesses and we would've had a Kingdom Hall there instead of the Cut 'n' Buff salon. Hairstylists don't go around knocking on your door at all times of day. The committee helps the town in all kinds of ways like this, and it starts by helping people make decisions. Ivy and Dogg weren't the first or last, but they were certainly the most ungrateful.

(Stockpile decisiveness and squander patience.) - The Committee

"This is the problem," Ivy said, cutting off Thatch and Mumford's debate. "All we do is talk about what the town is thinking."

Mumford shrugged his shoulders. "Well, there is another topic on the table. What's up with the two of you?"

Dogg looked at Ivy who stood expressionless. "Let me put it in terms you can understand, Mum. It's like a trade in baseball where there's a player to be named later. You know what you're giving away, but as for what's coming down the pipeline ... "

"To be honest, guys, I don't know how anything can be different for us in this town. There's no breathing room to figure out what we should do."

"Geez, four kids in the same boat," Thatch said, nodding to Ivy and Dogg. "But at least you two could both make a speech at that Save Fern rally tomorrow. Talk to the town directly about how you feel."

"Oh, God, that rally," Dogg said clearly already forgetting that he'd promised to champion Fern's safety. And in a display of Ivy's terrible influence, he continued. "Screw it. We can do something I thought I'd have to do alone."

49

We gathered in the empty lot at the corner of Manzanita Street and Colton Lane in the late morning shade of two giant pines next to Harold Adamson's yard, the same two pines planted by his mother ninety years previous. Some people carried signs— "Fear Not, Fern!" "Save our Girl!" "Today Fern, Tomorrow *Your* Child!"—others had cowbells or bouquets of flowers, stuffed animals and candy. There were old and young people, Brett Marks still in his third shift Denny's uniform, Margaretta Helms with her seventy-year-old mother Sophia and the two-year-old twins in a double stroller, the latter three looking gray as morning, Sophia because of Leukemia and the twins still sapped by Shigellosis.

Though we estimated nearly a thousand people responded to Jimmy Doggins' call for a rally to save Fern, he was understandably absent, given the unfortunate revelation of the previous night. And people were definitely talking about what they'd heard on the radio. Vince Bolton, who'd been the groundskeeper at Our Lady of Compassion for twenty-three years, told Gloria Valdez, "what that Jimmy Doggins needs is to be locked in a room and told what's what." And Marsha O'Riley, eighth grade teacher and an expert on the recorder went on forever about kids having kids and how Ivy was like a virus. "If she has that baby," she said, "all these young girls are going to think they can do it too. And if she doesn't have it, they'll think that's okay too." But as agitated as people were, it didn't seem to dampen the enthusiasm to let Ms. Colton know how the town felt about her treatment of Fern.

The committee hadn't time to meet to discuss Jimmy Doggins' admission that he had fathered Ivy's baby. At that point, in any case, we pretty much threw up our hands. As long as those two kids didn't end up together, there was still a chance to salvage things. Of course, we were upset at being forced to choose between the lesser of two evils. No matter what, our next Junior Mr. Mayor would have a moral cloud hanging over him . . . or her. How could either of these candidates speak at the annual interfaith picnic or represent Mudlick in any wholesome endeavor? The truth was, they couldn't, but since the whole town would be voting that day, we thought, given the alternative, Jimmy Doggins was still the better choice. Upset as we were, we reconciled the fact that the coming year would just have to be a very long salvage operation.

Jacob Alter, the committee member who'd gotten Jimmy to run in the first place, Jacob in his blue Hawaiian shirt and cut-off shorts acted as rally leader, elevating himself by standing on the post and rail of the Adamson's fence, his flip-flopped feet precariously holding his balance. "People," he said, "last night we saw evidence of a decline in the moral values of what Mudlick stands for." Jacob paused as a few affirmations and amens came from the crowd. "Up the street there is yet another example of immorality run amuck in our town." More cheers. "Only this time we can do something about it. We can save one of Mudlick's children. Onward!"

The marchers started up the street and someone initiated a chant that spread through the entire crowd. "Hey, hey! Ho, ho! Abigail Colton, let Fern go!" We walked and yelled filling both sides of Colton Lane under the partial canopy of Eucalyptus trees planted by Joseph Colton way back when he envisioned a stately drive up to his house. Now some of the thick old things with their peeling, orange bark and lopped off tops guarded a neighborhood rather than one man's private domain. And we made sure to leave a couple of our yellow notes on mailboxes where the owners weren't raking up the leaves and bark. But mostly we chanted our chant, walking by the beautiful Phipps home with its mound of purple bougainvillea partially folded over the tile roof. Elaine Tyler came out of her tiny white house using her aluminum walker. We couldn't have asked for a more legitimate endorsement. Her husband was killed in WWII, burned alive in a warehouse accident, and her son was shot dead in Vietnam. In her shaking hand she raised a miniature American flag as we passed.

Jimmy Doggins had a good idea and we wondered what the turnout might have been if he hadn't suggested the rally off the cuff, but had planned it as a real event. The votes he might have gotten then! Nevertheless, we were there in force, walking side-by-side, thick as a brick, yelling at the top of our lungs. We pictured ourselves arriving at the Colton house, hopeful Fern standing waiting desperately for us to rescue her, Abigail Colton helpless against the will of the town. But as we got closer to the Colton house, something odd happened. The people in the front stopped chanting, the sound dissipating until we were all dead silent and lined up, three deep, in front of the fence. Where we had expected to see Fern in her usual spot, perhaps waving at us, we saw the giant squid, shiny-slick with water, and most horribly, one of Fern's rooty legs sticking out of its mouth like the tail end of a sucked-up piece of green spaghetti. We were too late.

Gary Pomeranz dropped to his knees, holding the fence, and wept. Which isn't surprising because Gary was flung out of the Octopus ride at the Del Mar Fair when he was twelve and for the ten years following he had to wear a shunt in his brain to drain fluid. After Gary, other people started crying too, the entire gathering becoming a sobbing mass in minutes. Christina Dow, 1983 Ms. All County third runner up, threw her carnations over the fence and other bouquets followed, some going far enough to bounce off the squid's tentacles.

Jules Ziegler, who played Curly in *Oklahoma!* three times, made an honest attempt to begin a chorus of "Amazing Grace." And though there were a few people willing to join in, most were silent, staring at Fern's solitary leg and the squid as if this were a viewing before a burial. But even Jules couldn't sustain himself and his baritone throb dwindled away on the word "grace." Behind the giant squid, the Colton house was both bright and silent, the sun flashing off its white exterior as if refracting off steel. Ms. Colton had once again proven her total disregard for the town she grew up in.

After a few remaining minutes of silence, the crowd of people who had marched so loudly up the street, peeled away from the fence one by one and walked away quietly, except for the sick Helms twins who began shrieking almost simultaneously, forcing Margaretta and her mother to jog down the street. The committee stayed behind the longest, watching the faithful leave, wondering whether Ivy Simmons, Jimmy Doggins, and Ms. Colton had squeezed every last bit of optimism out of Mudlick and whether any of those departing citizens would show up at the Dime-a-Dip lunch and vote for a Junior Mr. Mayor at the V.F.W. in just over an hour.

50

People come running to a car wreck, and mostly not to help. Whether they admit it or not, they want to see twisted metal, fire, and most of all, casualties. As far as the committee was concerned, there wasn't any greater wreck that summer than the Junior Mr. Mayor election, which explains why the Dime-a-Dip lunch and vote drew more people than it ever had, a few thousand, so many that we had to set up emergency tables well into the softball field next to the V.F.W. hall and still we had people sitting on the grass, covering the concrete steps and leaning against trees, all of them with plates full of cold spaghetti, fried chicken, eleven different slaws, home-made pizza, four corn breads, cabbage rolls, goulash, corn on the cob, four lasagnas—one vegetarian, three bean salad, five bean salad, thirteen bean salad, cucumber and tomatoes in a vinaigrette, twenty iceberg lettuce salads, nine gelatin desserts pocked with fruit bits, Rice Krispy squares, dry fudge, chocolate cake, soupy ice cream, raspberry tarts, chocolate covered pretzels, and strawberry flavored angel food cake just to name a fraction. Each serving costing one dime, with all the proceeds going to help the candidates offset costs of their campaigns.

(To increase profit at Dime-a-Dip fundraisers, use small plastic spoons for serving.)   - The Committee

The gathered were somewhat subdued, understandably, on account of Fern, but Mudlick never had more people eating in one place at one time than the day of the election between Jimmy Doggins and Ivy Simmons. It wasn't the first time we'd seen this pair standing *together*, but people turned out to see them *together*. An expectation the committee did it's best to quash. If we were going to have to accept a tainted Junior Mr. Mayor in Dogg, we didn't need his pregnant temptress at his elbow. And yet, people couldn't help but wandering from the election outcome to the question of whether or not the pair would flaunt their immorality, *would they kiss?*

Ivy and Dogg's parents arrived early—Mrs. Doggins and Gwen Simmons—the two candidates were nowhere to be seen at first. Usually, the candidates would be circulating through the crowd, shaking hands, but after the display of the previous night, it didn't surprise the committee at all that neither had arrived for the lunch. Thatch and Mumford sat at conspicuously opposite tables, well aware of each other and exchanging the occasional smile. All the while, the polling lines were long, some people even eating as they waited to cast a vote.

Small consolation. We couldn't have asked for a nicer, clearer, summer day. The sun was bright but not oppressive and the breeze came up just when things seemed to be getting hot. Leaning up against the ivy-covered fence that separates the Oasis trailer park from the V.F.W. were all the "Save Fern" rally signs which were so vital just a couple of hours earlier, but now sat bent and useless. Of course, everyone was talking about Fern's murder and the radio program and where they heard it as if it was the day Kennedy got shot. But the general buzz of conversation changed noticeably, first at the far edge of the outside tables, the ones near third base. A general murmur coursed all the way up to the hall itself and the people who were inside came out to confirm what they'd just heard, that Abigail Colton and Viola were headed our direction.

Sure enough, not far down the street, the familiar denim outfit and bright white hair let us know that it was indeed Ms. Colton holding Viola's gloved hand. Viola looked as if she were dressed for church in her lavender dress, matching pillbox hat and impeccable white gloves. In her free hand she carried a large plastic tote which we would find out later contained a spiraled ham. As the pair approached, Janey Gilmore, who was about Fern's age, or had been, began to cry and her mother Pauline pulled the little girl to her side. Janey was feeling what we all were, that these two women were dangerous. They'd killed once that day already. But instead of rocks and bottles, boos and jeers, no one said a direct word to Ms. Colton and Viola as they parted the crowd and went inside the hall to set their ham on the table and fill their own plates

Cornelia Bowles, whose attendance was a surprise because her granddaughter, Suzy, was arrested four days earlier for growing sixteen, ten-foot-tall marijuana plants in her parents' finch aviary, Cornelia leaned into her husband Robert and said, "Someone should tell those women they aren't welcome here." And maybe we were all thinking that, but none of us did, perhaps because the pain of Fern's death was too recent. We just let them alone to fill their plates—Ms. Colton had two chicken legs, a cornbread, and three bean salad. Viola had some of her ham, and the same three bean salad—pay their dimes, and go somewhere to eat.

But Jacob Alter wasn't as quiet as the rest of us. He took to the podium covered with bunting set up beneath the flagpole, the flags already at half-mast. Jacob tapped the microphone, those of us on the receiving end hearing the loud thump thump sound of a pillow fight. "Excuse me," he said as the crowd bunched in front of him. "Every year this is a celebration of Mudlick's finest teen." The crowd laughed and Jacob grimaced to let them know he understood. "But today it's hard to keep our minds on this event. As you all know by now, we lost Fern this morning. And I think it would be appropriate to dedicate this lunch in her honor since, more than even our candidates, she has held our hopes and dreams."

Gabe Kinks of the First Baptist Church yelled an amen and a few others followed as general applause rose. Benita Frazier started a chorus of "In the Garden."

I come to the garden alone
While the dew is still on the roses
And the voice I hear falling on my ear
The Son of God discloses

Everyone but the Catholics joined in, not because they
didn't want to, but because for some reason they don't know
too many hymns like that by heart. The rest sang all the way
through to the end and there probably wasn't a dry eye among
us, especially as Benita took control of the final verse and lifted
her soprano voice above us all.

**(Two dimes worth of vinegar potato salad loosens the
vocal chords.)** - The Committee

Jacob raised his hand to keep the crowd silent. He asked if anyone wanted to come forward with a memory of Fern. Alice Uven
waved a wet handkerchief and rushed to the front. Her thin white
hair looked glassy and brittle in the bright sun. She took the podium
in a caterpillar green suit and white sandals that bunched her toes together like stacked wood. At first her voice wavered and she dabbed
the handkerchief to her eyes. "I've probably spent more time talking
with Fern than anyone in town except our dearly departed Pat Hunter," she began. "The day before she was taken from us she told me
all about how she wanted to be an astronaut." A few noticeable sobs
issued from the mourners. It was really hitting home what a brief life
Fern had, how little time we got to spend with her before Abigail
Colton snatched her life away.

"I haven't felt so at ease," Alice finished, "as the times I shared
with that little girl. God bless her." Again the handkerchief went to
her eyes as she stepped off the podium and wobbled back into the
crowd.

As Jacob stepped up to speak again he saw Ms. Colton and Viola
in the speckled shade of a pepper tree. They were scraping the last
few beans from their plates and listening to our impromptu service.
Neither of them looked especially distraught or even bothered by

the pain they caused. Jacob raised both his arms, squinting from daylight. "This hasn't been officially authorized," he said, "but I'm sure the committee would be proud to sponsor the construction of some sort of memorial to Fern."

"A statue," Martin Caywood yelled, an idea met with a great deal of applause.

Just as Jacob was set to fill in his idea, he saw a large black, gleaming Cadillac coming up the road. His silence, mouth slightly open as if there were a word caught in the back of his throat, and his focused gaze made us turn around almost as if we shared the same head. We watched as the car slowly made the curve around the park towards us until it stopped directly in front of the V.F.W. hall. The blackened windows gave no view of the passengers, though the driver, a shorthaired red headed woman in a black suit and tie sat mannequin still in the front, looking straightforward. We expected she would get out and open the door for her passenger, but nothing. We watched the door to see who might emerge. The committee checked among ourselves to see if any of us had invited a dignitary. No. We waited.

Though we couldn't see them, Mumford sat between Jimmy Doggins and Ivy inside the black car rented with the last of Jimmy Doggins' campaign money. At some point Mumford left the Dime-a-Dip to meet them. From their vantage point it looked as if the entire town had shown up for the election. "I didn't think there'd be this many people," Ivy said.

Mumford adjusted his big body, the leather seats squealing at each movement. He'd never worn a suit to any event for which we requested that attire. So, to spite the committee, on his last official day, he put one on, complete with white shirt, red tie and the Junior Mr. Mayor sash given to him during his inauguration. All he wanted since becoming elected was to be done with the whole thing. The feeling would have been mutual, but the committee wasn't sure if Mumford's ambivalence looked so bad considering what we thought we might be in for with our new Junior Mr. Mayor elect, whomever it was. "Bro, are you sure you two want to go through with this?" Mumford asked.

Jimmy Doggins smiled and reached across Mumford for Ivy's hand. "After today," he said, "I guess we can go through with anything."

We stared at the black car for two or three minutes wonder who had invited what dignitaries. Finally, the driver stepped out of the car, her red lipstick in severe contrast to her thoroughly pale skin. She opened the passenger door and Ivy emerged in jeans and a Let's Have Fun t-shirt which she filled out thoroughly. Her hair rested on her head in the old stringy way she used to keep it. She smiled and waved to the crowd but was greeted more with surprised recognition than actual enthusiasm. There wasn't any sustained applause or genuine cheering.

(Misplaced applause is infectious. Don't be a carrier.)
                                                      - The Committee
At that moment, to the committee, it appeared that Jimmy Doggins would likely win, and though he wasn't the candidate we thought we were getting, it would be easier, literally, to look beyond his role in Ivy's pregnancy than if she were elected.

Mumford stepped out in his dark suit, which fit him snuggly at the shoulders and rose a little high at his ankles. Lucille Otto shook her head. Of all of us, she'd been on him the most about representing Mudlick in a more dignified manner and there he was, obviously capable of trying what he would not try in 364 previous days. "No respect," she muttered, a sentiment those of us near her nodded to.

Finally, Jimmy Doggins emerged and everyone took a simultaneous and audible breath to the point of near silence, everything frozen except two male pigeons cooing for the attention of a female on the V.F.W. roof. We weren't surprised by the fact Jimmy Doggins wore one of Ivy's green Pride, Progress, and Preservation t-shirts but by the fact that he dyed his prickly hair to match and shaved it into a narrow, miniature Mohawk. Just weeks earlier we'd begun this campaign with a perfectly beautiful, blue-eyed, blonde teenage tennis hero and now we were confronted with something quite else, a young man who'd turned himself into some sort of punk rock musician type person. By comparison, even Ivy looked good.

"Well that's it," Lucille said in Gloria Valdez' ear. "They're just not taking this seriously."

Gloria frowned and shook her head, thinking what all of us were thinking, that it was a shame that, however it happened, Jimmy Doggins got mixed up with a girl like Ivy. She'd obviously changed him. It was that way with those Pink Ghetto people. They'd just as soon take you down with them than watch anyone succeed. All his life Jimmy Doggins was such a good boy and somehow Ivy got him in her bed, and look at the result. And people wonder why the committee is so necessary. Where are the parents in these situations?

The three of them, Mumford, Jimmy Doggins and Ivy, walked to the podium together where Jacob Alter remained, his mouth holding that unsaid word. Mumford shook his hand and looked out at the audience, shielding his eyes from the sun, searching until, in the middle, he found Thatch. From there, it was safe to offer an anonymous wink, and he did so. Jacob acknowledged each as calmly as could be expected and pointed to the folding chairs where they were to sit, the three of them Mudlick's sad version of Mount Rushmore, a gay man-boy in a too-small suit, a poor pregnant girl, and a talented young man going crazy and following the other two down a rat hole. Not a single person could take their eyes away, locking in on even the slightest hand movement between Ivy and Jimmy Doggins, any gesture that might end up in interlocked fingers, a hand on the thigh. When Ivy adjusted her position on the chair, she leaned toward Dogg and the crowd took a collective breath thinking they might see a kiss on the cheek. The committee was appalled at the distraction.

Behind them, in the hall, Rain Van de Kamp cast the last vote before the candidates' turn. She'd changed her name from Wilma when she discovered that her Dutch family also had Cherokee blood. After discovering that fact near her 50th birthday, Rain began wearing beaded moccasins and braiding her hair. As tradition has it, the final voter carries the ballot box to the podium where the outgoing Junior Mr. Mayor and the candidates cast their votes in public. Once Rain delivered the ballots to the podium, she stood and waved while the crowd applauded. They were that much closer to knowing who would be the next Junior Mr. Mayor.

Mumford voted first, followed my Jimmy Doggins, who smiled at the crowd as he raked his green line of hair with his fingers. Ivy was Ivy, stomping up to the box, marking her choice confidently, and shoving the ballot in the box as if the outcome were certain. Just as she took her seat, Gil Plummerman blew one of the air-powered horns he was famous for at the Mudlick High football games. The pigeons on the roof took flight at the sound as nearly all of us gave Gil a dirty look for startling us.

"All the votes have now been cast," Jacob announced, pulling his glasses from the pineapple pocket of his shirt. He read the same speech we read every year. "Ladies and gentlemen, the polls are now closed. In the tradition of these many years of Junior Mr. Mayor elections, let us now thank the outgoing Junior Mr. Mayor, Mumford Smith." Mumford stood and accepted the polite applause which Jacob interrupted by handing him the ballot box before continuing to read. "The votes are now in the hands of our outgoing Junior Mr. Mayor. The contest this year is between Ivy Simmons and Jimmy Doggins, two young people who have fought hard for the chance to represent Mudlick over the coming year with dignity and honor." Suppressed laughter bubbled through the crowd, even Ivy and Jimmy smiled, and Jacob looked up, frustrated. "I'm just reading what it says." He pushed his glasses up the bridge of his nose and finished. "The current Junior Mr. Mayor and the candidates will now retire inside to count the votes."

Mumford led the way with Ivy and Jimmy Doggins following. Everyone looked for an intimacy, a touched buttock or shoulder squeeze . . . nothing. As happened every year, they removed inside to the separate bar and dance area where a table and tabulating paper waited. Most years it took less than an hour to get the results. Once, when James Cowley ran against his twin brother Mark, there were a total of just thirty-five votes cast because most people weren't sure which brother they were voting for. We had that decision in twelve minutes, almost exactly. And though James won the election, we didn't know until years later that it was Mark who gave the acceptance speech.

This time with Ivy and Jimmy Doggins was different. We had no idea how long it might take them to count all the votes. The committee circulated through the crowd trying to get a gauge on whether or not the vote was still falling Dogg's way. Some were talking about how they had empty living rooms waiting for furniture that would never come. Many were filling up on a surprise desert. Kelly Burner, who was a year behind Ivy and Dogg, walked through the crowd passing out ice cream cups, the lids of which were stickered with her name in bright orange. "Kelly Burner for JMM!" Another young lady running for Junior Mr. Mayor. Ivy had started something that apparently wasn't going away.

There are some who might wonder why we'd be so concerned with who runs for Junior Mr. Mayor. And to those people we say that every election needs quality candidates and what's the point of a democratic process if just any old person can run?

As the committee tried to get an impression of what we had to look forward to the next year, we mostly found that people wouldn't tell us their vote. They'd scrape at the empty bottom of their ice cream cups and tell us just about anything else, but not whether they voted for Ivy and Dogg. Tyler Carmichael talked about the row of blisters he'd gotten the previous day from flipping pancakes in a skillet with too much oil

(Making raisin smiley faces in pancakes sets up unrealistic life expectations for children.) - The Committee

and Pamela Curtis revealed—though it was rumored long ago—the secret to her figure was that she'd had two ribs removed in a Mexican hospital. Scott Spencer who, at nine, was just there for the food, he told Gloria Valdez that his "stay-over Daddy" and his "real Daddy" got in a fight the previous night and his mom had to bail them both out of jail.

We learned all that, and more, but nothing conclusive about whom our next Junior Mr. Mayor would be. Like everyone, we stood, part of the thick buzz a thousand conversations creates. So as people milled about under the sun, occasionally looking at the door where Mumford Smith would emerge to announce the results, the committee itself realized that we had a unanimous impulse. Forced to vote for one, to the last of us we had voted for Jimmy Doggins. If Ivy had that child, none of us could bear sending her out as our representative, and if she had an abortion, well, what kind of message would that send to the rest of the Mudlick teens? What was then to prevent Kelly Burner from showing up pregnant for next year's campaign? Jimmy Doggins, though tainted now, was the logical choice and we took comfort in the fact that when you reasoned your vote, there was only this one conclusion and that the people of Mudlick were smart enough to see that Jimmy Doggins needed to be our next Junior Mr. Mayor. So the committee regrouped in the curve of four twisting junipers, odd shadows wrapping our bodies as we conferred and watched the door for the inevitable and only viable result.

51

An hour and a half passed. Kelly Burner's ice cream cups lay scattered everywhere, on the ground, in crooks of tree branches, and like tiny footlights along the platform's edge. The committee remained in its semi-shady spot among the junipers while most everyone else had retreated under the pepper trees or into their running cars, air conditioning going full blast.

Conrad Dalton seized the opportunity to retrieve the accordion from the trunk of his car, the instrument he planned to play at his daughter's wedding until her sudden and total liver failure during her mission work in Brazil three months before she was to be married. Of course, we heard "Lady of Spain," but he had worked in some new material, which at least was a relief, though not totally—"Copacabana" and the theme from *Star Wars*.

Observe the unwritten rule of limited sharing musical talents.)
                                                                    - The Committee

We endured the music and waited for Mumford to emerge with the results and then maybe, we thought, we hoped, this whole long summer and awful campaign would just disappear, just become a bad dream that startles you awake but which, by morning, gets reduced by sleep memory to a furry blue snake or a room full of tin cans.

"All I have to say," Gloria Valdez announced, fanning herself with an unused ballot, "is that we did our best and I hope this town appreciates it."

Dillard Phipps ran a thumb under one strap of his suspenders and we all looked at him. "What these people never understand is that we've got perspective." He clucked his mouth as if eating a grape. He didn't need to elaborate. We all knew exactly what he meant. The committee specializes in seeing what most people just pass over in their daily lives. We've developed a certain objectivity that puts us on the right side of things. And what's frustrating is that sometimes you get these people who haven't spent ten minutes thinking about something we're trying to accomplish and they come in with all their own ideas, most of which we've already thought of. It's a thankless job and one wonders why we volunteer for it in the first place.

"Damn," Jasper said as if answering some silent question he'd asked himself. "This's like a friggin' circus, or some Japanese monster movie where the good guy and the bad guy are still smashing the hell out of the city." He clomped a few steps, taking pains to crush the taller leaves of grass and Styrofoam cups below us.

"Monster movie," Gloria confirmed. "Ivy vs. Dogg."

"With a Cast of Thousands," Lucille added, surveying the crowd.

Jacket off, shirt tucked out with his tie undone and looped around his neck, Mumford finally emerged after three hours from the V.F.W. hall with the unsealed ballot box and a rolled up piece of paper in his shirt pocket. He walked back to the empty platform and took his place at the podium, scanning the crowd as it thickened in front of him. As if preparing for something momentous, Mumford unbuttoned his shirt and took it off, revealing a black t-shirt with neon pink lettering spread wide by his broad chest. The message read, simply, "Ivy & Dogg for Junior Mr. Mayor." It was just one more strange thing for people to laugh about, which they did.

Normally, the outgoing Junior Mr. Mayor would give a speech thanking the town for the previous year. Greg Appleton cried when he gave his. "In some ways I think my life has peaked," he had said. And he was partly right because two years later, at a Superbowl party, he fell off a fourth story balcony and broke his neck.

Mumford opted not to give a speech. Instead he took the rolled paper from his pocket and read the results. We crowded forward. "Three write in votes for Thatch Hutchison." Mumford pointed at Thatch and winked. "Ivy Simmons one thousand, five hundred and nine." We were horrified and worried that she'd gotten so many votes. Whether for dramatic effect or to clear his throat, Mumford paused. The committee was suddenly concerned. It sounded like enough to win. Mumford continued. "Jimmy Doggins, one thousand, five hundred nineteen votes."

With that, a mix of cheers and sighs of relief shot through the crowd as we all looked for the candidate to emerge from the hall. We clapped and cheered, but nothing. Mumford spoke again waving another, smaller piece of paper at us. "I have here a message from Jimmy Doggins. *Circumstances require me to respectfully decline the position of Junior Mr. Mayor.*"

The Ivy supporters yelled, throwing plates and hats in the air. Immediately the committee huddled to see what could be done. But Mumford wasn't finished. He burped into the microphone and we listened. "A message from Ivy Simmons. *Circumstances require me to respectfully decline the position of Junior Mr. Mayor.*" Now there was general confusion. People looked at one another and then at the committee as if any of us had a contingency. After all these years it looked as if we would have no Junior Mr. Mayor, which, in our mind, given all the problems, was inconvenient, a bit embarrassing even, but not a tragedy.

"Ladies and gentlemen," Mumford boomed, gesturing toward the center of the crowd, "with three write in votes, your new Junior Mr. Mayor is Thatch Hutchison." Applause, mixed with a couple boos, was limited, like the first solitary kernels of popcorn bursting in a pan. All of us stared in disbelief as Thatch, who looked equally confused, walked out of the crowd to the podium, and climbed the steps. Mumford stood waiting with the red and white sash, placing it over Thatch's head so that it hung across his body. "I didn't even vote for myself," Thatch said tentatively. And then with Mumford's hand on his shoulder he inflated. "But I've discovered the best way to run for Junior Mr. Mayor. Spend no money; launch no campaign. I accept the results of this election." To this, people offered more confident, if resigned, applause.

(The abandoned lead by default. Flee or follow.)- The Committee

Needless to say, we weren't happy. The committee worked too hard to allow this to happen. We would have to convince Jimmy Doggins to reconsider. How could he nullify the will of the people? How could he live in this town for the next year, facing all those people who supported him despite is immoral behavior? We didn't wait for Thatch to finish before we pushed through the crowd toward the hall where Jimmy and Ivy would wait until Thatch had completed whatever acceptance speech he could muster. But when we got inside, all we saw were the counting machine and three chairs around a table with a paper airplane sitting in the center. Ivy and Dogg had disappeared.

52

We look back on the day that Ivy and Jimmy Doggins ran away and it seems so vivid, after the crowd thinned Marlon Blake with that one wandering eye, in his green overalls removing the bunting from the platform in front of the V.F.W. hall, Mrs. Doggins leaning against the flag pole in a powder blue dress, arms crossed, one hand stroking her rice pearl necklace as she talked to Ivy's mother with that bright tattoo dedicated to her daughter, both of them shaking their heads calmly, pretending to not yet know their children would never step foot in Mudlick again, Thatch posing for newspaper photos with Mumford in his Ivy & Dogg shirt, the Junior Mr. Mayor sash on Thatch perfectly smooth across his torso in a way that Mumford never managed.

The committee watched this from a picnic table beneath a manicured olive tree, in the center of the table, weighted by a twig, one of nine-year-old Sarah Samms' crayon drawings of a smiling sun looking down on a frowning man built of ovals who looked on fire until Jacob pointed out the similarity to his Hawaiian shirt. It was as if she was our courtroom artist working in abstract. The three figures behind him, round and androgynous, like the sun, were all smiling, waving their plump hands. If these were Ivy, Jimmy Doggins, and Mumford, this little girl had captured the mocking attitude which had ruined the entire event.

(Confiscate Crayons—instruments of subconscious rebellion.)
                                                    - The Committee

Lucille Otto, in her precise way, asked the question most on our minds, the new question. "What shall we do if we can't convince Jimmy Doggins to reconsider?"

"Well we can't let that Thatch kid represent us," Jasper Carson said, pinched between crutches. "I'm moving the day that little homo becomes a spokesperson for the town I live in."

Lucille rolled her eyes. "No need for epithets," she said.

Gloria Valdez, fanned herself with a paper plate and twisted one end of her scarf. "How about a special election? Two new candidates?"

There was a general grumble among us and an agreement that running a new election would be time consuming, one, and two, an admission that our process had failed. And people need confidence in their community leaders. They need to know we can adapt to any situation, not just call a do-over when something appears to have gone wrong. So, we decided to see about talking to Dogg first, and if that failed, we'd have to work with Thatch, crossing off any events dealing with churches or children.

As it happened, however, we didn't get a chance to talk to Dogg. We watched as Thatch and Mumford finished the photographs, shaking hands with each other before Mumford roared off in his truck. But instead of leaving, getting the hint that we weren't quite ready for this new set of circumstances, Thatch walked over to our table. He had a surprisingly confident gait for someone who had just been outed and who was elected for an office he didn't run for. As he approached, a half dozen beatles swooped into the olive branches above us in a fierce argument before flitting to another tree and arguing again.

"So when do I start?" he asked, standing before us somehow changed, tan and relaxed in shorts that went past his knees and a t-shirt so tight we could see his nipples, already not our image of a proper Junior Mr. Mayor.

"Let's get one thing straight," Jasper started in.

But Lucille raised her powerful, if thin hand and he stopped.

"Young man," she said, "as you can imagine the committee is a bit taken aback by today's events. We've yet to decide a proper course of action."

Thatch slowly and barely nodded, squinting his eyes as if he were having an interior conversation. "I see," he said.

"And in your state," Lucille went on, "should you continue to be Junior Mr. Mayor, we'll have to modify your role."

Thatch looked at us suspiciously. "What state is that?"

"The homosexual thing," Jacob said, inspecting one of the hibiscus on his shirtsleeve before looking at Thatch. "We just have to be careful how we use you. No school visits or religious functions. Things like that."

"Listen," Thatch said, flushing, "you people have already caused me enough trouble. I'm not going to spend a year fighting you." We thought he was on the verge of quitting already, and all of us waited for a resignation, the easy way out. "So, this is the way it's going to be. Unless you want a year of really bad publicity, I'm going to do everything you would have had your precious Dogg do."

Jasper started laughing. "Dog do," he repeated.

Thatch continued. "I'm going to give a speech at the Junior Olympics, at the Boys and Girls club. I'm going to the Soroptimists, the Rotary and the Kiwanis. I'll speak at a Synagogue ground breaking if we have one. I'm going to show up with my sash whether you want me to or not. You've already hit me with the video, what else could you possibly do?" With that, he turned and stomped away before any of us could say a word.

So that is how it's going to be, we thought, this kid was already planning on coming in here and calling the shots. This is the problem when you tolerate certain kinds of people. It's okay if they just stay quiet and go about their lives, but they always want to throw their business in your face. We definitely weren't having a year of that, we decided right then and there. Jimmy Doggins was just going to have to change his mind, and maybe we could get him back to his old self as well.

We didn't know it then, of course, but Ivy and Jimmy Doggins were not in town. That afternoon Mr. Doggins found a map in his son's room, a route to Ensenada, Mexico highlighted in yellow, but after that, nothing, as if they would get to the town and just disappear. When he couldn't find Dogg's mother, he notified the sheriff; Jasper got wind of it too and told the rest of us. And Mr. Marxler came forward that he might have given Dogg the idea of "running for the border." It was clear to us that Ivy was forcing Jimmy Doggins to take her to Mexico for an abortion, confirming, of course, this was not the type of young lady suited to hold the office of Junior Mr. Mayor. Still, without absolute proof, all of Mudlick was asking *Where are Ivy and Dogg?*

We should have known we'd be snookered when Ivy's mother wasn't to be found either.

53

The Junior Mr. Mayor fiasco temporarily took a backseat to another tragedy. The memorial service for Fern was held on the shore of Mudlick Lake. It was an appropriately gray day and the lake was unusually still. It seemed strange that just a couple weeks earlier Jimmy Doggins' disco was blaring across this same park. It's funny how one location can transform itself to suit any occasion. People are not so flexible, apparently. Even the ducks seemed changed, more quiet, as if they understood the moment. And even though there were perhaps five hundred mourners, hardly anyone spoke. Pastor Davies Pone presided from a log and plywood decked raft floating a few feet offshore. Next to him on the raft leaning on an easel stand was a flat, wreath-like reproduction of Fern made of juniper. Wearing his familiar navy blue suit, Pastor Pone read to us from Isaiah:

> For the fields of Heshbon languish, the vine of Sibmah: the lords of the heathen have broken down the principal plants thereof, they are come unto Jazer, they wandered the wilderness: her branches are stretched out, they are gone over the sea.
>
> Therefore I will bewail with the weeping of Jazer the vine of Sibmah: I will water thee with my tears, O Heshbon, and Elealeh: for the shouting for thy summer fruits and for thy harvest is fallen.
>
> And gladness is taken away, and joy out of the plentiful field; and in the vineyards there shall be no singing, neither shall there be shouting: the treaders shall tread out no wine in their presses; I have made their vintage shouting to cease.

"We weep too," Pastor Pone said, wiping a tear from the corner of his eye. "We weep for our fallen Fern and the possibilities she held and the promise she represented."

(Scuff marks on shoes at a memorial are a sign of disrespect.)
- The Committee

The pastor invited anyone forward who cared to say something about Fern. At first we were all tentative, but finally Dillard Phipps walked up front and stood next to Pastor Pone. It was rare to see Dillard dressed in black, but he still wore suspenders, maroon with matching bow tie, all of it in contrast to his pale skin and white hair which he combed back for the occasion. He cleared his throat. "Lots of us got attached real quick to that little girl and I'm no exception. Some of us even had nice conversations with her. And I don't want to make anyone feel worse on a day like today. But the reason we lost Fern was because we weren't loud enough. We didn't protect her like we could have." Dillard paused and scanned the crowd, running his thumbs along the backside of his suspender straps. "I hope that next time some helpless child like Fern is in trouble, all of us will have the courage to step into whatever the trouble is and make it right. And for any of you who've doubted, this is the very work of the committee day in and day out." Dillard snapped one strap against his round chest and returned to the respectful applause of the mourners.

We really could have done more to save Fern from Abigail Colton. There were enough of us to shake down her gate and take Fern to safety. Clearly Ms. Colton didn't have Fern's best interest at heart. Clearly, she was just squid food as far as Ms. Colton was concerned. And when the stakes are so high, you can't futz around trying to convince someone to do the right thing, the moral thing. You just have to act and trust they'll understand later.

After Dillard's comments, no one else spoke. Pastor Pone removed the wreath made in Fern's image and lay it gently in the water, giving a small push so she would float further out in the water. His sons pulled him back to shore and we all spent a quiet moment watching this small, flat replica of Fern float in the greenish water.

Our brief silence was broken by Larry Yahn on the Bagpipes playing "His eye is on the Sparrow," our cue that the service was over. We filed silently along the lakeshore, watching this version of Fern so peaceful in the water, each of us praying that she found some peace and knowing that we'd see her goodness in the afterlife when it was our turn to go.

54

Whether out of jealousy or spite, some people just want to destroy the good others do. The committee only wanted to provide Mudlick with the best Junior Mr. Mayor it could find, and all we got for our efforts was grief. Immediately after Fern's memorial, a week to the day after the election fiasco we convened in the historical society room. We sat in our regular places in gray light pouring in from the overcast day, all of us in various forms of black. No one wanted to speak. Not even Jasper with his hobbled leg had much to say. It had been a hard week and in a rare moment it was clear the committee didn't know what its next move was.

After a while of none of us saying anything, Jacob Alter sighed and stood, walking over to the photograph of Joseph Colton. He gripped both sides of the gilded frame and brought the thing down to the ground where he turned it and leaned Colton's face toward the wall. The back of the frame had a yellowed newspaper column, Colton's surprisingly brief obituary. Jacob read it.

"Joseph Colton, land developer and former owner of Grand Mudlick Lodge passed away Tuesday after an extended illness. Mr. Colton was long one of Mudlick's leading citizens, continuing to reside in the town even after suspected arsonists burned down his famous lodge."

"Did it himself if you ask me," Dillard chimed in.

Jacob continued. "Late in life Mr. Colton was noted for his philanthropy and for the plants he collected throughout the world and which he donated to the city zoo and other local organizations.

"Joseph Colton is survived by his second wife, Helen Crosswhite Colton, and his son Collin, and his daughter, Abigail, who shares her father's interest in horticulture."

Jacob stood up. "Well, if he was a philanthropist, Abigail Colton certainly didn't carry that tradition on."

(Write your own obituary in case your family can't think of anything good to say.) - The Committee

We were all about to agree when there was a knock at the door. In stepped Ivy's mother, Gwen Simmons, in an ill-fitting black pants suit, and carrying a black vinyl photo album under harm. Behind her was Mrs. Doggins, also in black, but wearing a skirt and sweater. Though we had not seen them, they had both apparently been at the memorial.

"It looks as though we missed you at the service," Lucille Otto said, waving the pair to the two empty seats at the table.

"No," Mrs. Doggins said as they sat down, "we were at Pat Hunter's memorial. We were the only people there who weren't family." The committee looked at each other. Of course we were saddened it took days to discover her body, but none of us admitted that we'd heard about Pat's services.

"I wasn't particularly close with Pat," Mrs. Doggins continued in her quiet voice. "But we got to know each other when I visited Fern."

Gwen rattled around inside her suit. "And I went because she was a regular customer. Liked Schnapps now and then. Sometimes a light beer. Sweet lady."

"Anyway," Mrs. Doggins said, "we saw that you all were here and we wanted to tell you about the children."

We'd heard so many pieces of the puzzle over the previous week from different people we were certainly ready to hear what happened from the mothers. Gloria Valdez adjusted her gray scarf as the rest of the committee took their places. Lucille Otto sat closest to Mrs. Doggins and Ivy's mother. She placed both her hands flat on the table as if bracing herself. Then she nodded to Mrs. Doggins but Ivy's mother started first, slamming down the photo album in front of her. "First off, we don't even need to be telling you people nothing. You've made it hard enough on these kids." She drove her finger onto the center of the photo album. "And I've got a few things you ought to see."

"I assure you," Jacob Alter said, "that just like every year, we went into the Junior Mr. Mayor elections with lots of optimism." Jacob shifted in his seat as he tried to find the right words. His neck floated inside his collar as he moved. "But this year, as you know, things got, well, complicated."

"That's putting it fucking mildly," Ivy's mother said.

Jasper chuckled while Lucille and Gloria looked at one another mutually disapproving the use of a profanity.

Mrs. Doggins raised her hands as if to silence us all. "What Ms. Simmons is trying to say is that two teenagers ran away because of the activities of the people in this room. They should've come to their parents first, but it's not hard to see why they did what they did."

Gwen put her hand on the photo album as if she were about to open it, but just left her fingers stroking the edges.

"Wait a minute," Jasper said, flexing and unflexing his bicep. "Not to be impolite, but didn't this all start because your son couldn't keep his pants zipped?"

"As a matter of fact, Jimmy and Ivy are very aware of their situation."

Dillard Phipps, who seemed the least interested in this conversation, perked up. "So you've heard from them, I take it. Didya follow em? How far into Mexico did they get?"

"That's a story all itself." Ivy's mother smiled and checked her awkward looking bun with one hand. "They never went to Mexico. That map was just to throw Mr. Doggins off the trail for a while. They wanted to be alone."

"They're with my Sister in Northern California," Mrs. Doggins said softly.

"And the pregnancy?" Gloria asked.

Mrs. Doggins looked at Gwen and stood. She walked in front of the bright gray light of the window, crossing her arms and looking to Ivy's mother for support before speaking. "All you need to know is that the four of us had a nice visit with my sister and they've made that decision together." We spent an hour going over each event, hearing every little thing they knew *except* what happened with Ivy and Jimmy Doggins. We heard about Mrs. Doggins' accidental meeting with Ivy outside the Colton place when she was bent over with morning sickness, and about Gwen Simmon's pep talk with her daughter and Thatch, disgusting as it was. They told us everything. But when it came down to the one thing we deserved answered, they were silent. In order to come to some healthy conclusions and set future committee policy, we needed a response to one simple question; Did Ivy have her baby?

Finally, exasperated, but not nearly as much as we were, Gwen snatched up the photo album and took her place next to Mrs. Doggins, both of them smiling. "My daughter decided . . . " She paused. "Well, I guess she decided to piss you off."

"If you ask me," Mrs. Doggins added, "You people know way more about our kids than you need to. And you don't know nearly enough about yourselves."

Jacob Alter began to speak but Lucille Otto raised her hand. "To be sure, Ms. Simmons, the committee knows more about these children than we bargained for. We know about their suspect morals and we know about their homosexual companions. And quite frankly, I don't doubt if any of us could handle knowing much more, though based on their behavior so far we can make a pretty good guess as to how things are going to turn out." Even as Lucille said that, the committee was aware that the very two people we needed to know about most had somehow managed to conceal their true selves from us.

Ivy's mother leaned on the table, looking each of us in the eye. "Those are good kids you're looking down your nose at. Role models if you ask me." Again she slammed down the photo album.

"Role models? That's all we need," Jacob Alter said.

And this is the part we tell a little out of order to illustrate just how unreasonable these two women were, and how they clearly didn't appreciate the committee and all its good work. Clearly they didn't even understand their own children.

A few days after we met with Mrs. Doggins and Gwen, Vida Clark, though she wasn't on our side by any means, filled Lucille Otto in on a thing or two. Mrs. Clark had voted but not stayed for the results, and without realizing the importance of it, she'd seen Ivy and Dogg leaving town in a small white convertible. They were headed out on old route 20. Ivy was driving, Jimmy Doggins in the passenger seat, his short green Mohawk like a shiny strip of new sod. She could not see their faces, whether they were happy or upset, and she wondered what the election results had been, but wondered if it mattered. The fact they were in the car together, she thought, must have meant they were satisfied with the outcome. She would call Ivy in the morning and congratulate or commiserate.

The way Mrs. Clark tells it, she watched that white car go down the road, and though she couldn't quite put her finger on why, she herself became a bit sad watching as they sped away over that river of old asphalt throwing up its refracted heat. She watched until the car became a white sliver floating on a glimmering current, always on the verge of disappearing, but not quite.

What the committee likes to point out, especially in the light of Mrs. Doggins and Gwen's tantrum, is that their son and daughter left town without even a word to the people who helped them. To the end they showed their true selfishness. Didn't say boo to Abigail Colton, or Vida Clark, not a word to the kids that'd helped on their campaigns, not even a whisper to Mr. Doggins. The committee doesn't need to defend itself, but we were had just like everyone else and these two mothers were trying to make us feel responsible for the whole mess.

Months after that meeting with Mrs. Doggins and Gwen Simmons, we read in the paper that Jimmy Doggins won the high school state championship in tennis. But about Ivy, we never heard another word, never heard whether she kept that baby or not, nor if she and Jimmy stayed together, though we take note that Ivy's mother moved up north and Mrs. Doggins divorced her husband and left Mudlick too. And the more we thought about it, the more we were glad they all left. That last encounter with Ivy and Dogg's mothers summed up the whole experience for us. There are people like that who try to impose their values on everyone else. They don't care about anyone but themselves. They don't care who they hurt or what the consequences are and the result is the rest of us get pulled down with them.

(Remain open-minded to the fact you're right.) - The Committee

And without knowing the truth, we're forced to write our own ending, of which, as near as we can figure, there could be two. Ivy has that baby and Jimmy Doggins sticks it out with her and maybe it works for a few months, but then they realize they're kids and they're stuck and that life is full of consequences. Or Ivy doesn't have the baby, has it murdered, and maybe that seems right for the moment, and easier. But then she's 30 and suddenly thinking back about the twelve year old she might have been helping with her homework. Then her life is about regret, the same regret that will sweep over Abigail Colton for killing Fern. Every bad act leads to comeuppance.

And of course we wouldn't be the committee if we didn't admit to also being taught a lesson after the whole experience. We were rewarded for protecting our town. Ivy took her sideshow on the road and we didn't have to face the embarrassment she would have surely brought us. We turned back the onslaught, so to speak, defended the fort. Maybe the most important thing learned from all that business with Ivy and Dogg is that every day is a battle for what's good and right. There are plenty of people willing to take control of your life, people with a strange moral compass, and you have to fight back. The worst of it is they don't even know they're dragging everyone down the wrong path. If you ask, they'll defend their motives and act like their vision of the world is absolute. In the end, we learned what we already knew about people like them. You have to push back or get pushed aside. These people are the enemy and if you don't do something to stop them, if you don't make a stand, you deserve everything that's coming to you. So we ask one question of everyone now; When a mess like this happens again, what are you going to do to stop them?

And it's important to hear all this, to get your head on straight to avoid falling into the trap we almost did with Mrs. Doggins and Gwen Simmons. They marched into our meeting and lectured us on what fine children they had, and the truth is we were starting to feel kind of bad. It's evident now that we've come to our senses, re-examined events and put everything in its proper perspective so that it's clear the committee was right all along. But when Gwen Simmons opened up that photo album she almost had us.

Just before the photo album Mrs. Doggins looked at us in her quiet way. "Ms. Simmons is right, you know. This town would be a lot better off if we were all more like Ivy and Jimmy and less like you."

Gwen opened to the first page of the album where there were school photos of both Ivy and Dogg complete with missing front teeth; next a snapshot of little Jimmy Doggins blowing out candles at his Seventh birthday party, and on the opposite page, young Ivy looking up from a pile of Christmas wrap. Gwen continued turning the pages to photos of their elementary school election; a very blonde Jimmy Doggins with his first tennis racket; Ivy on her grandmother's lap, the two of them working at a junior high carwash. There was a photo of Ivy and Cole Clark Junior in his back yard, the balsa wood bridge he'd helped her with between them; Dogg giving lessons at tennis camp to tiny Charles Maxler; a newspaper clipping of Jimmy Doggins serving a championship point; an article about

Ivy collecting money for Cassandra Jenk's surgery, and a photo of them smiling nose to nose. There were the Junior Mr. Mayor campaign photos as well, Ivy at the hot dog stand, Dogg in his disco suit; the two of them posing together at the fishing derby, Ivy with her stringer of blue gill, Dogg with a bright thumbs up.

"Every picture of them has Mudlick in the background," Gwen said, jabbing a short-nailed finger at the album. "Their whole lives in this town. And now what?" She flipped several pages at once where there were no photos, nothing, empty.

The committee sat quietly around the table, séance-like. In our temporary shame, in that state before we came to our senses we didn't know what to say. In short order we'd remember our purpose, remind ourselves that if the right people don't speak up the wrong people rule the day. But just then, at that moment their little trick almost worked. We sat contemplating that black rectangle in the center of the table, its dark pages and the barren pages beneath those where photos of Ivy and Dogg's future might have been but were kept from the very people who deserved to know if we were right about them or not.

Gwen turned one page back to three photos of Ivy and Jimmy Doggins standing in front of Fern and the Colton house, everything bathed in morning light. Muted gasps escaped from our side of the room. As we stared at these misguided young people, Gwen and Mrs. Doggins grabbed their things and moved toward the door. But Mrs. Doggins paused before leaving: "Keep the album. It's the past you missed." We were alone with these final photos of Ivy and Dogg. In the first two, the trio of Ivy, Dogg, and a glistening Fern, send a grand wave to the camera, to the committee; and then in the last photo a gaze we should have noticed all along, Ivy and Dogg leaning forehead to forehead, not understanding that they are only pretending at love, and saying something they won't allow the world to hear.

Acknowledgements

I'm grateful to Sally Kim and PJ Mark, who first saw this town and topiaries a decade ago and didn't tell me to give up, and especially to Andrew H. Sullivan for adopting these kids in a most gentle and literary way. Gratitude also to Purdue University's College of Liberal Arts and my colleagues in the Department of English. I continue to be humbled by the support of my father, Yee-shing Leung, and my families in Lakeside and Louisville and beyond. Supreme appreciation to Tom Alvarez, Matthew Brim, Austin Bunn, Roxane Gay, John Gosslee and Charles Solomon. A special nod to Adam McOmber who boils my blood and brightens my days. Here's to the Lambda Literary Foundation, Vermont College of Fine Arts, Art Omi and the "Formative Three," Lindo Park Elementary, Tierra Del Sol, and El Capitan. And one final thank you, one last toodle-oo, to my dearest pal, Alice Estes Davis.

An excerpt from this novel appeared in a different form in *Ocean State Review*.

OTHER C&R PRESS TITLES

NONFICTION

Women in the Literary Landscape by Doris Weatherford et al

FICTION

Made by Mary by Laura Catherine Brown
Ivy vs. Dogg by Brian Leung
While You Were Gone by Sybil Baker
Cloud Diary by Steve Mitchell
Spectrum by Martin Ott
That Man in Our Lives by Xu Xi

SHORT FICTION

Notes From the Mother Tongue by An Tran
The Protester Has Been Released by Janet Sarbanes

ESSAY AND CREATIVE NONFICTION

Immigration Essays by Sybil Baker
Je suis l'autre: Essays and Interrogations
by Kristina Marie Darling
Death of Art by Chris Campanioni

POETRY

Dark Horse by Kristina Marie Darling
Lessons in Camouflage by Martin Ott
All My Heroes are Broke by Ariel Francisco
Holdfast by Christian Anton Gerard
Ex Domestica by E.G. Cunningham
Like Lesser Gods by Bruce McEver
Notes from the Negro Side of the Moon by Earl Braggs
Imagine Not Drowning by Kelli Allen
Notes to the Beloved by Michelle Bitting
Free Boat: Collected Lies and Love Poems by John Reed
Les Fauves by Barbara Crooker
Tall as You are Tall Between Them by Annie Christain
The Couple Who Fell to Earth by Michelle Bitting

CHAPBOOKS

Atypical Cells of Undetermined Significance by Brenna Womer
On Innacuracy by Joe Manning
Heredity and Other Inventions by Sharona Muir
Love Undefind by Jonathan Katz
Cunstruck by Kate Northrop
Ugly Love (Notes from the Negro Side Moon) by Earl Braggs
A Hunger Called Music: A Verse History in Black Music
by Meredith Nnoka